I0522506

BLOOD RECALL

BLOOD DESTINY, BOOK 11

CONNIE SUTTLE

Copyright © 2018, by Connie Suttle
All Rights Reserved

ISBN: 1-63478-023-X
ISBN-13: 978-1-63478-023-0

This book is a work of fiction. Names, characters and incidents portrayed within its pages are purely fictitious and a product of the author's imagination. Any resemblance to actual persons, living or dead, is purely coincidental.

This book, whole or in part, MAY NOT be copied or reproduced by electronic or mechanical means (including photocopying or the implementation of any type of storage or retrieval system) without the express written permission of the author, except where permitted by law.

Published by:
SubtleDemon Publishing, LLC
PO Box 95696
Oklahoma City, OK 73143

Cover art by Renee Barratt @ The Cover Counts

For Sharyn and Dolly—Stay strong.

To Walter, Joe, Larry, Lee, Dianne, Sarah and Mark.
Thank you.

AUTHOR'S NOTE

Warning!

Blood Recall contains references (and possible spoilers) to the following series:

Blood Destiny Series

God Wars Series

High Demon Series

Latter Day Demons Series

R-D Series

First Ordinance Series

BlackWing Pirates Series

If you haven't read these series, you may become confused, disoriented, or read things that will ruin the aforementioned series.

You have been warned...

CHAPTER 1

"They're two, and tearing into everything," I shook my head as Wynter ran through the arboretum, screeching at the top of her lungs while Wayne chased after her. "What they can't destroy with their hands, they rip to shreds with their teeth."

"So, they're werewolves, through and through?" Breanne sipped the tea we'd been served to hide a self-satisfied smile.

"It sure looks that way. For the past two months, I've started every conversation between Winkler and me with, 'your children,' followed by some form of damage report."

"Does it make him feel guilty?"

"Hell no. He grins and congratulates them on their newest mode of destruction."

"Have they destroyed anything that can't be replaced?"

"Not yet—but Connegar was recruited in making one mishap go away. He said, 'children make mistakes,' put the splintered chair back together and disappeared. Don't even get me started on the potty training fiascoes."

"Marking territory?"

"I said don't get me started. I don't know how Sandra has any hair left—because every day there's at least three hair-pull-worthy stunts performed by the werewolf twins."

"It's a phase," Bree waved a hand, as if that dismissed continuous damage at the hands and teeth of my youngest.

"You want something," I accused, changing the subject.

"Why do you say that?"

"Because that's how you roll."

"I rolled down a hill, once. In Texas. Prickly pear will make you rethink those decisions."

"Ah, Texas. I remember it well." I did—I'd spent plenty of time in Texas, with Winkler, Gavin and a whole bunch of others.

"I'm glad you said that."

"Said what?" I studied my sister while suspicions formed.

"That you remember Texas."

"I also remember the Alamo, but then lots of people do. What's going on?" I gave my sister a deliberate glare-frown.

"Well, there's a bit of a snag," Bree said, before sipping more tea.

"A snag?"

"As in a snag that happened because of rogue gods and timeline shifts," Bree sighed. "If something isn't done to set it right, then people could die before they're supposed to die and the timeline will be fucked and so will everything else."

"What are you planning to do about it?" I asked politely.

"I shouldn't do anything, or it could become worse."

"I don't like where this is headed," I began. "I have things to do and twins to keep out of trouble."

"You can bend time," Bree pointed at me. "Same as I can. Plus, help coming from you during this time will be welcomed, while a stranger showing up will be perceived as suspicious. In the extreme."

"So it's somebody I know," I drew in a breath.

"Several someones you know. When you figure this out, and you will, you'll be out for blood."

"Right. Where and when, so I can make a decision."

"Do you remember when you were sent to Refizan to help Dragon?"

"I do."

"Good. It's happening in Texas, right about that time. If you don't go, Winkler, Trajan and at least half the Dallas Pack will die. You see what kind of snag this is, now?"

"Fucking hell." I was already on my feet and hauling ass toward my suite to throw clothes in a suitcase.

～

Past, Dallas, Texas

Lissa

I only had sketchy information to go on; Bree had given me as little as possible to get me on my way. Here I was, too, in the mansion next door to Winkler's because it was currently for sale, the owners were out of the country and Winkler would end up buying it for me anyway.

Just in case, though, I asked Connegar and Reemagar to handle my occupation of it, and they'd made arrangements to lease it temporarily. They'd also made sure it was supplied with everything I'd need while I was there, and I owed them both a big hug and a kiss for it.

I'd have gone to Winkler's front door and rang the bell to let him know I'd arrived, but Kellee, in her pregnant splendor, was there and I sure as hell didn't want to get in the middle of that predicament. Too, Bree said I was only able to use the abilities I'd had at that time—outwardly, anyway.

Plus, the whole thing had to be kept from the Vampire Council, because let's face it—they thought I was far away and safe from Xenides and his army.

Asshole Xenides would be dealt with later—by the former me. This time, there were new assholes and my job was to eliminate them and keep them from joining Xenides' bunch.

Except I didn't know exactly who they were. Bree said I'd figure out.

Yay.

I held a current cell phone in my hand, rather than a comp-vid. I discovered I missed my comp-vid—a lot—when I dialed Winkler's private number and listened to it ring.

"Winkler, this is Lissa," I told his phone, in response to it asking for a message to be left. "Call me as soon as you can at this number. Thanks."

Tossing the cell phone on the bed in the massive master suite, I considered taking my clothes out of the case and putting them in the closet.

Except it could be a useless gesture—I didn't know what the problem was and could end up in Timbuktu for all I knew. Winkler had a private jet and used it often; I had the idea I'd be going with him wherever the trouble was.

In the meantime, I could go to the grocery store. I hadn't shopped for my own groceries in at least a century—somebody else did it. I had two credit cards Bree handed to me, courtesy of the Larentii, who were geniuses at that sort of thing. Grabbing my cell phone and stuffing it in the purse I brought with me, I misted to the nearest grocery store to stock my mansion in Dallas.

~

Austin, Texas

Winkler

"You've been hacked—pure and simple, and now we have thieves who've made off with two million while we're standing here scratching our heads."

Trajan spoke for me—since I was angry enough to tear into the bank president and a couple of flunkies who cowered behind him.

The bank wasn't covered by Winkler Security, but I had a safe deposit box there. It belonged to my father and I'd kept it all these years, when I should have put it in a more secure location.

And one closer to home.

Two million wasn't the only thing the thieves had made off with—they'd taken some of my mother's jewelry and a ring my father wore upon occasion. The ring had been passed down through centuries from father to son, and was worth quite a lot in its own right.

I didn't point out that the thieves could have walked into the vault and taken whatever they wanted, including a ton of cash, but the only thing broken into and stolen was the safe deposit box I rented.

The bank hadn't called me either, until mid-afternoon, claiming they hadn't detected the theft until then.

"We don't know what to say, and I'll look into getting your things back," the president warbled. The police were doing the usual—dusting for prints and searching security videos, but the cameras all failed while the thieves were inside the bank.

We had nothing to go on, no witnesses, and every outside camera lens had been spray-painted over or exposed to such bright light it couldn't record anything except that.

"Come on, boss, there's nothing we can do from here," Trajan took my arm. I needed inside the vault where the box had been to sniff around. I needed Lissa to get me in there in the worst way, but the vamps had her off somewhere and hidden, so nobody could reach her.

Attempting to cool my temper a few hundred degrees, I allowed Trajan to steer me toward the front door.

"I wish we could get Lissa on this," Trajan mumbled as we walked through the door and headed for the SUV. "She'd have it sorted."

"Just what I was thinking," I growled, letting the wolf show his displeasure. If Kellee weren't in the house, I'd probably go home and start throwing things before letting the wolf loose.

"Full moon in three days," Trajan whispered as we loaded into the SUV and buckled in. This was the worst time for something like this to happen, and I wondered briefly if it were by design before dismissing it.

Nearly three hours later and long after sunset, we were almost home when Trajan asked the question. "Want ice cream, boss?"

"Maybe a tub of ice cream. And a bottle of Scotch."

"Well, we have the Scotch, but we're out of tubs of ice cream. Here's the grocery store. We can load up and go home."

"What happened to all the ice cream?" I glared at Trajan.

"Don't look at me. Kellee went through two tubs in two days."

"Damn. Pull into the parking lot. We'll buy sixteen tubs. Maybe that'll last two weeks."

"If we're lucky."

We found a parking place, slid out of the truck and headed for the front door. Past those and to the left was the frozen food section.

And the ice cream.

Maybe Kellee's pregnancy was affecting me. They said fathers often had sympathy pains. Maybe hunger pangs, too. I sure as hell wanted some ice cream, ever since Trajan mentioned it.

Trajan was thinking, at least, and grabbed a shopping cart to load the ice cream. I heard its bad wheel clacking behind me as I headed for the frozen treats like a wolf on a scent. The glass doors were opened quickly once I arrived, and I began hefting half-gallon tubs of ice cream at Trajan like a quarterback doing lateral passes.

The fourteenth tub ended up on the floor at my feet however, when someone spoke beside me.

"Winkler, what the hell are you doing?" Lissa demanded. The tub of rocky road I was about to flip toward Trajan landed on the tiled floor with frozen thump.

CHAPTER 2

Lissa

"I left you a message. Maybe if you'd check your phone now and then," I accused while we stood in the checkout line to pay.

"Baby, I'm just glad you're here. It's like somebody answered a prayer or something," Winkler drawled. He wasn't handsome or anything, no matter where or when he was.

"Hmmph," I shook my head at him, attempting to shake away my thoughts. I couldn't cast a sly glance at this Winkler and meet him in the bedroom later.

"We ah, have things to tell you," Trajan said, piling tubs of ice cream on the conveyor belt.

"You need that much?" I lifted an eyebrow at Winkler.

"Kellee," he grumped softly.

"Like you won't be eating half of it," I poked his shoulder.

"Never said I wouldn't. I'd be buying half that if it was just for me."

"At least you're honest."

"Why are you buying groceries?" Winkler asked. "Did you come to cook for us?"

Uh-oh. I was still drinking blood in this time period. Food consumption and day-walking wouldn't come until later.

"Yep," I lied. "I know how you like to eat."

"Good. You staying at the house?"

"I'm next door—I managed to lease it temporarily. Don't want to upset things at home," I said.

"Probably a good idea," Trajan hefted the last tub on the belt and waited for the cashier to ring it up. "Kellee isn't pleasant at the best of times."

"I get that." I put a divider on the belt and started unloading my cart.

"Add this to my ticket," Winkler pointed at the groceries accumulating on the conveyor.

"Of course, Mr. Winkler."

"Ooh, you have fans everywhere," I wiggled my fingers at Winkler.

"How did you get away from—you know?" he asked, flashing a grin.

"They think I'm somewhere else, and I prefer to let them keep thinking that. You have to make sure that nobody says anything while I'm here, or I'll have to leave."

"You mean you escaped?"

"In a manner of speaking."

"Damn. Wish you could do that more often," Winkler hauled out his wallet to pay for everything.

"You and me both."

~

Dublin, Ireland

Ilya Kuznetsov

"Papa, you know what that program will do if they get their hands on it. Word is they've already sent out several to close in on their target. It'll be subtle at first, like always, and then they'll keep closing the noose until they get whatever they want."

My son was worried, as he should be. He and others like him

struggled secretly to keep Ukraine out of Russian hands, although that was becoming harder and harder, as time went on.

Here and there across the globe, people were turning against their own governments after finding themselves compromised by Russian intelligence, or in debt to Russian banks or other concerns. I knew the network was falling into place, as did Andrei.

I walked a narrow line between my work as a spy for Russia, and as a preserver for Ukraine, my homeland. My son and I lived dangerously as a result, and neither could afford to be caught.

We'd die if we were.

"How is Katya?" I asked.

"She's fine," Andrei waved a hand. "She wants to be involved in this, too, but she's too young."

"And it's too dangerous right now."

"Yes. We know about the *Klyki*, while she thinks they're a fairy tale."

"I curse the day their division was created. I would like nothing more than to watch them die. They kill too much and too easily—and more of the innocent die at their hands than the guilty."

"I agree. Where will you go from here, Papa?"

"I think I will follow those who've been sent after the target. I have some time—perhaps I might interfere?"

"I wish you luck and a safe return."

∾

Dallas

Lissa

"They took two million in cash, some jewelry and a ring that belonged to your father?" I studied Winkler's old photographs of the contents of the safe deposit box.

"While a pile of unmarked cash was nearby, just asking to be stolen," Winkler said around a mouthful of rocky road.

"You think they were targeting you, don't you?"

"I do." He scraped up the last of his tub of ice cream and stuffed it in his mouth.

"So do I. This makes no sense, otherwise."

"Will you get me into that vault after hours tomorrow night? To sniff around?"

"Why don't you let me go in alone—I can sniff while not materializing."

"What if it's somebody I recognize, but you don't?"

"There's that, I suppose. All right—I'll take us in, but if anything looks off, we get out fast."

"Agreed."

"Have you told Weldon about this?"

"Not yet. That call is next on my list."

"Good. He needs to be aware."

"Should I tell Tony Hancock?" I froze for several seconds at Winkler's words. "Look, I know he did everything wrong," Winkler held up a hand. "I don't have to bring him into this."

"Good, because I don't want him anywhere near it. Or me."

"He fucked up big time," Winkler stared at his empty ice cream tub mournfully.

"Oh, it's bigger than that," I sighed. I didn't add that Tony would gallivant all over England looking for me, or that he'd end up in Paris, just in time for Xenides to nearly kill him. Or that René would find him dying in a pile of rubble and make him vampire afterward.

Nope, didn't need to interfere with any of that.

Winkler didn't leave until almost dawn, so I ended up cooking a chicken fried steak for him. By the time he finally went home, I was so hungry I was ready to gnaw off a table leg.

I helped myself to the leftover steak and mashed potatoes and gravy before hauling my ass to the bed. I considered folding to the bank in question, but decided it could wait for when I woke, probably sometime in the afternoon.

If there was anything to find, I'd do reconnaissance before hauling Winkler in. Since I didn't know what we were dealing with, yet, it never hurt to be too cautious.

Especially if somebody were gunning for Winkler to begin with.

I was forced to wait for sundown and Winkler anyway; a wolf in the Austin Pack was murdered while I slept, and he was a business associate of Winkler's.

~

"He's been like this all day," Trajan whispered while Winkler stalked around my kitchen island and growled. "Elliott was a good friend, and an early investor in Winkler's security business."

"How did he die?" I asked, trying not to distract Winkler.

"Looks like another werewolf. Boss wants you to go sniff around the scene. We can go to the bank afterward."

"All right," I agreed. "Has he eaten anything?"

"Earlier."

"Good. We don't need a starving, angry wolf on our hands."

"You got that right."

"Come on, boss. No sense putting this off. Let's get in the truck and drive," Trajan said.

"Fine." Winkler strode toward the door like he was ready to hunt. I didn't blame him—I suspected that the theft and this murder were connected, and I needed to get to the bottom of it fast.

~

It takes at least three hours to get to Austin, especially when you're driving at excessive speed and get pulled over by the Texas Highway Patrol as a result.

"I am not getting you out of this ticket with compulsion," I reached into the front seat and poked Winkler in the ribs. "If you'd only gone five miles over the limit, he'd probably let you go. Twenty is a bit much. You're not totally indestructible, you know. If you wanted to get there faster, maybe the jet would have been a better idea."

"Your license and insurance verification, Mr. Winkler," the THP trooper was back, handing documents through the open driver's side window. "I understand a friend died, but you need to arrive in one piece." The trooper handed the ticket book to Winkler for his signature. "Slow it down, okay?" He tore off the ticket and handed it to Winkler while Winkler fumed silently.

"Jet's being worked on," Trajan mumbled from the passenger seat. "Can't fly for another day or two."

"Oh. I get the driving thing, now."

"Shut up, both of you," Winkler growled before putting the SUV in gear and pulling onto the road during a brief lull in busy, I-35 traffic.

"This is where we found him," Elliott Barnard's ranch foreman, also a werewolf, indicated the bloody patch of grass near a barbed-wire fence on Barnard Ranch's eastern edge. Tire tracks were nearby—from the police investigation and whomever had committed the crime, I assumed.

With only a near-full moon hanging overhead to light the scene, Winkler and Trajan were busy sniffing, while I studied everything the crime scene had to offer.

"Two werewolves," Trajan growled as I opened my mouth to say the same thing. "And a vamp," he growled louder, also before I could say it.

What Trajan didn't know, however, was who that particular vampire was. I'd scented him at least twice before.

"Ivan Baikov," I strode to Winkler's side and linked my fingers with his absently. "A really old, really Russian vampire. He didn't do the killing, but he was here."

Winkler's fingers tightened on mine as he turned dark eyes to me. A deep frown marred his features—no, he wasn't upset at the unexpected physical contact—he liked that part. What he was upset about was a vamp being here to backup two werewolf murderers.

"Know anything about the wolves?" he asked softly.

"No, honey. I've never scented them before, but I'll know 'em if I smell 'em again."

"Good. I'm counting on it."

"Tire tracks lead to the county road through that gate, over there," the foreman pointed out. "We've already sent trackers, but there's nothing to track once they pulled onto that road. It's just another truck mixed with hundreds of others."

"No description of the truck?" Trajan asked.

"Nothing. We didn't find Elliott until he didn't come home—he liked to roam the property alone, sometimes. We never worried about it, either, until now. Nobody's going out alone from now on."

"I need to make some calls," Winkler rumbled before pulling me toward his SUV. Trajan followed, after thanking the foreman and telling him we'd be in touch.

Winkler didn't say who he intended to call, but Tony's department was probably on that list.

"Call Bill Jennings," I whispered when Winkler opened the back door and waited for me to get comfortable before buckling me in.

"I'll call Bill," he growled. "I heard Hancock is out of the country, anyway." He shut my door before climbing into the passenger seat—I was glad he'd decided to let Trajan drive us to the bank.

Trajan ended up parking the SUV two blocks from the bank, so nobody would be suspicious. He'd wait in the truck while I misted Winkler into the vault where his safe deposit box was located.

I gathered Winkler into my mist and we were on our way to the bank, zooming invisibly through doors and past security cameras and alarm systems, until we flew straight through the vault door.

Three vampires were here, I informed Winkler as I stuffed both of us as mist inside his safe deposit box. I could feel his agitation—he couldn't answer me in the here and now, but I read his emotions easily. *I don't recognize any of them,* I added, before pulling out of the cramped space and hauling him out of the bank.

Cameras were recording everything in that vault, and I sure as hell didn't want to appear on anybody's digital recordings.

"What the hell?" Winkler growled aloud the moment he materialized on the SUV's front passenger seat.

"Three vamps. I don't know 'em. There are cameras recording everything in there, fur butt," I snapped the moment I materialized in the back seat.

"Fuck." Winkler buried his face in his hands. "Is there any way you can contact the ah, Council, to find out if they know of any visiting vamps in the area?"

"I'm not going to do anything of the sort. Send a message to Wlodek through Charles. Tell them about your friend being murdered, and explain that a vampire was on the scene. If these two things aren't connected, I'll drink wheat-grass juice instead of blood."

"Fine. What about doing an investigation on our own?" he demanded, dropping his hands. "If I talk to the Council, they'll send somebody if they don't have information."

"Now you're thinking," I said. "Let me handle this for now—at least the vamp part, while you concentrate on the wolf part of it. Together, we should be able to come up with something, if somebody doesn't start making demands soon."

"You think I'm about to be blackmailed?"

"I think it's a good possibility."

"Damn."

~

DFW Airport, Dallas, Texas

Ilya Kuznetsov

Baikov's vampir *is out of the country—B*. I read the text message as I walked through the airport toward baggage claim.

Bespalov never spelled out his name, and only used the most secure channels to communicate with me. He held an office in the government, and kept me apprised on a great many things, including the decisions made at high levels concerning the intended annexation of Ukraine.

"Hmmph." I pocketed my phone and stepped onto the escalator leading to the train that would shuttle me to the baggage area. Baikov's *vampir*—a member of the *Klyki*. That one was also named Baikov. I imagined that this fanged one had a distant, familial connection to the current General Baikov somewhere, but the human one was bad enough. He was the type to slice your throat open and laugh while you struggled to breathe or scream.

I'd never had contact with the *vampir* version. Who knew which might be worse? In most cases, the *Klyki* didn't work with their human counterparts; too many things could go wrong. I was thankful for that small piece of wisdom—it kept them from killing me and vice-versa.

Vampires could die in the sun—werewolves could die if shot enough times from close range. I didn't care which would be required; I was prepared to do it—even if it meant my death afterward.

Half an hour later, I left the airport in a rental car and drove toward a local post office. I'd asked an undercover associate at the Russian Embassy to mail two rifles to me and I needed to pick them up. The handguns he sent would arrive at my newly-rented condo the following day, through a different carrier service. "I love the U.S. and their fascination with guns," I said softly, turning a corner when the light flashed green. Being able to mail them through one carrier or another made my life so much easier. Ammunition would arrive by a third carrier, sent by the same associate.

After retrieving my package at the post office, I'd spend the rest of the day researching William Winkler and his business, Winkler Security. He was the target for the *Klyki*, unless I was very much mistaken.

～

Lissa

"Yes, I can cook, what do you want?" I asked as Winkler and Trajan followed me into my current home away from home.

"Chicken and dumplings?" Trajan pleaded.

"It's a good thing I bought a rotisserie chicken, or I'd have to say no," I said. "This way, the chicken is already cooked and all I have to do is throw it in the pot—after pulling the chicken off the bone."

"All right," Trajan grinned. I turned on the kitchen light and went straight to the huge, state-of-the-art fridge while Winkler helped himself to the wine and beer fridge under the counter. Who knew there was anything in there? My Larentii were much better than I was at this sort of thing.

He and Trajan went through a six-pack of *Dos Equis* while I cooked chicken and dumplings. Winkler offered me a beer. I offered him an appendectomy. We both declined.

They tore into the food the moment it was cool enough to eat, and ate the entire pot of chicken and dumplings I'd made.

"Kellee insulted the cook, and now we're having to make do by either ordering out, eating out or conscripting anybody in the house who knows how to cook," Trajan explained when he finished his last bowl and sat back, rubbing his stomach.

"No surprise," I shook my head and started cleaning the kitchen. Kellee, what I remembered of her, anyway, was a bitch with a capital B. Thank goodness her kids turned out okay, but she hadn't raised them. Winkler did. "What's on the agenda for tomorrow?" I asked Winkler.

"Elliott's funeral is in three days—two days after the full moon, actually, so there are arrangements to be made to take care of his widow. Elliott was the Packmaster for the Austin Pack, so there are complications. Debra doesn't want to stay in Austin after somebody else takes over; she wants to go to her brother's in Abilene."

"In other words, she doesn't want anything to do with the Second in the Austin Pack?" I asked as sweetly as I could.

"Well, uh, that may be an understatement, and Weldon may have to get involved. She's done her duty and had three kids rather than the required two, so I figure she can do whatever she wants—if she can manage to get out of town without Mick coercing her to stay."

"I take it he's not mated?" I frowned at Winkler. I'd forgotten how much I hated werewolf politics.

"Never has been," Trajan explained. "He's not the best, oh, how to put this—husband material."

"In other words, he's a misogynistic asshole, you mean?"

"Well, as Elliott's Second, he's the new Packmaster of the Austin Pack by default, and Weldon wants the transition to go smoothly," Winkler coughed into his hand.

"I am not protecting some asshole from a challenge," I snapped. "Been there, got the T-shirt. So done with that."

"There may be like, uh, three challengers," Trajan sounded uncomfortable.

"Who's the best choice?" My hands were now on my hips while I stared down two werewolves who were nearly comatose from eating a huge pot of chicken and dumplings.

"The youngest, but he may not be able to take on Mick, and then the other two. That's three fights in a row, and it won't be easy."

"Can't he wait until last?"

"Probably not a good idea," Winkler shook his head. "The one who takes Mick down will likely have the support of the pack behind him, and the new challengers, unless they also have substantial support, may go down under a new Second's loving jaws. The young one will have to prove himself to the pack, so they'll stand back and watch what happens."

"I need to upgrade my distaste for werewolf politics," I grumped.

"Still don't want to act as Gabe's Second—if I can convince him?"

"I'm trying to stay under the radar, remember?" I said. I thought about whacking Winkler with the dishtowel in my hand, but thought better of it.

"Well, let's see how things go. He may not want to make a challenge anyway," Winkler waved a hand, dismissing the idea.

"How old is he?" I asked.

"Twenty-seven," Winkler shrugged.

"Right." In werewolf speak, that meant he hadn't been out of diapers long. Didn't mean much to me—some were born old; others never reached maturity. "Last name?" I asked, just for the record.

"Billings."

Gabe Billings. *Billings.* Where had I heard that name before?

Oh, yeah.

"Is he related to Benjamin Billings?"

"Cousin, once removed," Winkler shrugged. "How do you know about Ben?"

"Just a casual conversation, that's all."

While I was doing a mental dance to placate Winkler, I was searching through future history, to see whether Joshua Billings, a werewolf I'd meet in roughly three centuries, was connected to Gabriel Billings.

He was—Gabe would become Josh's great-great-grandfather—*if he lived.*

"Will you let me know if Gabe decides to take on Mick in the first round?" I asked Winkler.

"Sure, but I thought you didn't want to be involved."

"Call it a feeling," I hunched my shoulders.

"I'll let you know."

"Thanks."

"Gabe's a good kid," Trajan interjected.

"Yeah. I have that feeling about him, too."

Somehow, in the timeline I'd lived before, Elliott hadn't been killed. At least not like this—he should have died later—twenty years later, actually, when Gabe challenged him.

But that was then. Something had changed, just as Bree said, and now I was here to keep the timeline from drifting too far off center to make a recovery. Fates of lives and worlds often hung in the balance.

Rather than hunting down Ivan Baikov immediately, as I felt I should, I had another wrench in the works to deal with—in the form of a young challenger for Packmaster of the Austin Pack.

Fuck.

"Tell me about this Russian vampire," Winkler said, changing the subject.

"I didn't like him before he made an offer to Wlodek," I said. "Something felt off about him and he gave me the heebie-jeebies."

"An offer?" Trajan was curious.

"They auction female vampires off to the highest bidder—if their sires don't have them locked up already," Winkler growled.

"Not much different from female werewolves," Trajan pointed out judiciously. Winkler turned a louder growl toward his Second.

"Honey, don't get your tail all fuzzed up," I told him. Everybody knew he'd picked someone different for his sister—she'd just decided to go against that decision on her own. I'd taken three bullets in the back for it, too, to protect her and her newly-married werewolf husband.

Just as Winkler would pick the wrong werewolf for his daughter in two decades, only someone else would prevent *that* blunder from happening. Winkler didn't have the best track record at matchmaking, but I didn't bother telling him that.

"I'll check in with Gabe," Trajan yawned and lifted long arms over his head to stretch. "Gotta sleep now, though. Full moon tomorrow night."

Uh-oh. Full moons saw plenty of challenges in the werewolf world. Things might be moving faster than I anticipated with the Austin Pack.

~

Kent, England

Wlodek

"Message from Dalroy, Honored One," Charles set a copy of an e-mail on my desk.

"Is it important?"

"He thinks it is. The Austin Packmaster was murdered yesterday, and the rumor is that two werewolves killed Elliott Barnard, while a vampire supervised."

I'd been toying with my gold pen while Charles spoke, disregarding the page lying on my desk. Until he'd said a vampire was rumored to have supervised the killing of a werewolf.

We didn't need a call from Weldon Harper while we were in the middle of attempting to trace Xenides' movements. We also didn't need the peace achieved between werewolves and vampires to be threatened again—we needed their assistance with Xenides. Word that a vampire was now interfering in werewolf politics and pack leadership could lead us in the wrong direction again.

If Lissa were here, I'd send her and Gavin immediately. She wasn't; she was in a place none of us could reach—by design. If Xenides managed to get his hands on her, we were all finished, vampires and werewolves alike.

"Put Dalroy and Rhett on this immediately. I want to know whether this rumor is true, and if so, I wish to know which vampire has chosen to place us in so much jeopardy. Kill the miscreant, if there is proof. I want information the moment it comes in from now on."

"In the States, the full moon is only hours away, Honored One. Should a vampire become involved in the succession in that pack as well," Charles didn't finish his train of thought, as I'd raised my hand to stop him.

"Understood. Have them investigate this matter immediately. I want proof, and I want that vampire dead if proof is found. If I discover that this one is in league with Xenides, you know how dangerous that could be."

"I'll inform Dalroy now, sir."

Charles swept out of my study without lifting even a slip of paper off my desk. I often wondered how he did that. Had Xenides made a play on a smaller stage, intent on turning small ripples into massive waves?

We didn't need another race war, and this could be the beginning. Lifting my private cell phone from a drawer, I dialed Merrill's number.

"Yes?" His cultured voice indicated he knew who was calling. "We have trouble," I told him. "A vampire may have ordered the murder of the Austin, Texas, Packmaster. Word from Dalroy is that two werewolves accomplished the deed, under a vampire's supervision. I dislike this possibility very much."

"Have Dalroy and Rhett been assigned to this? You know the full moon is coming for those wolves, and a challenge will be made, no doubt. Interference in pack leadership will not be well-received by Weldon Harper."

"I've already reached that conclusion, and yes, this has become Dalroy and Rhett's sole assignment—to get to the bottom of it quickly. If we need to send others, I'll attempt to find someone, as all my Enforcers and Assassins are looking for Xenides."

"You think Xenides may be connected to this, don't you?"

"I think it's possible."

"This isn't good," Merrill whispered, knowing I'd hear him anyway. "Will you keep me informed?"

"Of course."

≈

Lissa

I had no idea Winkler sent werewolves to guard my house, but there they were, patrolling the perimeter as I misted past them shortly after noon the following day.

It wasn't a bad idea—I figured he worried just as much about Kellee finding out I was there as anybody else who meant me harm. I was waiting for the screech to come if she did discover I was there.

She didn't care two cents about Winkler, but she'd pitch a fit if there was any other woman within reach. I had no intention of making any move in his direction, other than the few mistakes I'd made by touching him briefly.

In the future he'd be all mine, and I hadn't forgotten that for a minute. For now, though, I was starving, and Mexican food sounded like a great idea. Dallas has a lot of good restaurants, so I was headed for the nearest one as quickly as I could get there.

Materializing behind a nearby business where there were no

cameras or observers, I straightened my shirt and jacket before heading for the front entrance and some chicken tamales.

"Just one, today?" The smiling young man pulled a menu from a stack beside him and led me to a small table designed for two.

I was just about to open my mouth and confirm his headcount when I was tapped on the shoulder. Something squelched the scream I almost released as I turned like a puffed-out cat to confront the one who'd touched me.

I deflated quickly; Zaria had come.

CHAPTER 3

North of the Border Mexican Restaurant y Taqueria, Dallas
Lissa

"I'll have the cheese taco and cheese enchilada, please," Zaria handed her menu back to our server. I'd already ordered, asking for three chicken tamales.

I knew better than to ask how she'd found me, but she saw it in me anyway. "Bree knows—in fact, she suggested I come since, well, he's involved in this, too, and he shouldn't be."

"Who?"

"Ilya." She lowered her voice, knowing I'd still hear her.

"He's not involved with that idiot Baikov, is he?" I blurted.

"No. He's working against him, thinking he's indestructible in the face of a vampire," Zaria shook her head. "You and I both know you don't take a gun to a vampire fight."

"Why is he working against him—Baikov, I mean?"

"You don't know about the *Klyki*. He does."

"Fangs?" I blinked at the Russian word.

"The U.S. has vamps and wolves in special divisions; so do the Russians. Except that they have a bit of a twist to theirs. It involves the Lyristolyi drug."

"Fuck." I wanted to slap my forehead, but held back in case someone else was watching. I had a shield up; Zaria had a shield up. I doubted anybody would be able to read our lips past Zaria's shield—unless they were very powerful indeed.

"Where is Ilya now?" I asked.

"He rented a condo not far from here—he's gathering intelligence on Winkler, because he estimates that Winkler is Baikov's target—both the vamp Baikov and the human General version."

"For?"

"That infernal software, what else?"

"How did they find out he was successful?"

"The Kremlin has eyes and ears everywhere. The question is moot. What you have to concentrate on is protecting your wolf—and his Second and anyone else in his pack that's important to the future."

"And Ilya, too, I suppose?"

"Yes. If you want, I can help with all that. We just need to come up with a suitable cover for me—temporary, of course."

"Winkler needs a cook."

"I can cook," she agreed. "How do I get into the house?"

"You're a witch, the last I checked," I shrugged. "And you're good with people. Kellee won't pitch a fit around you—I think you can take care of that shit real fast."

"Ah, the pregnant bitch," Zaria leaned back in her chair. Our food was set in front of us moments later, iced tea glasses were refilled and we began eating while our server walked away.

"Kellee could become a target—if they want Winkler's cooperation instead of him dead," Zaria pointed out while cutting another portion of cheese enchilada to eat. "And I'm pretty sure they want his cooperation—at least until they get a handle on building and improving the software."

"Damn, this is complicated," I grimaced. "Do you know how many they've sent? I scented three at the Austin Packmaster's murder scene —two werewolves and Baikov."

"Only Baikov traveled here—the others are embedded and could come from anywhere," Zaria said. "Both vampires and werewolves."

"Does Wlodek suspect? That you know of?"

"He doesn't know about this. He's focused on Xenides, and that is enough to keep anyone distracted."

"So we have to destroy the Russian *Klyki*—well enough that they won't be able to regroup and cause more trouble, is that it?"

"For now. This entire situation is delicate in the extreme, and too many things could go wrong."

"I hear that," I agreed, discovering I was on my last tamale. They were really good, too. "We just have to find a way to work you into a job at Winkler's and between the two of us, maybe we can handle this without too much fallout."

"Keep an eye out for Ilya," she warned. "He may decide to attempt to warn Winkler, so it's up to you to get him and his wolves to stand down. He doesn't need to be torn to pieces while trying to help."

"That gives me an idea," I said while allowing a smile to curve my lips. "A really good idea."

❧

"She's what?" Winkler growled.

"A witch. She works as a trouble shooter now and then. And she can cook," I waved that temptation in front of Winkler.

"Why are you suggesting this?" He was still grumpy in the extreme.

"Because I can't help your ass during the day, or didn't you remember that?" I demanded. "She can, and she'll cook for you and your bunch until this is over."

"You know something, don't you?" His eyes narrowed as he studied me.

"I heard from her, actually, and this is something off the books for her—she thinks it's important—enough to get involved with no pay, unless you decide her services are worth something to you."

"Hmmph," Winkler expressed his skepticism.

"She knows things ahead of time, and has no trouble reading intent from the bad guys—it makes her valuable," I shrugged. "She told me that there's a vamp Baikov and a human Baikov, who's high in the

Russian military. Those two are connected and working for the Kremlin."

"Fuck," Winkler combed fingers through his hair in frustration.

"You wanted to know whether Wlodek and the Council were aware of this?" I pointed a finger at him. "Zaria says they don't know—that they're focused on Xenides, for obvious reasons."

"She knows all that? This I have to see," Winkler still sounded skeptical.

"Let me call her. We can meet her elsewhere, if you want, and you can decide. I trust her with my life, Winkler, and you should, too."

"Make the call. I'll run back to the house and get Trajan."

"You do that."

The twenty-four-hour restaurant wasn't crowded—it was nearly ten when we walked in and the familiar scents of coffee, pancakes and syrup greeted my nose.

Zaria was already there, with a booth large enough to hold all of us. I sat beside Winkler; Trajan scooted in beside Zaria.

"I didn't expect you to look, well, this young," Winkler snorted.

"Hmmph. Want me to change my appearance? I can, you know."

"Then do it," Winkler shrugged.

Zaria's face and body changed quickly. I knew, whether Winkler did or not, that Zaria now resembled her original self before she received the drug the first time—this was the author Harriett Majors, who was in her early fifties at the time. Yes, she and my mother had the same first name, originally. *Go figure.*

"Damn, boss," Trajan drew in a breath. Winkler didn't say anything; he just stared at the transformation in surprise.

"Can you uh, look that way while you're in the house?" Winkler finally found his voice.

"I can."

"Good. This way, you look like somebody's grandmother. Kellee won't have a fit about that—especially if you really can cook."

"I really can cook," she affirmed.

"You're sure?" Winkler turned toward me.

"As sure as I'm sitting here."

"All right—when can you start?" he turned back to Zaria.

"Tomorrow morning? I think I'd like to bunk at Lissa's place at night, though. All you have to do is call if you need me—and I don't already know that you need me."

"Sounds good to me," I said.

"Fine," Winkler agreed. "I'm not sure I have an open bed in the house anyway."

"Good enough. I'll be there at five tomorrow morning to cook breakfast. Do you have enough supplies, or should I get some?"

"Get enough to feed twenty-five—in three shifts," Trajan nodded.

"I'll help her," I offered. "I can get us to the store and back, so you won't have to worry about it. Now, go off to do your full moon thing. I know you're getting itchy."

"Come on, Traje," Winkler rose and stalked toward the door, leaving me and Zaria alone.

"That was easy," Zaria smiled. "Want pancakes?"

"I thought you'd never ask," I said.

"You think we got enough?" I stared at the mountain of food piled on my kitchen island. "These are werewolves we're talking about." We'd even restocked the wine and beer fridge, and then put even more beer in the fridge in the garage.

"We can get more if we need it," Zaria said. "I'm about to send it over to Winkler's and put it into its proper place," she added. "With power, of course."

"Sounds good."

Zaria lifted her arms and closed her eyes while everything on the island disappeared. "There, all done," she smiled at me. "Show me my bedroom," she said, while a large, packed bag appeared on the tiled floor beside her.

"This way," I said, lifting her and her bag into my mist and hauling her to the second floor.

~

Ilya

I watched as lights went out in the next-door kitchen, and only a second later, lights blinked on in two bedrooms upstairs.

Must be on a timer, I thought, turning back to the Winkler mansion. It was the full moon, and the werewolves were all gone for their monthly run. It was the perfect time for Baikov to move in and do some sort of evil.

Speak of the devil, whispered through my mind as a dark van pulled up and parked a block away. I moved farther into the shadow of the high wall surrounding the Winkler estate, waiting for someone to exit the vehicle.

The door opened, but I saw nobody leave. The door shut again, leaving a driver and one other in the van.

Vampires—all of them, I suspected. The wolves working for the Kremlin would be forced to make the turn tonight, just as the Dallas Pack did.

Hair stood up on my arm as a cold breeze passed.

A mister, the same voice entered my mind.

What? Why did I reply to my own imagination?

A vampire who can turn to mist—quite dangerous. Come. We will deal with this.

We?

Come.

Whether I wanted it or not, I was pulled into invisibility so fast I had no time to blink.

~

Lissa

I'd left Zaria to guard Winkler's house while I folded space to the

Austin Pack. If anything went down, especially Gabe Billings, I needed to be there to help him get back up.

Surprisingly enough, the entire Austin Pack was tracking two deer when I arrived and misted overhead. No hint of a challenge, and so far, they were following Mick's lead on the hunt.

They looked to be closing in on the racing deer in a wooded area, when shots rang out. *Bloody, fucking hell.*

~

Zaria

You see? I sent to Ilya, as he was gathered inside my invisibility. I'd borrowed the idea from Lissa, actually, and duplicated it so that I'd see another mister, just as she would.

The mist we followed was a malevolent violet, as he floated through Winkler's mansion, looking for a likely place to materialize. Security cameras were everywhere, so he'd have to search for a hidden spot to rematerialize.

I had no doubts he intended to plant cameras or bugs of his own, to gauge Winkler's response to—*damn.*

They're shooting at the Austin Pack, Lissa's mindspeech reached me. *I'm gathering as many as I can, but some of them are already dead. Others are wounded. I really need your help.*

Bring them to your yard; Ilya and I will be there shortly.

Ilya? Never mind, I see you're busy. See you in a few.

What is happening? Ilya demanded. I'd hear his thoughts, no matter when or where.

Stay calm; we'll have to force the situation, here, I replied. Extending power, I forced the vampire to rematerialize—much against his wishes, as it turned out. His fangs were out and he was slashing everything within reach with long claws as he blew through Winkler's home like a vampiric tornado.

I released his particles while he screamed, and all of it was recorded for the Dallas Pack to see later.

~

Ilya

"She's a witch." The red-haired woman informed me as I watched the sixty-ish woman who'd carried me with her tend to wounded werewolves. Those who weren't wounded—all from the Austin Pack, I learned—stood back while the witch worked on the others.

I blinked when bullets lifted from pierced bodies and slapped into glowing, waiting hands. "She heals, too," the red-haired woman said.

"So I see." My words were dry as hot, desert sand. "Who did the shooting?" I had an idea, but waited to see if she knew as well.

"We think it's vampire Baikov," she shrugged as we continued to watch werewolves being healed. "I've sniffed his evil before, you know. I'm Lissa," she turned and offered me a hand. "A vampire, in case you haven't guessed, and I'm also a certified member of the Sacramento Pack."

I blinked as I took her hand. I may have cursed softly in Russian under my breath. "I think something similar all the time," she said to my untranslated *holy shit*. "The van got away," she added, although I'd already guessed it.

"You may as well stay here with us—if they find out you're tailing them, you'll need more than a cache of guns to deal with the blowback," Lissa went on, as if she were discussing the weather. "Besides, I believe Winkler would like to hear all this directly from someone who actually knows who *they* are."

"I will have to stay out of sight—I cannot be compromised," I replied.

"I think we can handle that. Zaria can make you look any way you want, to stay under their radar."

"Is that her name? Zaria?"

"For now," Lissa shrugged. "She's undercover, just as I am."

"Strange." I shook my head. Before tonight, I never dreamed I'd be traveling inside a witch's invisibility, or see someone kill a vampire so easily.

I'd never known that vampires could become mist, either. "Can all vampires turn to mist?" I asked.

"No. Only a handful can, and they're so special, they're usually kept under wraps and hidden except in special circumstances. There will be an attempt at retaliation for this one's death; you can count on it."

"Did you know this one?"

"No. Zaria sent images and his scent before doing away with him; I had no idea he existed before tonight."

"She sent you his scent?"

"You watched her separate particles, and you're asking about that?"

"I see your point," I admitted. "If General Baikov learns his weapon has been neutralized, he will certainly retaliate."

"So you know the human version, huh?" she asked.

"Oh, yes. We have a mutual loathing for one another. He wants Ukraine back, for numerous reasons. I dislike his possessiveness toward my people."

"I understand completely," she agreed. "Look, I think Zaria's done."

She was; the last werewolf patient rose and limped toward the others, disappearing among their numbers.

"You can sleep out here if you want," Zaria indicated the huge yard surrounding the house, "Or you can sleep inside where it's warmer and there's plenty of food and water. You're not in danger, here—not tonight. We'll see that you get home tomorrow if that's your choice. For now, consider yourselves guests of the Dallas Packmaster. Good choice," Zaria's voice held approval as the lead werewolf headed for the open front door.

"I'll go grab blankets and water bowls," Lissa said. "Want to help?"

"Of course," I tossed out a hand in a helpless gesture. "Why would I not want to feed werewolves on such a night?" I didn't keep my native accent from escaping, either—these two women already knew who and what I was.

～

Winkler

"What the fuck happened here?" I demanded as Trajan and I walked into the lower level of the house at five that morning. Yes, we were naked and covered in deer blood, but we usually came home that way.

Half the lower level looked as if a hurricane had blasted through, leaving broken lamps, crushed furniture and shredded drapes in its wake.

"A misting vampire happened," Zaria didn't even bother noticing our nudity. She held a spatula in one hand while the other was covered by an oven mitt. "Don't worry, I got rid of him. I just haven't had time to clean up the mess he left behind. I'll handle that after breakfast."

"Where's Lissa?" I demanded.

"Well, probably seeing to the Austin Pack over at her house," Zaria replied with a nod. "A few got killed before she could mist them away from the shooters."

"Shooters?"

"Somebody attacked the Austin Pack last night, probably to show you what you're dealing with," Zaria shrugged. "Look, if you want pancakes and every kind of breakfast meat you can imagine, then get yourselves and the rest of your pack cleaned up and presentable to eat. Then you can pass out while I remove the debris."

"It's okay to bring Kellee in," Trajan yelled over his shoulder.

Members of my pack filed in, with Kellee at the center, protected by a tight knot of trusted werewolves. "Is there food?" Kellee whined.

"Fuck," I growled. "Feed her first," I said. "The rest of us will be right back."

"Who are you?" I heard Kellee demand of Zaria.

"I am Zaria," I heard the reply. "Sit down, shut up and eat while I find you something to wear."

*

Ilya

"Your bags and belongings are in your bedroom," Lissa led me to a door on the third floor. "Your bedroom will be shielded while you sleep, so don't worry about that for now."

"I'll be able to get out?"

"Of course. Nobody will be able to get in if they mean you harm, that's all. Come nightfall, Winkler will be over here, asking questions. You can help answer them. Get some rest if you can."

After closing the door behind me, I found my bags on the bed and my cache of weapons atop a wide dresser nearby. If I needed more, perhaps my new contacts could get them for me.

I considered a crossbow wouldn't be a bad idea—if it were loaded with wooden darts to stop a vampire.

Bullets would do for werewolves; I'd learned how effective they were the night before.

My bedroom had an en-suite bath, so I dragged my shirt off and headed in that direction. A hot shower sounded good before my attempt to fall asleep.

~

Lissa

"I had to be creative," I said as werewolves picked through a pile of sweat pants and T-shirts. They were human-looking now, and ready to put on clothing after visiting the showers in the available bathrooms throughout the house.

Debra, the lone female, wore something I'd swiped from Zaria's closet—she was taller than I and was the closest fit to our lady guest.

"I can't thank you enough," Debra sighed over an empty breakfast plate. Zaria had cooked enough for an army, and sent half of it to my house with power to feed the Austin Pack.

"I'm glad I got there when I did," I told her. "I don't know who you lost, but I'm sorry I didn't get there for them, too."

"Hmmph. Mick didn't need to be in charge anyway," she said, turning her head to gaze out the kitchen window. "Dawn is coming soon," she remarked.

"I know," I said. "I'll have to go to bed. If you need anything and

Winkler hasn't sent somebody over after breakfast, then contact Zaria at Winkler's house. She'll do what she can."

"You're the one who saved us," a young werewolf walked in, combing fingers through drying hair.

"This is Gabe," Debra introduced him. "He got hit last night, but your friend Zaria saved him."

"Thank goodness," I reached out to take his offered hand. "I was worried about all of you."

"You the one belonging to the Sacramento Pack?"

"Yeah. That's me. I'm here undercover, so don't let that out, okay?"

"Secret's safe with us," Debra said. "And it will always be safe with us."

My cell phone rang, then, curtailing further conversation. It was Winkler. "You have ten minutes before I have to go to bed," I told him.

"Be there in one," he replied before cutting off the contact.

"Winkler is on the way," I told Gabe and Debra. "Tell him what you know of the attack. We'll find these bastards if it's the last thing I do."

Winkler arrived in less than a minute; he'd ran the whole way, looked like. "You look tired," he announced first thing.

"We've had a busy night," I frowned at him.

"I get that. Debra, Gabe, how are you?" He turned to my guests.

"I'll let you talk—I need a shower before getting in bed." I patted Winkler's back before heading toward the stairs and my second-floor bedroom.

~

Winkler

"We were about to run down two deer," Gabe explained. "They ran into a wooded area, and that's when the bullets started flying. Mick went down immediately; as did a couple of others. Some of us were hit, too, but still trying to run out of that trap. That's when Lissa came and lifted us away. I can't recall too much after that—Zaria says they almost got me in the heart with one of the bullets. The others lodged in my shoulder and hip."

"How many did you lose?" I asked.

"Seven," Debra answered. "Without Lissa's help, it would have been a lot worse. We had shooters on three sides in those woods, if I heard correctly. We can go back—we'll have to, anyway, to recover bodies."

"If they left them there," I huffed.

"You think they'd take them?" Gabe sounded confused.

"Anything's possible, kid," I said. "Word is we're dealing with Russian vamps and weres, so we have no idea what they might be up to."

"You're kidding?" Debra sounded shocked.

"Not kidding. Have that information on good authority," I said. "I figure we'll get confirmation on it later. I'm warning you all now; if you go back to Austin, keep your wits about you."

"I think I'll go to my brother's right after the funeral," Debra sighed. "This—I didn't sign up for any of this."

"I know," I reached over and patted her hand. "You deserve better than this, and I mean that. If you want, I can arrange for somebody to drive you and your things to Abilene."

"I think I'd like that," she admitted. "I just hate leaving the younger ones here to fend for themselves."

"Deb, we'll be okay," Gabe attempted to reassure her. "Besides, Mr. Winkler, here, may need our help tracking those bastards. Had to be vamps or humans, don't you think? Wolves would be running into the pack and taking us on that way. These were shooting at us and hitting us, too. Sounded like AK-47s to me."

"The choice of werewolf assassins everywhere," I growled. "We'll go looking at the site after Lissa wakes tonight," I said. "Why don't all of you get comfortable and rest through the day? We'll get you wherever you want to go tonight."

"I like that idea," Debra agreed.

"I'll have food sent over for lunch and dinner," I said. "Call if you need anything else."

"Thank you, Mr. Winkler," Gabe said.

"You're more than welcome, kid."

~

Zaria

"How the hell did you get Kellee to sit there and be polite?" Trajan whispered after Kellee left the table and wandered toward her bedroom to sleep.

"I look like everybody's grandmother," I said. "You don't disobey Grandma, or you don't get any treats."

"Well, hell, I'd have dressed up like a grandma if it would have that effect," he drawled.

"Come on, now. She can smell testosterone from a quarter-mile away. Besides, aren't there stories about wolves dressing up like grandmothers?"

"Those are fairy tales. Wolves almost never dress up like grandmothers to lure in little girls."

"Of course not." My fists were firmly planted on my hips as I pretended to glare at Trajan. He laughed.

Winkler's boots scuffed across the kitchen tile as he walked in. "Austin Pack lost seven last night. Mick was one of them," he said, sliding onto a barstool next to Trajan. "Any bacon left?"

"Yeah. I saved some for you," I turned to grab the leftover bacon from the warming oven. "Want anything else?"

"Nah. I just need something to chew on while I consider what to say to Weldon when I call."

"He won't be happy," Trajan sighed. "Damn, I'm tired."

"*He* won't be happy? I'm not happy," Winkler tapped his chest. "I don't think anybody involved in that mess is happy, either. Mick would be pissed, except he's dead."

"Look, if you two are gonna trade complaints, I'm gonna fix your house and then go grab some sleep," I said. "You ought to consider the same."

"Will we be safe?" Winkler demanded.

"I have a shield around both houses. You're good for now."

"I think I'd like to hear how you do that, but it can wait," Trajan yawned wide enough to crack his jaw.

"Awesome. You know where to find me and all that shit," I said, stalking toward the destroyed portion of the house.

~

Lissa

"My love?"

"Huh?" I had to swim through several layers of deep sleep to reach the surface, believing through half of it or more that Reemagar's voice was only a dream.

"I bent time. You've slept for eleven hours. Time to wake, my love, and face the night in Dallas."

"Oh, great," I slapped a hand over my face. "You could have saved that for later—after three cups of coffee, maybe."

"I believe Zaria said something similar to Valegar, when he woke her to cook lunch," Reemagar kissed my forehead. I still hadn't opened my eyes, but it was him—I could smell the sunlight on his skin. "Wake now, you are needed."

"Larentii, stating the obvious since time began," I mumbled.

"We are quite handy in that way," he agreed, a smile in his voice.

"Stop grinning," I cracked an eye open to check.

"My Lissa, always unwilling to wake."

"Not unwilling—unless it's somebody else waking me. I do fine on my own, you know."

"Of course you do."

"Okay, now you're just patronizing me."

"We excel in it."

"Right. How is she—Zaria?"

"Valegar bent time for twelve hours with her. She was rested, albeit somewhat grumpy when she was wakened."

"I can't blame her a bit. Not after the night we had."

"I understand."

"See previous, patronizing comment."

"Come now, your wolf is pacing, waiting for sundown in Dallas. I must get you back."

"Where am I?" I came fully awake, then, to find myself in Reemagar's arms on the Larentii homeworld, while he stood naked in sunlight, soaking it up like a sponge. Since I was naked, too, I considered having words with this particular Larentii mate.

"That will have to wait, my love. We go back now."

I felt like a ruffled hen when I dropped onto the floor in my suite, while Reemagar disappeared before I could thank him or hurl insults. Frankly, the jury was still out on which one of those wanted to come out of my mouth first.

Hastily gathering clothes from the closet, I got dressed as the sun slipped below the horizon, and I misted downstairs the moment I heard Winkler shout my name.

CHAPTER 4

$\mathcal{I}$lya

Zaria had come back to Lissa's house to cook for the Austin Pack, so I volunteered to help. I love to cook, and four hands are better than two when you cook for twenty or more.

"I can't believe you put this together so fast," the young werewolf complimented us as we placed rare steaks on plates and set them out for waiting guests.

"It took a fast trip to the grocery store," Zaria shrugged and pulled another sizzling steak off the grill. Huge bowls of salad lined one side of kitchen counters, along with baked potatoes and asparagus. Surprisingly, the werewolves were eating all of it—with much butter and sour cream on the potatoes.

William Winkler walked into the kitchen with Lissa beside him. I was grateful—he'd been shouting her name only minutes before.

"Want one?" I asked the Dallas Packmaster, offering a steak fresh from the grill.

"You need to ask?" He took the plate and helped himself to a potato and salad. "Sit down when you're done and we'll talk." He pulled a barstool toward the breakfast bar.

"I think we're done, now," Zaria turned off the grill, allowing the vent to continue pulling hot air away from the kitchen.

"Good. Pull up a chair and talk to me."

Lissa had already found an empty barstool; I found two more so Zaria and I could sit. Zaria was having a potato, salad and asparagus, while I had the last steak cooked.

"This is really good," Winkler stuffed steak into his mouth.

"It's the marinade," I shrugged. "I learned how to make it from the chef at Frederica's in New York."

"You're kidding." Winkler stopped chewing for a moment.

"No. I enjoy cooking. It makes me happy."

"Hell, even I have to grease palms to get into Frederica's," Winkler grumbled.

"You don't speak the chef's native language. I do," I grinned. I figured it was difficult enough to one-up the Dallas Packmaster.

"Well, that explains it," Lissa grinned at Winkler. "Honey, you just need to speak Czech, that's all."

"I'll get on that immediately," Winkler grinned back at her.

I knew it then; he was in love with this vampire. She loved him, too, but there was some sort of barrier between them. I imagined it had to do with Winkler's pregnant wife. I knew little of werewolf politics, and perhaps this wasn't the best time to ask impertinent questions.

"Do we have plans to go to Austin?" Zaria asked.

"We do. I'm sending Debra to her brother's after the funeral, so she'll be out of danger, I hope. The others want to help us investigate. We'll see how that goes," Winkler shook his head. "We'll be picking up bodies, too, if they left them behind."

"You worry that they didn't?" I asked.

"I worry about a lot of things."

"Yes. I can see that you do."

"Tell me about the Russian vampire."

"Baikov is the one I'm familiar with. I don't know names of others, although there are many, if my sources are correct."

"That's the one you met?" Winkler turned to Lissa.

"Ivan Baikov, yes," Lissa nodded.

"Ah. A first name. I didn't know that, only the last," I confessed. "His human descendant, the General, is called Kornel by his friends—or those he identifies as friends."

"That's a Czech name, isn't it?" Zaria asked.

"I'm surprised you know that, but it is. Now you know where I get some of my information—the chef at Frederica's hears from his family, and they hear about Baikov's family. Good to know the right people, eh?"

"I'd say so," Lissa breathed.

"He is dirty, that one. I don't know which Baikov I'd rather face in a fight—because both are bad as they come, I believe."

"Tell me about the wolves and vamps working for the Kremlin," Winkler changed the subject.

"Ah. They are known in the secret circle as *Klyki*—fangs," I explained. "Hardly anyone outside the Kremlin knows of their existence, as you can imagine. They are sent on special assignments, when a normal person would have difficulty in persuading, capturing or killing a target. You, they wish to persuade," I told Winkler. "Otherwise, they'd have attacked your pack last night. They're showing you what can happen, without getting too close to your heart, you understand."

"So they want something."

"Yes. Something you have, or perhaps your cooperation. We should find out soon enough."

"Hmmph," Zaria sniffed.

"You know what it is?" I turned to her.

"I know what it is."

"I suspect the same, more than likely," I told her.

"What do they want?" Winkler frowned at both of us.

"They want your recognition software," I said. "Yes, we have known for more than a year where it came from. Do not ask how we came by the information—I do not know, and that knowledge puts many at risk on both sides. Just know that they now want it, and they want you to show them how to use it, so they can change and improve. Do not take this as an insult," I held up a hand to quell Winkler's protest.

"And their attack against the Austin Pack means they also know what you are," Lissa tapped Winkler's arm to pull his attention and his snarl away from me.

"Yes. They have learned this, or their werewolves have informed them. You are not unknown to them, yes?"

"Fuck." Winkler pushed his chair back, the legs scraping the tiled floor with an irritating rasp.

"Have you talked to Weldon, yet?" Lissa caught Winkler's arm as he stepped away from us.

"I did, but I'll have to call him back."

"Who is Weldon?" I turned to Zaria.

"Grand Master of all werewolves," Zaria said softly. "He'll have to be informed that there are Russian werewolves working against other werewolves."

"Ah."

"For now, we have no names to give him, so he can investigate and level charges," Winkler pulled his chair back and sat again.

"Perhaps this is why I haven't heard names, either," I said. "Those must be kept quite secret for this reason."

"Wlodek would send Enforcers, if he knew what Baikov was up to. Probably a good thing he doesn't know," Lissa said.

"Wlodek?"

"Head of the Vampire Council," Zaria said.

I turned and leveled a curious gaze at her. "Until now, I'd say a witch with your talents was an impossibility."

"You haven't seen anything, yet," Lissa sniffed.

"Come on, let's see if everybody's done eating," Winkler rose again. "We need to get on the road. Plane's fixed, but I can't carry that many. We'll have to convoy."

~

Lissa

Zaria, still looking like a grandmother in her sixties, with light-brown-going-gray hair and a decent figure, climbed into the back seat of Winkler's lead SUV. She moved to take the middle seat while I scooted in beside her and shut the door. Ilya took the window seat on Zaria's other side; he was in his late fifties at least, but I didn't doubt for a moment he could hold his own in a fight.

As long as the fight was with another human.

How are you holding up? I sent to Zaria while looking out the window. Trajan drove; I watched the walls around Winkler's house recede behind us as we drove down a side street that would eventually take us to I-35.

He won't meet the other me in this lifetime—I'm the only survivor of that dead timeline, she returned. *This isn't going to be easy.*

I'm having a hard time keeping my hands off Winkler, I confessed. *He's the same—and not the same.*

I feel that way, too. Feeling familiar, and having to take steps back from behaving that way.

Does your Ilya know you're here now?

I didn't talk to him about it, but there's always the possibility that new memories will come unexpectedly.

I hope it doesn't change anything.

That makes two of us. By the way, we're being followed, she said. *Dalroy and Rhett are three cars behind our last vehicle. Two more vampires— unfriendly ones—are behind them.*

Fuck.

"Mr. Winkler," Zaria said aloud.

"Zaria?" Winkler turned in his seat to see what she wanted.

"We are being followed. We can allow them to keep following, or I can lay an illusion, making them think that other vehicles are yours while we become invisible—for fifteen minutes. They'll lose us and then wonder how it happened."

"Do it." Winkler's eyes turned silver in the light of a passing car's headlights—it was too soon after a full moon and the wolf was more present than usual.

"We are now invisible to all," Zaria announced after glowing for a moment. "Tell the others to follow your lead; I'll make sure a path opens for all of us."

Winkler was on his phone immediately, passing a message to seven vans behind us. Trajan took advantage of the invisibility and hit the gas, bumping the speedometer at eighty-seven.

Like a train, we passed unmolested through Fort Worth, which was a minor miracle. Traffic, no matter if you took I-35E or I-35W through Dallas or Fort Worth, was heavy and challenging.

Ten minutes past Fort Worth, Zaria announced that we were visible again. Our speed slowed, vehicles somewhere behind us looked normal again and four vampires were likely wondering what the hell happened.

"That's a tidy trick," Ilya spoke for the first time, glancing behind us to see the other vans, all with identical sets of headlights, following us.

I didn't tell him that Zaria had employed Larentii power to do it. Most of the people in the car had no idea what a Larentii was, and were still skeptical about witches.

Whatever it takes to get us through this, Zaria's mindspeech sounded grim.

Dalroy and Rhett may be in danger, I replied.

They were—from the other two. What I did kept them from being shot at on the road. They've already pulled over to discuss our disappearance. They know where we're headed, so they'll probably decide to make their way to Austin anyway. The same goes for the other two. I'll let you decide what to do with them when they show up.

"Winkler," I said. "When we reach Austin, send the other vans to a separate location. Zaria will make them invisible when they leave the convoy. We'll proceed to the crime scene. We may have guests before our investigation is over."

"I would welcome them," Ilya patted the shoulder holster under his jacket. I had no doubt that there were rifles in the back of the van, too.

"Ilya," I leaned around Zaria to look at him. I could see him clearly in the darkness, while he squinted to bring me into focus.

"What is it?" he asked.

"Our guests won't be human. If you shoot, make it fast, all right?"

"I'll make it fast, then get out of your way."

"Good." Zaria leaned her head back and shut her eyes for a moment. "Just don't get shot or clawed to death," she added.

∾

Kent, England

Charles

"Honored One?" Wlodek sat behind his desk, frowning at the latest expenses incurred by Enforcers who were hunting Xenides.

"Charles?" Wlodek lifted his dark eyes to mine, a question glinting in their depths.

"I just heard from Dalroy. He and Rhett say that they were following Winkler's convoy out of Dallas, when two other vampires you have listed as deceased pulled out of a side road ahead of them. They were also following Winkler. Dalroy says they managed to place their vehicle in between the convoy and the rogues, but somehow thinks he and Rhett were recognized."

"What about the convoy? Has anything happened?"

It was a good question, and one I'd asked myself. "Dalroy is somewhat confused on this part; he and Rhett swear that the convoy disappeared after they left Fort Worth city limits, and no trace of them can be found anywhere. He is confident that they are returning what's left of the Austin Pack to Austin after they were attacked during the full moon by snipers. Seven were killed in that attack, and there's been no word how the others escaped and ended up in Dallas."

"Snipers?"

"Dalroy suspects other rogues, Honored One. He is concerned that he and Rhett may not be enough to handle this."

"I have no others to send, Enforcers or Assassins," Wlodek said after going silent for several moments.

"I can go. You know I can be quite discreet."

"How will I get all this done?" Wlodek indicated the papers strewn across his desk.

"Honored One, I suggest that if these troubles aren't dealt with,

45

paperwork will be the least of our worries. Besides, Rolfe is adept at filing and computers; he merely doesn't talk about it."

"He can fill in if necessary?"

"Of course."

"Then you have my permission to go to Texas. See that you return, young Charles."

"I will return, I promise."

"Good. Order the jet to take you tomorrow. If you leave now, you can spend the day with your sire, Flavio, and then board the jet shortly after night falls tomorrow."

"It will be done as you say."

"I will let Flavio know you are coming," Wlodek lifted his cell to make the call.

"That won't be necessary." My voice had deepened, and none, including Wlodek, could refuse my compulsion when I employed it against them like this. "Flavio will not be involved; I will make my own way there."

"Yes." Wlodek's eyes unfocused for a moment, before clearing as I strode out of his study.

～

Austin, Texas

Lissa

"How much time do you think we have before they get here?" I asked Zaria.

"They're forty and fifty miles away, respectively, with the rogues in the lead."

"That's not good."

She and I were examining the ground where two vampire snipers had set up, their rifles no doubt fixed with night scopes for shooting running werewolves. They'd likely set up downwind, too, so they wouldn't be scented before getting their first shots off.

"Are you seeing anything?" Ilya walked up, then. Yes, the moon shone brightly overhead, but we were beneath trees, which had hidden vampire snipers.

"I'm smelling plenty," I told him. "This was a sniper's nest for two vampires. I figure there's at least one more, maybe two, from the reports we've gotten."

"Any evidence left behind?"

"No bodies, and that bothers me," Zaria said. "If there was a spark of life, or anything else left of those werewolves at all, then that can be used against us."

"Blackmail," Ilya nodded.

"Among other things," Zaria said, her words chilling.

I thought you got rid of all that stuff before, I sent to her, meaning the drug.

I did—all that I could find or knew about. That doesn't mean that more wasn't hidden behind Sirenali bones, somewhere—you know Liron is still active in the here and now.

"Fucking hell." I tossed out a hand and started walking toward the other side of the wooded area, where Winkler and Trajan were sniffing around. Did Bree know all this when she sent me right into the middle of it?

She probably did. I was grateful Zaria decided to help; if she hadn't come, I'd be hard-pressed to handle everything myself. That didn't include finding a hidden cache of the Lyristolyi drug surrounded by Sirenali bones—an impossible thing unless we could force the information out of someone who knew about it.

Maybe Ivan Baikov knew. I made a mental note to track him down ASAP.

"Find anything?" I asked when I reached Winkler's side.

"Two nests—one straight ahead, the other opposite to the one you found," Winkler rumbled, anger in his voice. "I'm surprised they didn't kill more than seven."

"Two snipers in each nest?"

"Three in the one straight ahead," Trajan said. "Although I can't say for sure whether all of them handled guns."

"True. Let me go sniff around to see whether any of them were Baikov. He's kinda on my last nerve right now."

Sure enough, vampire Baikov was one of the three straight ahead —likely calling the shots, no pun intended. Why they'd chosen rifles rather than claws was still up for debate, but we had more werewolf survivors as a result of that decision.

Perhaps that was the point. They'd hoped to gather the wounded, perhaps—for the reasons Zaria worried about. I'd foiled part of that plan, by picking them up and hauling them out of there. I wondered how Baikov explained *that* to his boss.

They'd also discovered that we'd had the survivors of the Austin Pack in Dallas; that's why they were tailing us when we left Winkler's mansion. That meant somebody in the Kremlin knew it, too.

When would they begin their blackmail campaign, and what form would it take? Winkler stood to take more hits before that happened, and I didn't like that in the least.

I heard Winkler's cell phone buzz on silent from where I stood, twenty yards away. His answer was a tersely barked, "What is it?"

I'd misted to his side, only to hear Ace tell him his father's grave had been dug open and vandalized, along with the bones beneath it.

～

Zaria

"What just happened?" Ilya asked when Winkler lifted his face toward the moon and howled, even in human form.

"Nothing good," I told him. "And we're about to have company. Get your gun out, shooter-boy. We need all hands on deck."

"You're mixing ground troops with naval ships?"

"Semantics," I snapped before flinging an invisibility shield around all of us. The rogue vamps had arrived, and they were barreling down on us while Winkler shared his grief with the sky.

～

Lissa

Baikov isn't here, I informed Zaria while misting outside the shield she'd placed. The four rogue vamps were confused—for a second time in four hours, unless I missed my guess. Yes, our van was still parked half a mile away—they'd probably stopped there first.

Now, with claws and fangs out, their eyes red and glinting in the moonlight, they searched for their quarry—who'd disappeared from sight, sound and scent.

They'd followed our scent up to this point—Zaria left that intact—to further their disorientation, no doubt. The night before, the Austin Pack had disappeared. Tonight, their intended quarry disappeared, too.

We waited, watching as they spread farther out, hoping to regain our scent. *Ilya says he recognizes two of them as former KGB agents, Zaria* sent to me. *He says they were listed as deceased.*

I suppose that's true—up to a point, I agreed. *Dead during the day, at least. Do we need any of them for anything?*

Save the last one for me, Zaria said. *Do whatever you want with the rest.*

Heads coming off now, I sent and went to work.

❧

Ilya

I dropped to my knees in amazement as three vampire heads were lifted off their shoulders in less than two eye blinks.

The fourth vampire began to run, only to be frozen in place when Zaria lifted her hands to stop him.

There he was, caught in mid-stride, one foot barely touching the ground when Zaria approached him, dropping the shield around us.

Lissa reappeared, too, shaking ash from three vampires off her claws before retracting them. If the Kremlin learned of her and Zaria, they would demand that they be killed or turned to their purposes.

Zaria had left one of the former KGB operatives alive—probably by design. His eyes were the only thing he could move when I stood before him—he recognized me just as I recognized him.

"So, not dead after all," I spoke in Russian. "That will be remedied shortly."

"What are you going to do?" Lissa asked Zaria.

"I'm going to freeze him in a block of ice," she shrugged, as if it were something she might do every day. "Then you're going to cut through the ice surrounding his neck, and I'll send both pieces where they'll do the most good."

"Where might that be?" I turned to Zaria.

"I think General Baikov needs to cool down," she said.

Lissa stifled a snicker, while Trajan didn't hold back a laugh. Winkler, still upset over the news he'd gotten, stood by, waiting for the two women to get on with their plan. I had an idea we would be visiting a gravesite somewhere before the night was over.

Winkler

I should have been astonished when the vampire was encased in a solid block of ice, frozen while still in a running pose. Instead, I was mired in anger and depression. Why would they think I'd cooperate if they tore into my parents' graves? They'd been buried together, since they'd died within a few days of one another.

With disinterest, I watched as Lissa sliced through the top of the ice, leaving the block containing the head barely disturbed and still atop the portion containing the body.

Zaria raised her hands again, and the ice and the vampire it contained disappeared. I hoped Baikov was sleeping when it dropped onto his bed beside him. He deserved if after stooping to grave desecration.

"Dalroy and Rhett are coming," Lissa hissed at Zaria. "What do you want to do?"

"Leave the ash—take the van," Zaria said, before transporting us, van included, to the gate of the Wilburn Ranch, where my parents were buried.

"Call and tell them you're here; we'll drive in like we're civilized and all," Lissa patted my back.

"What the hell just happened?" I demanded.

"Zaria transported you. It's one of her tricks," Lissa said.

"Fuck me," I growled and hauled out my cell phone.

Austin, Texas

Charles

"I have no idea what happened here," I heard Dalroy tell Rhett. Both had claws and fangs out when I walked from between two trees in the wooded area.

"It's me—Charles," I held up a hand. "The Honored One thought you needed help."

"We do. Three vampires died here tonight, and there's no evidence of who's responsible," Rhett shook his head. "Did you do this?"

"I could have," I replied. "Only Wlodek and I will ever know," I added.

"I—see," Dalroy sighed. They'd ask no more questions about it, assuming I'd either accomplished this feat or witnessed it. "What now?" He lifted an eyebrow as his eyes met mine.

"We'll be tracking the other vampires and werewolves the Russians have sent against Winkler," I told him. "And providing assistance to those who are already here to help."

"Would that explain some of the ah, unusual things?" Rhett asked.

"Perhaps. Tomorrow evening, we'll arrive at Winkler's home and discuss plans. This—all of this, mind you, is known only to Wlodek and me, so it is as secret a mission as we can keep it."

"I understand. This information will go no further."

"Good. Take me to the nearest safe house, and we'll consider swapping rental vehicles before the night's out. The enemy likely knows what you are currently driving and will target it."

Wilburn Ranch, outside Denton, Texas

Lissa

"This is a mess," I closed my eyes in disgust. Bones, bits of fur and a few other grisly things were strewn across the site. They couldn't have done anything more upsetting if they'd tried.

The scent of vampire was all over this, and Ivan Baikov's was one of them. I should have stomped his feet when I danced with him at the Annual Meeting, asshole that he was.

"How many?" Winkler demanded. He smelled vampire, just as I did, but more than three or four and the scents were more difficult for him to sort. He wasn't in the mood to sort them, either; not when I could give him the facts much faster.

"Seven. Who knows how many participated or how many watched?" I said. "Although I imagine Baikov wouldn't want to dirty his claws, so he probably supervised, just as he did in Austin."

"This all comes back to him, doesn't it?" Winkler turned to Ilya.

"More than likely." He spread his hands, letting Winkler know that he didn't like what they'd done any more than the rest of us.

"I want to know what was taken, if anything," Winkler snapped.

"You can wait for tomorrow and your werewolf forensics team, or you can let me scry it," Zaria suggested softly.

"Do it." Winkler flung out a hand and turned his back on the scene before striding away.

"What do you need?" Trajan asked Zaria.

"I need to put all of this back together, then see what we're missing," she replied.

"She can do that?" He turned to me.

"Yeah. I've seen it done before, actually." I had, only I'd seen Erland do it, instead of Zaria. Zaria's method would probably be more elegant than Erland's, even, but either way, it would get done.

~

Ilya

She looked to be a few years older than I, with hair going gray. Her movement belied her age, however, as she moved her hands gracefully, commanding each bit of fur, bone and sinew together, exactly as it should be.

Trajan, the tall werewolf, watched with just as much fascination as I, while a werewolf and a human body formed beneath the moon that night. By the time Zaria was done, we understood what was missing—ribs, from the male werewolf. Winkler's father didn't have the proper number of ribs. They'd shredded the rest of him and his lady wife, who'd died in human form, to hide their deed as long as they could.

Except we knew, and much faster than they could imagine we would.

"Does he want to see them before I lay them to rest again?" Zaria pointed her question at Trajan.

"I'll ask," he said and loped away.

Winkler was back in less than five minutes. At least everything looked better than it did when he left. "Should we say something, boss?" Trajan asked softly.

Winkler couldn't answer—he was choking on emotion. I understood why; his father forced him to challenge because he'd grown too old to hold the pack, and knew a challenger would come soon. He gave the pack to his son, by throwing the fight and forfeiting his life.

"The blessings of light and love follow you into your next life," Zaria lifted her hand while golden sparks of light fell upon the bodies. "May you find those you've left behind again, and hold joy in your hearts upon that meeting."

With that, the bodies were lowered into their graves once more, while grass, flowers and the sweet scent of roses washed across the earth-filled spaces.

Winkler lifted his head and howled for the second time that night.

CHAPTER 5

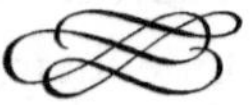

*D*allas, Texas
    Ivan Baikov

"What do you mean, he woke next to a dead vampire? Vampires turn to ash when they die."

"The ah, report is that the vampire was frozen in a block of ice—actually, two blocks of ice—the head was in a separate block."

"That is not possible. They become ash quickly. Too quickly to be frozen after death. If he were frozen before death, he could break out of the ice easily. Cold means little to us. This tale is absurd."

"I will have him speak to you himself regarding this matter, then."

"Tell my nephew to call me himself, next time. I dislike speaking to his subordinates."

"You have made that statement before, and I apologize for following his orders this time."

"Hmmph. See that he calls me. I wish to hear this story myself. The way you tell it, it is preposterous."

"He ah, says there was a note with the body."

"Then I await his call."

"As you say, sir."

"Hmmph." I punched the button to end the call, sick as I was of looking at the imp's pasty face on my phone screen. Kornel would explain this mess to me personally, and apologize for telling the imp to call me to begin with.

At that point, an image came through, causing my cell phone to beep. I opened the attachment to see it better. The note was written in Russian.

Greetings, General, it began. *We would like very much for you to halt your pursuit of William Winkler and any others connected to him. We've returned this vampire to you; the other four we've caught are now ash, including the mister. Continue at your own risk—you have been warned.*

Zaria.

Zaria? I knew of none by that name. "Hmmph," I said again and shut off my phone. A woman was responsible for my mister's death? Well. We would find this Zaria, and teach her a lesson she would not forget—until her death came at our hands.

∾

Lissa

"Damn, I'm tired," I said, while pouring a cup of coffee and adding cream.

"Here," Zaria held out a bottle of honey.

"Thanks." I dumped a generous dollop of honey into my cup and stirred before sipping. Sundown was almost on us, Zaria had been cooking for werewolves most of the day and looked exhausted to me. She'd left dinner for them in warming pans, which the housekeeper promised to clean up afterward.

"Bend time and get some sleep," I suggested. "While I wake up from a bad nap."

"All right—I'll be back in an hour." I watched her disappear, wondering where she'd go so she'd feel safe. After seeing the grave opened and body parts strewn everywhere the night before, my sleep had been filled with all sorts of bad dreams—dreams of being up against more than we thought we were.

And, as my dreams had a habit of being true or mostly so, I was worried. I thought this would be a walk in the park. Things were sliding sideways, however, and Winkler was at the center of the maelstrom.

Why did they take his father's rib bones? Three were missing. Why? The same question had haunted my sleep, too, and still there was no glimmer of an answer.

I hoped Zaria was able to rest; we needed to discuss all these events when she came back, and she needed a clear head to do it properly.

As did I. Taking a sip of my coffee, I waited for its magical waking properties to manifest.

"The boss is irritable, with a capital I," Trajan said softly when he walked into the house an hour later. "Where are Zaria and Ilya?"

"Ilya is upstairs in the shower. Zaria is still asleep, I hope. Not only was she out all night, but she cooked all day for your bunch, too. I hope Winkler remembers that come paycheck time."

"We uh, may have a line on another cook," Trajan cleared his throat. "Boss mentioned the same thing about Zaria—says she's too valuable to us elsewhere, although her cooking is more than fine."

"Thank goodness," I let my shoulders droop in relief. "She needs sleep just like anybody else."

"She won't have to carry that disguise if she stops cooking and stays over here," he added.

"I'd say that's up to her," I said.

"Yeah."

"Lissa?" Winkler called out from the front door. "There are three people out here who want to see you."

"What the fuck?" I slid off my barstool quickly and headed toward the front door.

"Problem," Zaria announced as she ran down the stairs and breezed past me. No, she didn't look like Harriett Majors any longer.

She looked like the dark-haired, bright-blue-eyed Karathian witch, Zaria.

"You know about this?" I followed in her wake, expecting the worst.

"Just now. Come on," she stopped to grab my arm and pull me forward. "Let's go tell dear old Dad how nice it is to see him."

Terrified that I'd find Griffin at the front door, my posture stiffened so much I was marching straight-legged toward waiting doom, only to find Charles, Dalroy and Rhett at the door instead.

Dear old Dad.

Zaria's dad.

Charles.

≈

"We've taken out five vamps, but Baikov isn't one of them," I explained to Dalroy, after he asked the question.

"I should have known you were involved in all this—it explains everything," Rhett grinned. Ever since we'd met in Kansas City that first time, he'd hoped we'd see one another again, somewhere.

"Well, don't get your hopes up too high," I cautioned. "I think this is worse than I imagined at the beginning."

I studied Zaria—she'd not said a word after Charles' arrival. I wondered if arms crossed tightly meant she and Charles were having a mental sparring match, instead. Ilya, whose widened eyes indicated the only surprise he was willing to reveal at Zaria's new appearance, soon settled in to join the conversation.

"We haven't come across the werewolves, either, and I know he has some," Winkler interjected. "We got their scent twice, now, but no sign of them since the full moon. Weldon is flying in tomorrow," Winkler went on. "He doesn't like the looks of this, either, so I sent the jet to pick him up."

"Do you three want to stay here?" I asked Charles. I didn't bother to discuss that the Charles I knew in the past had never indicated he thought I was anywhere else. This one knew where the current me was, and that the future me was here, sitting at the kitchen island two chairs down from his.

"I think it's safer—I worry that the safe houses may have been compromised with this many vamps involved. They can't attack during the day, but the werewolves can."

"Weldon may want to stay here, too, just so he won't have to hear Kellee's tantrums," Winkler sighed. "Will you have enough space?"

"That'll fill all but one bedroom," I said. "We have enough room."

"There's something else," Zaria said.

"What's that?" Winkler turned to her.

"I can cast a spell so Lissa and our other vampire guests can walk in daylight. We don't have to confine our activities to night hours only, if we don't want to. I'll remove the spell the moment this is over," she held up a hand. "I don't want word of this to get out, you understand."

"The wolves will be pissed," Winkler confirmed.

"Then we just won't tell them. Present company excepted," Zaria said.

"Are you sure this will work?"

"I've seen it done," I confirmed. Actually, I'd done it a time or two on Le-Ath Veronis, getting a sire to a comesula on the light half of the planet to perform a turn—after a deadly accident when time was extremely short.

"I'm willing to try it first," Charles grinned.

The schmuck.

"Your eyes will be shielded, too, enough that your brain will believe you're in darkness and your body's urge to shut down won't be such a problem," Zaria went on before approaching Charles first. "I warn you, though, your body clock will fight this all the way down."

Does he actually need it? I sent to Zaria.

He has to separate himself from this body to appear in daylight for now. Breanne will give him her blood later and eliminate that problem.

He can do that? Separate himself?

Yes, although he looks like he does in the future when that happens. His corporeal body—this one—is left behind somewhere, so he can go out during the day. It expends a great deal of power.

Yeah. I knew all about a humanoid body being affected by the amount of power it could actually contain. I used to have to separate my spirit from my body and let it fly free to recharge. Once I was promoted to a higher echelon in the Hierarchy, it was no longer necessary.

Charles, in the here and now, was dealing with the same problem. He knew he'd gather more power eventually, but he'd have to either change his current body or leave it behind to do so. In essence, he'd recreate himself, just as I'd been recreated during my promotion.

I hadn't done it myself; I'd went to sleep the same old Lissa, and awoke the brand-new Lissa, capable of holding myself together while expending massive amounts of power.

When I was new to my earlier power, Ashe had held my body together so I could visibly wield enough of it to make an impact. Without that help, I'd have blasted my own body to atoms with the energy I'd expended on the High Demon world; it was like building a spider web to hold back a speeding train.

That's when I realized something important. Yes, I was one of the Mighty, now; I'd been promoted.

Just as Charles, Breanne and Ashe had likely been promoted—or had promoted themselves—into a higher echelon. Yes, people still called them the Three, or the Mighty, but they never referred to themselves like that.

Not anymore.

Remind me to have a talk with my sister when we go home, I sent to Zaria.

I'll be interested in her answers, Zaria replied. Well, all Zaria had to do was look at me to determine what I was thinking—unless she blocked it. Fortunately, she blocked that sort of thing much of the time.

I didn't want to consider what Zaria might actually be—in the final analysis. She held the entire Metal Library inside herself, and I still didn't fully understand its purpose.

"What's the plan for tonight, then?" Winkler asked.

"I did research before retiring for the day," Charles said. "There has been an uptick in the number of flu-like cases reported by physicians. It stands to reason that Ivan Baikov and his vampires are feeding off the population rather than leaving a blood trail in the form of bagged blood shipments. I had to do some coordination of reported cases, but the usual idea of hitting bars and other places where many gather in one place appears evident."

"Did you narrow it down to which bars?" I asked.

"Six, in different parts of Dallas, two in Fort Worth."

"Does this mean we split up tonight?"

"That makes sense," Charles shrugged. "Nobody goes alone—anywhere. Stay in touch as best you can."

"I'll take Lissa," Winkler raised his hand immediately.

"Rhett and I will go," Dalroy offered. They'd opted out of the daylight spell Zaria offered.

"I will go with Zaria," Charles said. Zaria frowned but didn't say anything.

"I suggest that Charles go with Trajan, while the only human travels with sure protection," Ilya countered.

"Hear that?" I turned to grin at Zaria. "You're sure protection."

"I'll put that on my resume," she laughed.

Charles wasn't happy, but he acknowledged that Ilya was correct—he needed protection against vampires if he came across any. He might get one shot off before a single vampire was on him, and more than one vampire was a definite death sentence.

"Let's split these bars up, then," Winkler said. "Lissa and I can take the two in Fort Worth; the rest of you take two each close together, if you can."

Bar locations were sorted quickly, before we walked out the front door. "Are the shields still up around the houses?" Winkler mumbled as he led me toward a waiting van.

"Yes."

"Good." He rolled his shoulders to remove kinks. He was still upset about the night before, and frankly, I needed to speak with Zaria about his father's bones and what might be done with them.

She had far more experience with the drug than I did. Maybe they were pointing their machinations in that direction, and I didn't like it one bit. Telling Winkler about it, too, could cause more problems than we could deal with.

For now, that shit was on a need-to-know basis, and I hoped Winkler would never need to know.

"It's kinda nice to have just the two of us in the car," Winkler sighed as he shut the driver's side door and started the van.

"Yeah. I feel like I've been on edge for a month, and I've only been here a few days."

"If you were really on your own, without the Council hanging over your head every minute, I'd take you to the beach and we'd relax."

"Sounds great, but that's not in the cards."

"I know. Since Charles is here, does that mean Wlodek knows you escaped?"

"Not in a manner of speaking. Charles keeps some things from Wlodek. I know that, now."

"You sure you can trust him?"

"With my life." I realized I meant it, too.

"What about the other two?"

"They know to obey Charles. If he says not to talk, they won't."

"I always thought Charles was nothing more than a well-organized flunky."

"Well, we all thought that. Turns out, we were wrong."

Really, really, wrong.

~

Charles

Zaria had barely looked at me the whole time we were in Lissa's kitchen. I'd hoped to bring her out with me so we could talk in private, but instead, I was with Trajan, Winkler's werewolf Second-in-Command.

Zaria and Lissa thought I was the current Charles. That body was in sleep stasis elsewhere, while I attempted to help in the here and now. I only changed my appearance to resemble the current Charles, to keep things simple.

Frankly, things were anything but simple, and they had a lust for power—from both rogue gods and men—stamped all over them. Trust Liron and perhaps others to make this sideways grab at power while the Vampire Council was distracted by the threat posed by Xenides.

Had the General in this timeframe been aware of Liron's dealings beneath his radar, he'd have removed that threat and carried out Liron's plans himself. Or, he may have subjugated Liron more than he did and together, they'd have destroyed everything.

It made me grateful that Liron, in his own lust for power at the top, kept his dealings away from the General's prying senses.

The General was adept at scheming, but Liron was even better.

"So, how's the mess with Xenides going?" Trajan asked as he steered our van toward the first of two bars on our list.

"About the same," I replied. "We track him; he eludes us. For him, it's a game with a sick prize at the end of it."

"Glad I'm not in the middle of that, then," Trajan grimaced.

I didn't tell him he was in the middle of something that could turn out to be so much worse.

~

Zaria

While summer days in Dallas are generally rated as hot, hotter or hottest, the nights can be slow to cool down. Pulling the collar of my silk shirt open by another button while the SUV's air conditioner blasted at full speed, I considered things. "Why so quiet?" Ilya asked softly.

"Thinking—about where all the trails lead in this mess," I replied.

"Yes. I think about that, too. I believe things are more complicated than I originally thought."

I almost said *that's what I love about you*, but bit the words back. Instead, I said, "Can you make spaghetti marinara?" It was one of my favorites that he cooked for me in the future.

"Of course. I have a special recipe. Would you like some? I noticed that you don't eat meat."

"That's true—it's why I asked."

"I'll make it for you tomorrow, if we have time."

"Good, because those werewolves are all about their animal protein, meaning I can't eat everything they do."

He laughed, and that was a good sound. I was surprised at how well he knew the Dallas area, but didn't ask. If I lowered my blocking shield to read him I'd learn why, and didn't want to pry into other parts of his life. He could tell me those things in his own time, if he wanted me to know.

The sad truth was I loved him, no matter where or when or how we were, and that would always be. It didn't matter that he was in his late fifties, with a bit of gray in dark-brown hair. The cynical glint still shone in the depths of dark-blue eyes in this existence, and the wry smile would follow him in any guise.

"Do you ever get the feeling that you've known someone you just met forever?" Ilya asked out of the blue.

"Once," I agreed. "It was like there was no learning curve—that anything we did was exactly what the other wanted—for the most part." I had memories of Krav Maga lessons that I hadn't wanted, but somebody else told him to teach me, so there was that.

"Who was it?" he asked.

I was so tempted to tell him. "I'll tell you someday. How's that?"

"Someday means you intend to stay in contact. That suits me."

"Sounds like a deal, as long as you promise not to teach me Krav Maga."

"You don't want to learn?"

"I have no aspirations in that area. In fact, it was a New Year's resolution, once—never to learn. Frankly, people have attempted to teach me how to physically protect myself, with mixed and rather disappointing results for them, of course."

"You rely on your ability to keep you safe?"

"Generally speaking, yes."

"Good enough, as long as it continues to keep you safe."

"So far, so good. Besides, I know a few defensive moves—I learned those during all those previously-mentioned failed attempts at hand-to-hand."

A familiar, wry smile curved his lips in the dim light of the van's interior. "At least you're not completely helpless," he teased.

"Those are fighting words, Mister. If you weren't a fellow coffee-lover and spaghetti marinara maker, I'd turn you into a gecko. Don't ever trade insults with a witch, dude, unless you want to shave scales instead of skin."

His shoulders began to shake—he struggled to hold the laughter back. It failed to work, and he guffawed.

"Here we are," he turned into the parking lot of the first bar, still chuckling. I went still.

"Hand on your gun," I whispered. "They're coming."

~

Lissa

It was a trap. They knew we'd look into the matter, and they were content to wait for us to arrive.

Except they didn't expect Winkler to have anyone except Trajan at his side. The moment we'd stepped out of the van, they attacked. I had shields up or Winkler would have gone down quickly.

We have three trying to get past my shields, Zaria reported in mindspeech, while I blinked at the four attempting to get past my own. Winkler stepped backward until his shoulder bumped mine before giving all four whirling, striking vampires the finger—with both hands.

I have Dalroy and Rhett en route to your location, Charles informed me. *Trajan and I are about to deal with three who are waiting for us. They won't expect an attack from the outside where you are, so keep your shields up until they're dead. They want Winkler more than anything, I believe, and they've just upped their game to achieve that end.*

No shit, Sherlock, I replied, my sending dry.

"At least Weldon isn't here to see this," Winkler shook his head as four vampires moved so swiftly around my shield it looked like an attack of whirling, black-leather trench coats. The clicking noises of their claws against the hardness of my shield was becoming annoying, however, just before they all became winking sparks and floated away on the warm, night air.

Zaria and Ilya had arrived before Dalroy and Rhett.

~

Charles

Trajan and I parked three blocks away and went in quietly, while I shielded us against sight and sound.

We found our three vampires waiting in the shadows near the back door of the bar, behind a dumpster, which covered their scent.

It was a good move and worthy of a shrewd opponent, but I'd seen this tactic before. I'd read too many Enforcer and Assassin reports to be surprised by any of it.

Let me take the two on the right, I sent to Trajan's werewolf, who blinked under the moonlight at my ability to send mindspeech to anyone, let alone a wolf. I'd lay compulsion when this was over, and nobody would recall a thing about it.

With a brief dip of his chin to show his agreement, we crept forward. I let Trajan leap on his target first before flashing in and decapitating the other two, who'd been taken completely by surprise.

It took a little longer for Trajan to dispatch his vampire, but I left him to it, and he had two, inch-deep claw marks across his ribs to show for his trouble when he was done.

"It's not bad," Trajan assessed his wounds once we were back inside the van. He jerked his clothing off the back seat to get dressed while I drove the van out of the parking lot.

"Zaria can fix it," I said. "We'll go back now. I think Zaria and Lissa will take care of the other bars after sending everyone else to the house, first."

~

Lissa

We saved the second bar in Fort Worth for last. Someone was coordinating the attacks, too, because every bar Zaria and I went to after the first ones, we found that the number of vampires increased.

Baikov is doing this—they're all communicating, by cell or some other way—he had a mister; it stands to reason he'd have mindspeakers, too, Zaria sent to me as we floated inside my mist over the roof of the last bar.

Like most of the others, the roof was flat and covered in a waterproof substance. Smoke from the grill, which smelled of steaks and burgers, flooded out a vent.

I can't get a lock on them by Looking, I admitted. *They may be inside mist somewhere, hiding, or inside the building, waiting for us to come in. I can usually see another mister's mist unless he's blending in really, really, well with something else.*

This may be by design, then, Zaria agreed. *If they're protected by Sirenali bones or bone dust, then they're hoping to make a big score, you can bet on it.*

Big score, as in taking us or Winkler?

Or the number of civilian deaths—maybe both.

You're not doing anything for my level of confidence, I huffed.

Whatever we do here, I get the feeling we need to remain invisible.

That makes two of us. I have a creepy feeling about all this.

Then let's go inside and get this over with, Zaria heaved a mental sigh.

Yeah.

~

Winkler

"You're not worried about them?" Weldon demanded of Charles.

"They're strong and extremely talented. If anyone can deal with what Baikov and his cronies dish out, it will be those two."

Weldon had arrived not long after we'd gone on our mission earlier, and waited inside Lissa's kitchen for us to get back. Now he had words to aim at all of us for returning and licking our wounds, both to our physical bodies and our pride, while leaving the heavy work to the women.

"Grand Master, I believe Mr. Winkler is in far more danger than any of us realize," Charles went on. "Please, this would have been Wlodek's choice as well as mine in the same circumstances."

"I don't know Zaria at all, so I have no idea what she can do. Lissa I have full confidence in, but we know there are weak spots. If human lives are placed in danger, she'll do everything she can to protect them, including risking her life for theirs."

"Please wait until you meet Zaria before making such judgments," Ilya held up a hand.

"What's this Russkie doing here anyway?" Weldon tossed out an insult and a hand.

"I am from Ukraine," Ilya hissed through clenched teeth. "My goal is the same as yours in this—take down Baikov—both versions if possible."

"He's useful, in that he's given us information we wouldn't have on the enemy, otherwise," I said, rubbing my forehead to relieve the tension. "I'd never heard of the *Klyki*. Have you?" I pointed my question directly at Weldon.

"No. Hell, no," Weldon stalked toward a barstool and sat, anger in every movement. "What about Wlodek?" he snapped at Charles.

"We didn't know either, until recently, when the Austin Pack was attacked and we sent Dalroy and Rhett to investigate. This is moving rather fast, and we'd be having a difficult time dealing with all of it without Ilya's information."

"All right," Weldon slapped his hand on the bar. "Do we have anything to drink in this place?"

"Whatever you want," Trajan dipped into the under-counter fridge and pulled out a case of beer while I headed for the liquor cabinet.

"Sorry about the Russkie thing," Weldon apologized to Ilya while popping a lid off a beer bottle.

"I'll have Scotch, if you don't mind," Ilya said. I handed him a bottle and a glass for both of us. "Make mine a triple," I told him. "I have a headache."

"Best home remedy ever—to make more headache," he spoke in his native accent and poured my glass first.

"To headaches," I clinked my triple-shot against his double before we both drank.

~

Lissa

I still don't see anything, but the hair is standing on my arms and the back of my neck, figuratively speaking, I sent. And I'm itching like crazy, and that's never a good sign.

See through everything, Zaria said.

Like X-ray vision?

Yeah.

As if they knew they were spotted the moment we did just that, misting vampires blew the entire wooden bar apart, flinging patrons standing around it outward with splinters, nails and glassware acting as shrapnel against anyone else in the place.

Someone here had learned my trick.

How?

I knew how.

Tony and Lawrence Frazier, the fucker who'd taken my blood.

Some of it had fallen into Russian hands, and now it was turned against us. As if that weren't enough, Russian-controlled werewolves burst through the door, firing semi-automatic weapons into the crowd.

I screamed the entire time Zaria flung us back to my mansion, and was still screaming when I materialized between Winkler and Weldon.

CHAPTER 6

*Z*aria

"It's all over the news," Ilya growled angrily as I healed what was left of the ugly claw wounds across Trajan's left side.

"I know."

Winkler and Weldon were holed up in the downstairs media room, watching everything on the enormous screen there. Lissa was upstairs in her bedroom, seething. I'd gotten enough of a look at the werewolf attackers to realize they didn't know much—they were under Ivan Baikov's vampire thumb and were good soldiers, willing to die to carry out his compulsion-laced orders.

I'd said that last part aloud while Ilya and Trajan listened. "The misting vampires had some of Lissa's blood, or something close enough," I said. "Humans turned vampire for a short amount of time, to achieve a desired result. If Lissa had appeared to fight them, she'd have been fighting herself, in essence—or herself times four. That's how many were there."

"Bloody, fucking, ball-bending hell," Trajan cursed. Ilya didn't understand what I was saying—not completely. I'd explain it to him later and told him that in mindspeech. He nodded while Trajan pulled his shirt back on with jerky movements and stalked toward the media room to let Winkler know.

"This is bad, isn't it?" Lissa misted into the kitchen and materialized on a barstool.

"Yeah. It's bad, and it could get worse," I said. "Don't ask," I held up a hand. "Saying it may release the idea into the atmosphere, and we don't know who may be listening."

"What do we have to drink?"

"There's some good Scotch left," Ilya offered.

"I'll have some." Lissa buried her head in her arms on the granite bar.

"Want some, too?" Ilya lifted an eyebrow in my direction.

"Not now. I need to think," I said.

"You okay?" Winkler strode into the kitchen and laid a hand on Lissa's shoulder.

"Winkler, things aren't looking so good." Her voice was muffled since she didn't raise her head to answer the question. "How many died?" she asked as Winkler massaged her neck gently.

"Thirty-four. Seventeen are in critical condition at area hospitals; only twelve got out with superficial wounds. They're being questioned by the police after they were treated and released. All the attackers got away, of course."

"Of course."

"What exactly are we dealing with? If I may ask, now?" Ilya said.

"Lissa's blood is special," I told him. "Her talents of misting, mindspeaking and such can be transferred temporarily to anyone who receives some of her blood. Not long ago, her blood was stolen by an asshole, who has evidently sold it to the highest bidder. In this case, it's the Kremlin, or someone with ties to the Kremlin."

"General Baikov."

"In all likelihood, yes."

"How much do you think they have?" Winkler asked, taking his hand from Lissa's neck.

"Who knows?" Lissa lifted her head and blinked at him. "We can't really gauge it, since I don't know how much he took to begin with. He took it during the day, while I was unconscious."

"A violation of the worst kind," Ilya rumbled. "Taking advantage when the victim is helpless."

"So we're dealing with a finite source, we just don't know how finite?" Winkler began.

"Unless they've found a way to reproduce it," I said, speaking my worst fear aloud.

"How can that be possible?" Winkler frowned at me.

"For now, don't assume anything is impossible. We could get into deep trouble if we do that."

"Just like the deep trouble people at a bar got into tonight," Lissa accepted the glass of Scotch Ilya offered her and drank.

She knew, just as I did, that it could happen again—and again after that, until the ones behind the attacks were either dead or got what they wanted.

What are you thinking, daughter? Charles walked in to ask.

I think all this is connected to Lissa's blood and the ribs of Winkler's father, I replied. *And it could be connected to bits and pieces of countless others, too.*

Lissa

"At least you're comfortable talking to me," Charles sighed as he handed me a cup of coffee later. "Zaria may never feel that way."

I'd settled onto a lounge chair around the indoor pool at the back of the house. There was no water in the pool—why keep it full and maintain it if nobody lived in the house most of the time?

"Charles," I turned my gaze on him as he settled on a chair next to mine, "All her life, she had no idea who her parents were. She knew she was adopted, and although her adoptive parents loved her and she cared for them, I think she felt there was something missing."

"Just as you did." He leaned back in his chair with a sigh.

"I worried that the monster married to my mother was really my father, although deep down, I suspect I knew otherwise. It caused some damage, as you well know."

"Major, irreparable damage," he admitted, closing his eyes. "I suppose I never considered that—outside the fact that she was taken care of and loved."

"I'm surprised you call her Zaria instead of Corinne," I observed.

"Larentii name themselves."

"I see. So, even though Nefrigar and the others call her Corinnelar, she's really Zaria."

"Yes. And Harriett before that. Harriett Majors, the best-selling author, raised by adoptive parents."

"Yeah—I read her books back in the day—when she was still human, or we thought she was. Now, what do you think she knows—or suspects about all this? Charles, you and I know where all my blood went during the original timeline."

"Yes. This has the hint of rogue interference. You suspect that yourself, as does Zaria."

"But there's something else that she's referred to."

"You understand that Zaria is probably more knowledgeable of the Lyristolyi drug than any other being, as she's had it administered twice. In addition to that, the Larentii probably have a better grasp of its workings than the Lyristolyi ever did. I believe this is why Breanne asked her to come help you. What appeared routine at first has twisted into something far more sinister."

"How long can they continue to make vampires like me?" I demanded, causing Charles to open his eyes and focus his attention on me. "The effects of my blood only last for a short time. It isn't as if they can just recreate those talents whenever they feel like it. They'll run out of what they have soon enough."

"Zaria did say it had to do with your blood and the ribs of Winkler's father," Charles grimaced. "But I suspect we'll have to find her to get a full explanation."

"Fucking hell. Where is she?"

"She bent time to think and rest, I believe. Lissa," Charles said, his voice turning deadly serious, "This isn't the time for you to hold back on the things you couldn't do before. No, don't come out with guns blazing," he held up a hand. "Use what's needed when it's needed."

"Zaria is already doing that," I turned away, letting my head drop against the back of my chaise. "And I've used my shields several times." I stifled a yawn.

"I hope we don't lose anyone who's important in all this," Charles rumbled as my eyes closed. I needed sleep—in the worst way.

Weldon sipped a traditional cup of black coffee as I walked past him into the kitchen, looking rumpled after sleeping several hours on a chaise rather than a bed. I felt every ache and pain from not sleeping on an actual bed, too. Charles had been gone when I woke.

"That witch must be something, to allow you up before sunset," Weldon said after swallowing a mouthful of coffee.

"Hmmph. Zaria's kind of special," I said, pulling out a coffee mug and pouring myself a cup. I added cream and sugar to my coffee before taking the chair next to Weldon's.

"I thought you guys didn't do that sort of thing unless forced to do so," he said while I sipped delicious, warm brew.

"Zaria," I said and kept drinking.

"I'd say you're special, too, but you should know that already," Weldon remarked, his eyes focused on the huge refrigerator opposite his seat at the island.

"That's me—special Lissa," I agreed. "Want something to eat?"

"I'm a werewolf. I always want something to eat."

"In that case," I slid off my chair and went to the refrigerator he'd stared at to see what was inside.

"You're having ham and eggs and didn't invite me?" Winkler strode into the house an hour later.

"And biscuits and gravy. Want some?" Weldon asked, helping himself to his fourth biscuit.

"You don't even have to ask." Winkler settled on a barstool while I fixed a plate of food for him.

"Any word from the Austin Pack?" Winkler asked before stuffing half a biscuit covered in gravy into his mouth.

"Since two of the prime candidates got killed in the massacre, I have plans to meet with a delegation here tomorrow, to talk about it," Weldon said.

"Is Gabe one of those coming?"

"He is," Weldon confirmed. "Do you have a stake in this, somehow?"

"Only about half of a stake, if that," I said. "I like Gabe and don't want to see him go down, that's all."

"A true Alpha knows when to time things properly," Weldon shook his head and spread blackberry jelly on his biscuit.

"Well, that doesn't always work out so well when they shove Seconds forward, now does it?"

Weldon's hands stilled for a moment as dark eyes focused on me. "No, I suppose they don't," he agreed and went back to his food. "Not without a lot of help, anyway."

"We've certainly had help—or I wouldn't be sitting here right now." Winkler paused in his food consumption to reflect for a moment.

"Same here," Weldon nodded.

"Did you ever get rid of that deer head in your spare bedroom?" I teased. "It's creepy, sleeping under a dead deer."

"Kathy Jo got rid of it," Weldon grinned. "She said the same thing. It's in storage, though, so it didn't go far."

"Right. Because somebody, somewhere, will want to hang a carcass on the wall again."

"It's not the whole thing," Winkler pointed out.

"Of course not. It's just a head, with creepy, glassy eyes. Dusty, too, if I recall."

"Dead creatures, hanging on walls to impress your guests, usually do anything but," Zaria offered her opinion as she scuffled into the kitchen wearing bedroom slippers, pajamas and a robe.

"Says the vegetarian," Winkler teased her.

"We have opinions, plus, we only hang pictures of vegetables on the wall, instead of actual peppers we've stuffed," she teased back. "Is there more coffee?"

"Yep," I said. "Want some eggs and biscuits to go with it?"

"Oh, yeah," she nodded, slipping onto a barstool.

"What are you talking about?" Ilya walked in, completely dressed and ready to bash heads. "Good early evening," he leaned in to kiss Zaria's cheek. She smiled and only pretended to push him away.

"We're discussing stuffed deer versus stuffed peppers," Weldon shrugged, as if that would explain everything.

Ilya poured coffee, then helped me cook eggs for Zaria and himself before sitting beside her to eat.

~

Kremlin, Moscow, Russia

Kornel Baikov

"Is there enough blood and marrow to complete the process?" I asked my chief scientist.

"Barely, but yes. Next time, I suggest taking larger bones."

"How quickly can this be done?"

"Give me two weeks. The others will be ready before then."

"Excellent. I'll inform my uncle. What about the women? Will they be ready?"

"They are under careful scrutiny. Many of them failed to survive, as I told you before. Once the others are ready, they will be briefed on their new abilities. You understand that the life expectancy of the women will only be a few months, at most, and they will become incapacitated before the end comes."

"Then we'll kill them at that time while creating more. This synthetic process you've developed has quite the hint of genius about it. I and my department are very pleased."

"We're working on the synthetics for some of the others, and progress is good. We may have the breakthrough needed within a week."

"Very good. How is our supply of the powder?"

"It only takes a small amount sewn into the clothing to achieve the desired results," he said.

He couldn't measure that himself, and neither could any human. We had our own barometer, who called himself D'slay. He barely spoke Russian or English, and often cursed in a language I'd never heard.

Making the dust required lives, however, and more than sixty prison cells and mental ward beds had been emptied to provide them so far. It saved the government money in housing and other related expenses, so we were given permission to take as many as we wanted. We were instructed to make our selections from political prisoners first, so that is how we'd proceeded. We'd turn to the prison camps next, and empty them if we had to.

The rumor that the dust was ground-up bones failed to disturb me in the least. Besides, it took more dust to conceal a jet than it did a person, so it was carefully measured out to D'slay's specifications. "Continue with your work," I waved the scientist out of my office. "Keep me informed when everything is ready."

"Of course."

~

Dallas, Texas

Ivan Baikov

"The noose is tightening," I reported to my nephew. "We killed thirty-four initially. Two more died during the day. I'd say it was a good effort from our new recruits. They learned their lessons quite well. They still believe they must obey my compulsion, too."

"Too bad you couldn't capture the werewolf in all the chaos, but we understood it would be difficult when we made our plans."

"There was only a brief sighting before the mindspeaker who reported it was killed," I said. "I believe the werewolf was taken to a safer location after that. Once we begin sending the ransom notes, he will understand we have only toyed with him so far."

"Has anyone been back to the house?"

"We cannot breach the wall of security he has around it. I suspect some new, electronic shield which vibrates so much my people cannot pass through it. At least that is what they report when they come back to me—that something disrupts their thinking and shoves them back every time."

"Ah, another bit of technology to add to the long list of his inventions that we want for ourselves," Kornel spoke possessively.

"I agree. We will have these things and soon," I promised. "When will our newest recruits arrive?"

"I hear they'll be ready in two weeks or less. Once they arrive, they should be eager for your command."

"William Winkler won't have the stomach to face what we send against him; I'd bet my life on it," I said.

"He'll command anyone working for him to stand down," Kornel laughed. "And, if the first ones we send fail in their efforts to take him, we send in the females and see what he does with them. We'll have him, one way or another, Uncle, and the world will be ours."

"Hmmph. The world will belong to the one in charge of Russia. Will that be you?"

"I have no need to be President of the Russian Federation. Let him be blamed, if blame is leveled. We will control everything, with or without him."

~

Lissa

"You're not going to believe this," Winkler settled on a barstool at my kitchen island, still dressed in the suit he'd worn to Elliott Barnard's funeral earlier in the day.

"Believe what?" I asked, pulling out a bottle of beer and opening it with a tip of a claw.

"Thanks," he said, taking a deep pull from the bottle before setting it back down and shaking his head.

"The Austin Pack presented a proposition to Weldon today, right after the funeral. They all like Debra—a lot. At least all the ones who survived the sniping incident. They asked Weldon to put her in charge for now, because there's nothing she doesn't know about running the pack. She chose a Second, too, with the stipulation that when he's ready to take over, she'll step aside and leave him in charge. Anybody wanting to challenge will do so when that takes place—out of respect for Elliott and Debra."

"Seriously?" I blinked at Winkler in shock. "Wow. Democracy comes to the Austin Pack. Who'd a thunk?"

"Guess who she chose as her Second?"

"No idea," I said.

"Gabe. The wolves in the pack like him, too, and, as he's a CPA in his day job, he can keep the records and finances in line while Debra does the other stuff."

"Way to go, Debra," I slapped my hand on the island.

"Weldon says as long as the pack holds true to this pact they've formed, and everything is kept up the way it's supposed to be, he's fully in favor of it."

"So we just have to keep the Russians from attacking them again," I said.

"Weldon said the same thing. There's something else."

"What's that?"

"Bill Jennings says he's coming to Dallas to talk about all this. Word is that he wants to look into the killings at the bar in Fort Worth, too, but probably doesn't know they're connected. Yet. So far, only the Texas Bureau is investigating, but if they get wind of foreign influence in this, the FBI will show up and things could go south really fast."

"Damn. I hope Bill doesn't tell Tony anything." Winkler thought I didn't want to see Tony, and that was it. He had no idea that Tony's future depended on leaving him right where he was.

"I thought you could fix things like that when Bill got here."

"I suppose I can, although I don't like doing that to friends."

"Then wait and see what he says before doing anything."

"I'll do that. What are the odds that we can keep him from informing the President and any other government agencies if he suspects Russian involvement? I figure Ilya's face may be on a secret, spy-wanted poster, somewhere."

"No idea."

"So we're back to compulsion."

"Maybe."

"When will he get here?" I asked.

"He's coming in late tonight and getting a hotel room. He'll call for an appointment tomorrow."

"How safe do you think he'll be in a hotel?"

"No idea. Why?"

"Fuck." I buried my face in my hands. *Zaria?* I sent mindspeech.

What do you need? she asked.

Bill Jennings is on his way, and planning to stay in a hotel tonight. Do you think he's safe?

I don't want to take that chance.

I think the same. I'll tell Winkler to bring Bill here. We can put him in the last bedroom.

I'll make sure it's ready.

Thanks.

"Get a message to Bill," I turned to Winkler. "He's staying here with us. I don't want them to target anybody else we know, and Bill's too important."

To the future.

~

Ilya

"Can you explain the shield around these homes?" I asked, following Zaria toward the stairs after checking the only remaining bedroom on the third floor.

"I have to make it appear to be something technological, rather than a spell," she told me as we took the first steps downward together.

"What does that mean?"

"A spelled shield only holds certain people back. I had to add something to it, making it appear more mundane. They'll feel a vibration when they get close enough, and hear a buzzing in their heads, like they're too near a high voltage electrical source or something."

"Something that Winkler could create, perhaps?"

"That's the idea—that he's holding them back with his own technology."

"Is something like that possible?"

"Not without affecting people on both sides of it," she said. "That sort of power grid would drive everyone inside the houses insane after an hour, so it isn't practical, and it would have to be turned off to allow anyone through it."

"And I suppose the power source could be compromised, leaving it open for invasion."

"Exactly. They don't know how it's powered right now, but they'll come looking soon enough. They just won't find anything."

"This means that some of their experts will come, once they fail to find the source," I spoke my thoughts aloud.

"I'm afraid that's true. Do they have anyone here in the States already?"

"They may have some embedded here and there. They will be Americans, perhaps, who have been won over or blackmailed. We must be careful to identify them before they get too close."

"All I need to do is look at them."

"Are you serious?"

"Absolutely. Come on, marinara boy. I want spaghetti."

∼

Lissa

"Thanks for going to the funeral with me today," Winkler said when Ilya and Zaria walked into the kitchen.

"You're welcome," she shrugged. "Ilya's going to cook spaghetti. Want some?"

In two hours, we had spaghetti marinara, Bolognese, and alfredo, with crusty garlic-parmesan bread and salad to go with it.

Trajan and Weldon joined us for the meal, after informing us that Jimmy, the new werewolf cook at Winkler's, had made meatloaf for dinner. It was good meatloaf, by all accounts, but no werewolf ever turned down extra food when it was offered.

I ate with the others while Winkler stared at Zaria and shook his head. She merely smiled at him and kept eating.

As we were cleaning the kitchen, Bill called Winkler. Winkler practically demanded that he come here, first, and stay with us while in Dallas. "He's on the way," Winkler turned off his phone. "Any beer left in the garage to restock the fridge?" he turned to Trajan.

"Yeah—the fridge out there is still full."

"Let's bring some in. Bill may want a drink or three while we tell him what we know."

I let my shoulders sag—I really didn't want to place compulsion on Bill. He was one of the best people I'd ever met, although he'd been too by-the-book when I first met him.

He'd be a better Director than Tony ever was, when his turn came. We just had to make sure his turn would come. Not only for his sake, but for Ashe and Breanne's sake, too.

"He may want to arrest me," Ilya said, confirming my thoughts.

"Nobody is going to arrest you," Zaria shook her head at him. "How would you like to look? Temporarily, of course, so Bill and Baikov won't know you."

"Brad Pitt?" he joked, his subsequent smile very much on the wry side.

"Hmmph." Zaria glowed. In moments, Ilya looked like Brad Pitt's older brother, with thick blond hair going slightly gray, his eyes a lighter blue, and a dimple creasing his left cheek.

"Oh, yeah, Brad Pitt the elder," Winkler nodded in approval. "Nobody will know you, now."

"Can you leave this?" Ilya pointed to his face. "You know, to improve my street cred?"

"I knew it would go to his head," Zaria poked him in the ribs.

"He knows what street cred means?" Winkler asked. "I had to look it up six months ago."

Ilya bit back a laugh.

"Lissa, are you feeling itchy?" Zaria asked.

"I sort of am," I confessed.

"Let's go get Bill."

"I think you're right." I gathered her, Winkler and Ilya into my mist and flew toward DFW Airport.

This is about to get crowded, Zaria informed us as I dropped us neatly in the back of a shuttle van, which held Bill, one of his agents and a vampire driver.

I'll get the driver, I told Zaria. *Can you handle the not-so-loyal agent?* I could smell the treason about him, even while I was mist.

How about you handle the driver and I'll transport the rest of us to the house. We may want to ask agent-boy some questions before we hand him over to somebody else.

I think that's a great idea. You transport them the second the vamp's head comes off.

I can manage that.

Thank you.

You're quite welcome.

Don't mention it.

No worries.

I think I was giggling mentally the moment I decapitated the vampire. I know I was laughing the moment I materialized in my driveway with Winkler and Ilya.

Ilya already had a choke-hold on the agent while Bill, a look of shock on his face, reached for his shoulder holster.

"It's okay, Bill," I held up a hand to reassure him. "Your driver was a *vampus non gratis,* and this guy may have sold you out." I narrowed my gaze on the agent, who swallowed uncomfortably in Ilya's grasp.

"I hope you can get to the bottom of this and fast, then," Bill walked forward until he was facing his agent. "I'll need to make a report and decide what to do with him afterward."

"He's had compulsion laid, so it may not be totally his fault," Zaria joined Bill in front of the agent. "I'll have to look into the matter."

She disappeared, making Bill and the agent gasp.

"She'll be back," I shrugged. "Bill, we have food and beer in the kitchen. Agent-boy needs to tell us what he knows."

With Winkler's help, Ilya marched the agent into the house, Bill and I close behind. "Lissa," Bill said softly, "I thought you were in England."

"I'm supposed to be. Everybody else thinks that, including most vamps. I needed to handle something going on here, so don't tell Tony anything about this. Not only am I pissed at him, he needs to stay right where he is."

"All right," Bill said, as if he were accustomed to keeping things from Tony all the time. "I need a beer while we have a conversation with my agent, there."

"He sold out before compulsion was placed this time," Zaria reappeared, a tub of movie popcorn in her hand.

"Oh," she said, looking down at the tub. "He met his contact at a movie theater. Got paid for his time, too. I have the bank account info if Bill needs it."

"Tell me who she is," Bill frowned at me.

"Zaria," I said, and smiled as she offered me popcorn.

CHAPTER 7

*L*issa

This is better than the movie they picked, Zaria said as she and I ate popcorn with our wine. Bill ate leftover Italian and the others had a beer while the agent sweated on a kitchen barstool. I'd told him to sit there and answer all of Bill's questions honestly, after Zaria gave the name of his Russian handler.

Bill recognized the name when he heard it. Things went downhill for his agent after that.

What were they watching? I asked.

A cheerleader movie, and it was kinda awful.

Not surprised, I said.

"What is the most sensitive information you passed to your contact?" Bill demanded.

"That William Winkler designed the recognition software we use."

"That's fucking above your clearance and paygrade," Bill snapped. "How did you come by that? Only a handful of people know."

"The White House knows," the agent laughed hysterically. Bill, anger suffusing his body, rose from his seat and stalked toward the living area while pulling his cell phone from a pocket.

"Fucking hell," I sighed.

"So, you're the source of all my troubles, then?" Winkler's face was now inches away from snitchy-pants agent.

"I-I was only a go-between on that," the agent babbled. "I read the information passed to me from a White House staffer, but I wasn't supposed to. My guess is that it came from someone higher up."

Probably a bit too high, I sent to Zaria.

Possibly. I can think of two who might be involved. Either one spells treason. Neither are the President, but in his inner circle, so to speak.

Just what I was thinking. I didn't find anything out of the ordinary for this one—I've met him, actually—more than once.

"We were hacked," Bill pocketed his cell phone as he walked back into the kitchen. "I think they're screwing around with Winkler, now, because they couldn't get past his firewall to steal the program months ago. This is very similar to when they attempted to get it while he was developing it."

I didn't realize Bill and Tony knew about that, but it made sense. Somebody had offered Phil quite a bit for Winkler's program—and his head.

"So they found out my software wasn't a failure, and they've come back to me, then," Winkler growled. "And people have died because of it—just like last time."

For Winkler, that hadn't been very long ago. For me, it had been centuries. "We need to actively hunt vampire Baikov; he's the closest threat," I said.

"I agree. Where do we start?" Bill turned to me.

"Easier said than done," Zaria said. "Unless I miss my guess, he's clothed up to his neck in Sirenali bone dust."

"You'll forget you heard that," I pointed a new obsession at snitchy-pants. "Bill, has the President hired any upper level staffers recently? I don't keep up with the news much."

"He has a new Chief of Staff—the one you've met decided to retire."

"Under heavy persuasion, no doubt," I grumped.

"You know, now that you mention it, I did find that unusual for him, but people cave under the pressure of the oval office all the time."

"Anybody else?" I asked. "That has access to the President and is relatively new?"

"Couple of assistants, maybe."

"Good. We may need to have a conversation with all those people."

"I can get us on a plane in an hour."

"Winkler?" I turned to him.

"I sure as hell want to put them on the hot seat," he rumbled. "And we can drop this fucker into the Mississippi River when we fly over it," Winkler breathed into snitchy-pants' face. "Weldon is heading home tomorrow, though, so he won't be with us."

Snitch-agent pressed his back against the chair he sat on, turning his head in an attempt to escape Winkler's snarl. He knew Winkler could tear him to shreds without expending much effort.

"Baikov will likely figure out where we're headed," Zaria offered. "Winkler, we need to get everybody out of both houses, Kellee included, then send Weldon home and put the others somewhere safe. I'll leave the shields up, but we need to leave a trail of breadcrumbs for Baikov to follow, rather than causing more mayhem in Texas while we're gone."

"I think I agree with that," Bill's forehead creased in thought as he considered our options. "Is there a way to get the others out so they won't be seen?"

"Yes," Zaria and I said together.

"I hate military jets," I complained as Zaria buckled in two seats down. Winkler had plunked into the seat between us with a proprietary snort and sat there like he'd just taken charge of the entire operation.

He wasn't pleased about being hunted again for the software he'd created, and he wanted to deal with the situation immediately.

I worried that it wouldn't be nearly as easy as luring vampire Baikov into a trap and offing him along with his head. Ilya and Charles were coming with us; Dalroy and Rhett stayed behind to protect the others at Winkler's Port Aransas beach house.

Zaria and I transported them there; I'd laid compulsion on Kellee to mind her manners and stay in the house until the whole thing was over, unless Winkler said it was all right to go out. It was for her own safety, and Winkler asked me to do it.

Things were changing every second in the timeline, and we didn't need Kellee fucking things up more than they already were.

Somewhere on Refizan in the current time, Dragon and I were killing Ra'Ak spawn. Where I was, things could become much worse than that. Zaria, upon occasion, would wear a worried frown, and that troubled me more than anything.

She knew a great deal about timelines and how they could go from snarled to totally fucked up if somebody didn't intervene to set them on the right track again. We hadn't drilled down to that conversation, yet. A part of me was glad, or I'd have even more trouble sleeping.

We landed at Joint Base Andrews around three in the morning, local time. Winkler and Trajan had gotten some sleep on the way; Ilya and Charles had stayed awake and had quiet conversation during most of the trip.

I tuned them out after a while; Charles certainly wouldn't tell him anything he didn't need to know, or that couldn't be erased by compulsion later.

"I have rooms in a hotel not far from the hill for all of you," Bill said as we gathered our things and deplaned. Two black SUVs waited to carry us and our luggage to the designated address.

"Lissa, will you and Zaria ride with me?" Bill asked. Winkler frowned, because he wanted me with him.

Instead, Winkler, Trajan and Charles rode in the second vehicle, while Ilya joined us and rode with Bill. "I'll set up meetings tomorrow evening, if that's convenient for you," Bill told me as the vehicle pulled away from the jet.

"Bill, you can set something up earlier, if that's better for everyone," Zaria said. "I can see to it that Lissa is awake and protected."

"I really don't understand how you can do that," Bill said, shaking his head. "But if you can, then I can put something together for early afternoon."

"That sounds good," I told him. "It'll keep Baikov away from us during that time—and any other vampire he thinks to send after us. We can deal with werewolves easy enough—and humans, too, if it comes to that."

"Good. After we question the people involved in this, I hope we have a clearer picture of whom to hunt," Bill agreed. "I'd like to get on that fast, before they figure out we know anything. I'll set up a meeting with the President, too, but that could be short and sweet after the initial interviews are over."

"Whatever you need, Bill," I shrugged. "We'll be right behind you every step of the way. Just make sure this is kept secret, and no photos get out."

"I'll see to it."

I'll see to it, too, Zaria sent to me. Not only did she want to protect us, but Ilya, Winkler and the others as well. I wanted what she wanted, and would add my shields and protections to hers.

The hotel was a nice one; apparently the State Department used it frequently, and Bill had made arrangements to use their account to put us up. Zaria didn't have a problem with it, so I figured we wouldn't be outed by anyone involved.

I also wondered how far behind us Baikov was, and if he were already in D.C. Since neither Zaria nor I could find him by *Looking,* we could only guess at how long it would take for him to follow our trail.

Is there any way we can track somebody dressed in Sirenali bone dust? I sent to Zaria.

I have someone working on that. If they come up with anything, I'll know and pull in the process to help us in the here and now. We don't need more of this shit to deal with in the future-past. And, if there's a live Sirenali passing his blood to others to produce more Sirenali bones, then we have to find him or her, too, and dispatch them.

Huh? This was something new to me.

V'ili was doing the same thing, almost—he'd cloned many Sirenali from himself, plus, a few humanoids were given the Lyristolyi drug to create more

Sirenali to clone. Then, all those Sirenali clones were rendered mute and sold to criminal factions all over the Alliances. After years of making clones of other clones, the process broke down and past that point, most of them were born sick. That's when they started allowing them to die, or began killing them outright to provide bones and bone dust to hide stolen goods and such. Much of Cayetes' wealth was provided by that cottage industry, if you can call it that.

Oh. Now I understand.

I did—and it terrified me. *Do we need to narrow down his bloodline? This Sirenali's?* I asked.

Good guess—yes, we do. If we find Baikov, I'm hoping we can extract bone dust from what he's wearing and reverse-engineer this. The trouble is, of course, that we may not have enough time to do all that. And, if there's more than one Sirenali, we may be screwed anyway.

Damn.

Agreed.

When we pulled into the hotel driveway, my mind was whirling with the problems we were facing. *Are we going to be able to sleep?* I asked Zaria.

I intend to ask Valegar to help, she sighed. *We can't fight off the Cossack horde without rest.*

Well, you're right. Will you ask Valegar to contact Connegar for me?

Already done.

～

Bill

I knew Lissa could mindspeak. Zaria evidently could, too. They'd held a private conversation between them on the way to the hotel. A part of me wanted to participate. Another was afraid to be involved in it.

I decided if they wanted me to know, they'd tell me and let my curiosity go. "I'll be staying here, too," I said as we stepped out of the vehicle and pulled back to allow a hotel employee to load our bags onto a cart.

"Bill, have I told you lately how awesome you are?" Lissa smiled at me.

"Why, no. Feel free to say it as often as you want."

"You're awesome, too," Zaria patted Ilya's arm. Maybe he felt left out, even if he never moved a facial muscle to indicate it. *Damn, he was a good spy.*

I knew who he was, even with the disguise. This was the famed Russian spy that we'd nicknamed *the Blacksmith*. I didn't say anything because Lissa and Zaria trusted him in this and frankly, he was on our side against the Baikovs.

We could return to our opposing sides after this, but for now, the enemy of my enemy was definitely my friend, and he had inside intel that I didn't.

"Order room service if you're hungry," I told the others. "I'm having a snack while I make a few calls."

Lissa

Zaria knocked on my door two minutes after I dressed in my pajamas. "I have warning shields around both people Bill wants to question," she said. "In case Baikov decides to have them offed before we can get to them."

"Good idea," I said. "Do you need any help with that?"

"No. I suppose Baikov's too slick to go himself—that would make things really easy for us."

"From what I've seen so far, he doesn't like to get his claws dirty."

"You've danced with him, so you know what he looks like," Zaria pointed out. "I think we can resurrect that memory and give Bill something to send through that awesome software Winkler designed."

"Um, can we isolate those images? I doubt Wlodek's current self would appreciate anybody outing vampires from the Annual Meeting."

"Don't worry. We can do anything you'd like with the final product."

"What do I need to do?" I asked.

"Just think about that night. I'll see it in you and can recreate it on this." She held up a thumb drive. "It'll look like you were wearing a camera while you danced, that's all, because that's how it will appear to me, initially."

"Initially?"

"I can extrapolate from your memories," she shrugged. "I could probably put the entire ballroom scene together if I wanted—it's like stitching images together from your peripheral vision. I don't need to do that."

"Maybe I'd like to see that sometime," I said. "It would be nice to get clear details from that night—I remember being terrified during most of it and wasn't paying attention to minutiae."

"Then I'll commit it to memory and give it to you later," she smiled. Her smile was a tired one, as was the one I returned to her.

"There. All done," she said, handing the thumb drive to me. "Give that to Bill later. I'm off to get some sleep."

Instead of walking out the door, she folded space.

"My love?" Connegar now stood in her place.

"Honey, I am so happy to see you," I told him as he lifted me in his arms. I stroked back a lock of his hair before leaning my head on his shoulder.

"Come, then," he murmured. "We will bend time and you will sleep."

∼

Ilya

I didn't even jerk when Zaria's hand covered my mouth, waking me. "Someone is about to attack the Chief of Staff," she whispered. "Do you wish to come with me?"

"Of course," I said, not bothering to hide my native accent.

"Good."

"Let me get dressed," I flung back covers. I only wore boxer shorts and now had an erection, thanks to Zaria's nearness.

"No time," she said. The glow about her was swift before it disappeared, and suddenly I was fully dressed.

"Your weapon," she handed a nine-millimeter pistol to me and then flung both of us to an unknown location. We were just in time to jerk a terrified man away from a window before bullets sprayed through it.

"Those are just the warning shots," I hissed in Steven Gorham's ear as I dragged him farther into the room. "There are others in the house already."

"What?"

In the dim light, his eyes were wide with fear. "This is the price you pay for selling out your own government," I admonished.

Near his bedroom door, Zaria had positioned herself, waiting for those in the house to come bursting in, bullets flying. The Capitol Police guards, stationed outside, were already dead, although more were on the way.

One of them coming up the stairs is vampire, Zaria's words sounded in my head.

"I hope you can take care of that one, then," I said softly.

"Huh?" Gorham couldn't help himself.

"They sent a vampire to destroy you, did you know that?" I shook him by his collar. "I should let him have you."

Gorham's legs buckled beneath him—he knew what he was up against, now.

I'll let them in, Zaria said. *You shoot the two werewolves. I'll deal with the vampire.*

"On it," I replied.

The door blew open—no doubt the vampire's work. I was forced to ignore the vampire's disappearance in a flurry of winking sparks, so I could shoot the two werewolves in the head who trailed behind him.

∾

Zaria

Steven Gorham, about-to-be-former Chief of Staff, spent the rest of the night at our hotel, handcuffed to a bed while some of Bill's trusted agents guarded him.

The crime scene was still crawling with Capitol Police. Good thing I'd staged the scene so it looked as if one of the dead officers had been inside the room protecting Gorham, while the attackers tried to kill both of them.

In the officer's case, they were successful, along with killing three fellow officers stationed outside the residence.

The story was that Gorham called Bill, and that Bill went to get him after the attempt on his life. Lissa's compulsion was needed for that, and nobody knew Gorham was in handcuffs inside his hotel room.

"Did you get any sleep?" Lissa walked up with two lattes in her hands. She gave one to me. "Not much, I'm afraid," I confessed, sipping the latte. "Damn, that's good," I said and thanked her for the drink.

Ilya in the clear? she asked.

Yeah. I changed bullets to make it look like they came from the dead officer's gun.

Brilliant.

Desperate is more like it.

"Ladies," Ilya walked up, a cup of black coffee in his hands.

"Nice work last night," Lissa told him with a grin.

"Eh," he shrugged.

"I'm surprised they didn't go after the assistant," Lissa said softly.

"The same crew was supposed to do just that. We sort of interrupted their plans. I figure when Baikov wakes tonight, he'll be so pissed he'll destroy something."

"Perhaps that's why his distant relative, the General, has a volatile temper, too," Ilya suggested.

"I imagine he inherited it," I agreed and sipped more of my latte. "Lissa has images of the vampire version," I added. "You can probably view those with Bill later."

"Good. I'll compare the human version with that one. Human

Baikov hates being photographed, but I know what he looks like well enough."

"We're counting on that," Lissa nodded. "Bill needs the info."

"In this, I am happy to oblige. If you could help eliminate the *Klyki*, I would be eternally grateful. Too many Russians and Ukrainians are dying at their hands."

"We'll be happy to honor that request," I patted his shoulder. "But only because you asked."

"You tease me," he grinned.

"Honey, we're just getting started," I smiled at him.

Lissa stifled a snicker.

∾

Lissa

"I thought daylight wasn't an option for you," the President smiled at me.

"It isn't. This is Zaria's talent," I told him.

"Bill said as much. I wasn't sure whether to believe him." He winked at Bill, who stood behind me in the oval office.

"Well, then, shall we see what my Chief of Staff and his assistant has been up to?" His face darkened at those words—Bill already told him that Gorham had sold us out on Winkler's software.

Winkler, Trajan, Ilya and Zaria were in a room nearby, waiting on us to finish our preliminary conversation with the President. They'd join us for the questioning, which Bill and the Joint Chiefs intended to do.

I'd already placed compulsion on both to answer truthfully, so we'd get to the bottom of this quickly.

At least they hadn't been obsessed; Zaria confirmed that with a relieved sigh. If they'd had obsessions laid, we wouldn't get anything from them.

That led me to believe that the Russians only had one actual Sirenali who could lay obsession. Zaria thought the same; if they had others, there would be someone already in the U.S. laying obsessions left and right.

That didn't mean they weren't reproducing more Sirenali with the aid of the drug, and then killing them for the bones or bone dust, just as Zaria feared.

We walked out of the oval office and were joined shortly by the others. An aide led us toward a conference room, where the Joint Chiefs waited for the questioning to start.

Ilya, are there people disappearing in Russia without explanation? I sent to him as we walked through the White House.

"All the time," he leaned in to answer. "Nothing unusual about that."

"Damn," I said aloud. *I was hoping we could pinpoint the source of some particular bone dust,* I added in mindspeech.

"Then you should look at prisons, orphanages and hospitals for the mentally ill—people vanish from them all the time."

I'll revisit that topic later, when we're in a more secure place, I sent.

He smothered a laugh. We were in the White House, which was supposed to be very secure. With the Chief of Staff's recent peccadillos, that wasn't completely true.

Winkler couldn't help growling at Steven Gorham as we were offered comfortable chairs on one side of a long table. The President sat at the head and waited until everyone was seated before turning the Joint Chiefs loose on Gorham and his assistant.

"How much did they pay you?" The Secretary of the Navy demanded of Gorham. Gorham had been sweating during an hour of heavy questioning. His assistant, a younger man who wanted a career in politics, sat beside him, his eyes wide, like a deer's in bright headlights.

"Six million," Gorham confessed unwillingly.

"You could have held out for more," the Army Secretary half-joked. He, like the others, couldn't believe what they were hearing. The Russians had attempted to take the software, and when they couldn't hack it, they'd gone looking for its creator, to take him or her instead.

According to Gorham, they already suspected it was Winkler's software, but they wanted confirmation. He'd handed it to them without a qualm.

Winkler's fingers gripped mine under the table—he'd made sure to sit next to me.

"Did you think you wouldn't get caught?" the President demanded.

"I was assured of it."

"Because they were planning to kill you before you could say anything, you ignorant twat," Zaria snapped at him.

No, she wasn't supposed to speak at the meeting. Nobody chastised her; instead, most of them chuckled as Gorham shifted uncomfortably in his chair.

"I need to go to the restroom and get a drink," he whined.

"Very well. We'll take fifteen," the President waved a hand.

We filed out of the meeting; I wanted more coffee. The same held for the rest of our party—we headed for a nearby room that held a coffee urn, bottled water and various pastries.

Zaria's head lifted as she pulled a paper cup from an available stack.

Shields up, she told me and held the cup under the spigot to get coffee.

I have no idea who'd walked into the place with a hidden bomb earlier, but it detonated in the men's restroom while guards stood outside, waiting for Gorham and his assistant to take a piss.

"They knew, somehow, that we hadn't gotten to the question of whether he'd seen any of his collaborators, and we hadn't spoken to the assistant at all, yet," the President grumbled.

At least the news programs were all saying the President wasn't anywhere near the bomb when it went off, but they were already reporting that the Chief of Staff and his assistant were dead in the blast.

Do you have that information? I sent to Zaria.

Of course I do. Their mistake was in not obsessing them. They thought their compulsion would hold. You blew right past that, when you couldn't have before.

Will you show Ilya what you saw in them?

Yep. and Bill, too. I'll have images after we leave here today. The assistant was the one who saw the handlers—Gorham thought to keep his hands clean of that so he arranged to have snitchy-pants agent pass the file to the assistant, so the assistant couldn't say for certain that it actually came from Gorham. Gorham could subsequently look innocent while his assistant took the fall. Too bad that went sideways.

The Joint Chiefs are in a snit, now, I reported. *I overheard that conversation with the President. They want every staffer in this end of the building questioned about the bomb.*

Well, you can't really blame them. If they'd been in the bathroom with the treason brothers, they'd have been killed, too.

Did you have something to do with it? That they wouldn't be killed?

Maybe. I'll never tell.

Oh, come on. You can tell me.

Well, I figured the enemy had a final ace up his sleeve, and some way to off Gorham and company. This way, I have everything from him and his assistant while the enemy still thinks he's safe. I had to remove the ah, urge to pee from the Joint Chiefs—until this was over.

Have you noticed we think alike, sometimes? I asked. *I was figuring they had a way to come after them before all was said and done. I worried they'd kick down the door and come in with guns blazing.*

That was the backup option if the bomb failed, I think.

I took care of that option, Charles' voice sounded in our heads. *And I removed the compulsion laid on the Secret Service agents ordered to do it.*

Nice, I sent to him.

Thanks. Zaria's sending didn't sound half as perky as mine did.

Plus, Charles was supposed to be asleep in his hotel room, as he was an ordinary vampire—or so Bill thought. Instead, he was awake and taking his own measures to protect us.

You really need to work this out with your daughter, Charles, I sent him a private message.

I know. I'm working on it.

Just tell her who her mother is and get it over with.

Well, that's more complicated than it sounds, he admitted.

Why's that? Is her mother some big, bad criminal or something?

Uh, no. It's just that there's ah, more than one.

More than one criminal?

More than one mother.

Fucking hell, Charles, what did you do, mix DNA?

Sort of. I'll tell you about it later. I just can't right now, all right?

And those two mothers don't know, do they? Am I right?

No, they don't know, and it's more than two.

Charles, if Zaria doesn't knee you in the ba-doobies over this, I will.

I'll be sure to wear protective gear when I tell her, then.

You do that—and you better hope it works if she's pissed.

I figure she will be. Saying sorry over this won't go far, I don't think, because I care about her—and the others involved, too.

Right. Start practicing your apologies now, and make sure they're damn good ones.

"We're cleared to go for now," Bill arrived and interrupted the mindspeech with Charles.

Zaria had her head turned away; she probably knew Charles and I'd been engaged in a private conversation.

"What are the chances we can get real food?" Winkler rose from a chair and stretched.

"I second that," Ilya spoke up.

"I know a good steak place," Bill said. "Let's go."

CHAPTER 8

*L*issa

"It's tofu," Zaria explained as Ilya examined the salad she'd ordered. "It looks like chicken chunks, but it's not."

"Are you sure you're getting enough protein?" he continued to frown at her food.

"I am," she smiled at him. I think his heart melted, right then and there.

"Do you think nighttime Baikov has arrived, yet?" Bill pointed his question at me.

"Probably," I answered. "Although he may think his concerns are eliminated with Gorham's and his assistant's deaths."

"They're in pieces at the morgue," Winkler said, cutting into his massive, rare-cooked T-bone. "I'd hope that would satisfy anybody, since he failed to kill them last night."

"His would-be assassins are dead, too," Trajan pointed out. "What do we know about them?"

"I'll be paying them a visit," Zaria said.

"Why in heaven's name would you do that?" Winkler asked.

"Zaria can see things others can't," I explained. "I'll go with you, if you want," I told her, leaning around Winkler to meet her gaze.

"Sure. Maybe you can tell things from their scents."

If Zaria said that, then I figured I *would* be able to tell something from their scents. I didn't speculate and I didn't ask—I was hungry and set about eating the prime rib on my plate. Worry can ruin any good dinner, and I wasn't going to let it interfere this time.

"Bart Orford and Lester Briggs. Henchwolves," I closed my eyes and breathed a bitter sigh. Somebody had either cloned them or had used the Lyristolyi drug to recreate them. It was another blow against Winkler. Soon enough, I figured they'd contact him about joining their ranks, just to stop these attacks.

Winkler knew Bart and Lester just as well as I did, and a growl sounded low in his throat as we examined the bullet-riddled bodies at the morgue.

I'll have to take you back in time to sniff the vampire before I offed him, Zaria sent.

You think I'll know him, too?

It's possible.

"They're fucking with us," I gave Bill a hard stare. "Big time."

"Are you sure you don't want Tony brought into this?"

"No," Zaria and I both snapped.

"Tony needs to be where he is," I held up a hand. "I'll explain that better to you someday."

Zaria and I excused ourselves to go to the ladies' room half an hour later. She bent time the moment we shut the door behind us.

"They'll pass right by us here," Zaria said as we stood near the steps of Gorham's townhome. We were so heavily shielded nobody could see or hear us. Sure enough, two minutes later, Lester, Bart, and a vampire walked past us.

I drew in a deep breath and felt like screaming. Before I could open my mouth, Zaria sent us back to the restroom at the restaurant, while I almost hyperventilated inside a stall.

I should have known.

I should have.

The vampire? He had Saxom's stink all over him—and was one of his direct turns. Xenides had thrown in his lot with the Russians this time around, and events were slipping and sliding away from the norm at such momentum, I had no idea whether we could stop them.

"I was afraid of that," Charles shook his head when I told him later. "All it would take is one or two short meetings between Ivan Baikov and Xenides, then havoc would arrive."

"Then we need to track Baikov—if we can," I said. "Even Zaria can't find him, and that's a problem for everybody."

"There's the blood supply," Charles suggested.

"It could turn into another Fort Worth incident," I said.

"That's probably what he's hoping for—to convince Winkler to come to him voluntarily."

"I'm surprised Winkler hasn't heard from him already."

"I was wondering about that myself, unless Baikov wants to up the ante."

"In what way?"

"Well, think about it. They have your blood, but likely a limited supply of the real thing. Evidence points to you being with Winkler, does it not?"

"They'll try to blackmail both of us?"

"I would, if I were them."

"Fuck."

"I figure they don't really have good intel on Zaria, or they might demand her, too."

"Like they'd get that," I huffed. "If Zaria is threatened, look for the entire Larentii race to show up at once."

"They don't know that."

"Probably a good thing."

"I agree."

~

Zaria

"What's wrong?" Ilya tipped my face up as I sat in the hotel lobby, thinking about everything that could go wrong with what had already gone wrong. Now, Ilya was asking what was wrong.

"Too much," I said.

"Tell me." He sat on the bench beside me while Bill and Winkler received messages at the front desk.

"Honey, that's impossible. It falls into the *I can't believe this* realm, and you really would question my sanity."

"Hmmph." He pulled my head onto his shoulder and kissed my forehead. "You should hear about some of the things I've seen," he murmured against my hair. "When I was younger, I'd have said the *Klyki* were an impossibility. I know better, now."

"How much do you believe in aliens?"

"It's possible, I suppose."

"It's a fact," I sighed against his collar and closed my eyes. "They're helping the Baikovs—and the Xenides in the world."

"Xenides?"

"A vampire whose goal is to destroy the planet we're standing on. Saxom, Xenides' alien sire, commanded Xenides to do it, shortly before Saxom was killed."

"This is revenge?"

"Saxom's revenge. His vampire child has no way to refuse his sire's compulsion."

"How can an alien be vampire?"

"All vampires have alien blood, honey. The first ones here came from another world in the beginning."

"You're frightening me."

"Same goes for the werewolves. All alien when they first arrived. They have a purer bloodline than the vamps do."

"Next, you'll tell me this is also true with the shapeshifters."

"Yeah. That's true, too."

"You are almost asleep. Shall I carry you to your room?"

"I'll walk."

"Come, then, they are going to the elevators now."

~

Bill

"They want you *and* Lissa?" I read Winkler's message a third time. It also clearly stated not to go to the police. Well, I wasn't really the police—not the normal definition of it, anyway.

"It probably wasn't hard for them to figure out that she's handling some of this mess on my behalf," Winkler said. "What with the Austin Pack's disappearance, and the vampire getting killed in my house, although that was Zaria and not Lissa."

"Then they have no idea Zaria exists," I blurted. I was concerned about Ilya knowing—but only for a moment. It didn't take a genius to realize he cared about her, and there was no way he'd sell her to the Kremlin. "You think they'll find out about her, too?" I added. "Surely not—unless she tells them herself," I attempted to quash my own fears.

"Um, she may have already done that," Winkler confessed.

"How?"

"She ah, dropped a dead vampire, frozen in ice, on General Baikov's bed."

"Get Lissa on the phone. I want to meet with her and Zaria. Bring Ilya, too, if he's willing to come."

"If Zaria comes, he'll be here."

"I get that idea, too."

~

Lissa

"This is vampire Baikov?" Bill asked as he replayed the recording of Baikov dancing with me at the Annual Meeting.

"Yes."

"Looks very much like the human General Baikov," Ilya watched the images intently.

"I can recreate those images you have of him—if you're willing to think hard about them," Zaria offered.

"I will be happy to oblige. He refuses to allow himself to be photographed, likely because of the software. He has no wish to become a target, when he very much deserves to be one. Too many innocent deaths lie in his wake. Journalists, political prisoners and many others—all dead, thanks to Baikov."

Bill knows who Ilya is. Ilya knows that Bill knows, Zaria sent to me. *I'm leaving the disguise in place, so vamp Baikov and company won't know who it is.*

Well, at least we won't have to hide his spyness from Bill, I replied. *Besides, this association could work out for both of them in the future.*

It could. We'll see. Right now, it's expedient for them to work on the same side.

"Zaria?" Bill turned to her expectantly.

"I'll have it for you tomorrow. Ilya and I are both too exhausted to do this for you tonight."

"Tomorrow, then. I'll run this through the software by that time," he held up the thumb drive.

"Good enough," I said. "I'm tired, too. Bill, you ought to get some rest while you can."

"Don't worry, this will take ten minutes, then I'm out for the night."

The shield I have around the hotel will keep us safe through a nuclear holocaust, I told Zaria. *Go to bed, I've got it this time.*

Thank you.

"We found Ivan Baikov—entering the U.S. in Matamoros," Bill said at breakfast the following morning. "Since he was headed for the Dallas area, it makes sense to come across somewhere on the Texas border."

"I'm sure compulsion played a part in that," I said, sipping coffee. "No swimming or climbing needed for that asshole. Was he disguised?"

"Yes, and we've zoned in on his documents, which look just like the disguise. His mannerisms and the way he tilts his head while listening to someone helped us nail him."

"Any hits after that?"

"He likely dropped the disguise, so we're still working on that. We're focusing on the Dallas area mostly, and branching out to suburbs and smaller cities as we go."

"Sneaky asshole," I sighed.

"Most definitely. I've asked to have him tracked here in D.C., too. He's here, somewhere, I'd bet my life on it."

"You're right," I agreed. "He's following Winkler, no doubt about that."

"I'm going to get coffee," Zaria arrived at our hotel breakfast table.

"They'll bring some to you," Bill pointed to an empty chair.

"No—I think she wants a specialty coffee," I told Bill. "I'd like a caramel mocha, if you're going."

"I'll get it. Will you order a cheese and tomato omelet for me?"

"Sure will," I grinned at her. She was about to fold space to the nearest Starbucks and frankly, I hadn't had a caramel mocha in a while.

"I'd like a flat white, if that's on the menu," Bill reached into his pocket for money.

"Don't even worry about it," Zaria patted his shoulder. "Tell Winkler and Ilya that I'm bringing theirs, too."

I watched her walk toward the restaurant entrance. Somewhere, probably a bathroom, she'd disappear and then reappear with a tray full of drinks.

"I really like her," Bill said.

"I do, too." I didn't admit that I was coming to feel more than like for her. Zaria and I could have been sisters; we often thought alike on so many things.

"Trajan is guarding Charles' room," Winkler sat next to me at the table and lifted a menu.

"Zaria is bringing something for you from Starbucks, so don't order coffee," I told him.

"Is she bringing something for me?" Ilya's voice held a sliver of hope.

"She said so," I told him. "Sit down. When you decide what you want, I need to order a tomato and cheese omelet for Zaria, too."

"Traje says the Denver omelet is excellent," Winkler perused his menu. "I think I'll have that and a ham steak on the side."

I figured Zaria had herself shielded from the restaurant staff as she blithely walked in carrying a cardboard tray loaded with drinks. "Here you go," she told Bill, setting his flat white in front of him.

"Caramel mocha," she held out my cup. "Triple capp, no foam," she handed Ilya a large cup, "and a double shot hazelnut latte for you," she set a cup in front of Winkler.

"What did you get?" I asked as she took the chair next to Ilya.

"Vanilla latte. What else is there?" she grinned and lifted her cup to drink.

"For anyone else, I would call that wimpy coffee," Ilya teased.

"Honey, call it whatever you like. You're not the one drinking it."

"We haven't ordered yet," Ilya told her. "You can order for yourself."

"Well, all right, then," she said. Our server arrived in less than two minutes, she and the others ordered and we talked while they ate.

"There they are," Zaria pointed at the large screen at one end of the meeting room. She'd given Bill information on where Gorham's assistant met with the spy. Thankfully, there was a security camera at a business across the street, which caught the meeting at the edge of a park. She and Ilya had already given a thumb drive containing images of General Baikov—Bill had those running through the software while we turned to other things.

"Damn, that's grainy," Bill squinted to see better.

"His name is hidden," Zaria frowned. "That means he's obsessed."

"His name is Zukov," Ilya said. "Peter Zukov. His nose has rubbed many times against General Baikov's posterior."

"Wait, who's that?" Winkler asked. A third party had joined the other two.

"Kelvin—well Kevin Miller," I said. "I'd recognize that little fucker anywhere."

"He's dead," Bill began. "In Kansas City."

"They've reverse-engineered the drug for sure," Zaria hissed. "How the fuck? Never mind, I know how the fuck." She disappeared before any of us could stop her.

∾

Zaria

Trajan thought Charles was sleeping. Inside my father's bubble of sound-dampening solitude, I'd interrupted his Zen thought period by screaming at him about Liron's alliance with Xenides, and the reverse-engineering of the Lyristolyi drug.

"You know he's throwing these low-level threats at us to cause chaos, don't you?" Charles didn't turn a hair while I'd shouted about unholy alliances.

"Well, it's working," I hissed.

"He's got worse coming, daughter. Much worse."

"That's just what I'm afraid of." He knew, just as I knew, that Baikov could reproduce Lissa with the blood he had. Just as he could reproduce anyone whose blood or DNA he could come up with. And he could cover them all with Sirenali bone dust, because he could reproduce those fuckers, too. If Xenides learned of it, he'd want a cloned Lissa for himself—if not more than one.

"Ilya said that people disappear from prisons, mental wards and orphanages. They're probably drawing on those resources to create duplicates. We have to go hunting, I think," Charles leveled hazel eyes on me.

In reality, he was taller, with dark eyes and hair. This version seemed so—benign. Harmless, even. He was a master of manipulation, after all.

The Mighty Mind, or Wisdom. One of the Three.

My father.

"We have to go hunting." I tossed out a hand and disappeared in front of him.

~

Lissa

"What do we know about Kevin?" Bill asked. He wanted to track Kevin and Peter, and didn't seem to care which one we found first. I figured he hoped they'd lead us to Ivan Baikov, just as I did.

"He likes comfort food," I said. "And plenty of it."

"Full moon is too far away to use that to track him," Winkler grumbled.

"We'll use that as a last resort," Bill said. "The message you have says thirty-six hours before they strike again. I figure they may send Kevin, along with a few vamps, to take you in—if you agree to hand yourself over," he added.

"Did they explain their threats if he doesn't turn himself over?" Ilya asked.

"Of course not," Winkler snarled. "That's what they always do— make you afraid of what it might be."

~

Zaria

I sat on the same park bench where Gorham's assistant met with Peter Zukov and Kevin Miller. Across the street was the diner, whose grainy images we'd looked at earlier.

Burgers, Hot Dogs and Chili Fries, their sign proclaimed, beneath *Al's Fifties Pit Stop*. It was a popular greasy spoon, I'll give it that. The lunch crowd had arrived; the restaurant was filling up fast.

"Well, how-de-do," I breathed as Kevin Miller walked into the place behind two truckers. Looks like Kevin wanted everything on the menu; he was hungry.

Lissa, I sent, I have my eye on Kevin Miller at Al's Fifties Pit Stop, across from the park bench. Feel like a burger?

~

Lissa

Well, the old saying was true. The way to a man's heart—and every other part of him, too—was through his stomach.

Winkler didn't say a word as he and I walked into the diner first, followed by Bill, Ilya and Zaria.

Would this Kevin recognize us, or was he in the dark about the real Kevin's demise? *Time to ask questions and find out.*

Kevin sat on a stool at the counter, between two truckers. *He's being guarded by them,* Zaria informed me.

I can get all three, I replied. *Bill, where do you want them?*

"There are holding cells in the basement of my building," he said, his voice soft.

Good enough, I sent.

I'll handle their disappearance, Zaria said.

Good. I went to mist, and in seconds had three men gathered up and flying toward Bill's office building.

~

Bill

I still have no idea how Zaria does what she does, but there wasn't even a blink as the three barstools were emptied of their occupants and three images appeared in their place.

We watched as all three solid images slid off their barstools and headed for the door, opening and closing it as if they were corporeal.

Three waiting customers rushed toward the available seats, covering them quickly.

"Food must be good here," Winkler quipped as we followed Zaria out the door. In less than a block, she transported us to the holding cells, where Lissa paced outside while two mean-looking men dressed as truckers shouted at her. Kevin Miller sat sullenly on the bench at the back of his cell. He didn't like being locked up—that was clear.

"Shut up," Lissa barked at the two men, who went silent so quickly it was frightening. "Sit down," she snapped at them. They obeyed, backing up to their own benches and plopping down.

"He doesn't have Kevin's memories," Zaria moved to stand beside Lissa. "He has no idea he was made from the blood and tissue of a dead werewolf."

He looked up when Zaria said Kevin, however, so they'd given him that name.

"Does he recognize me?" Winkler asked.

"Only from photographs," Zaria replied. I struggled to determine how she knew all that just from looking at the little fucker.

"Do you remember who you were before?" Zaria asked.

"Kevin Miller," he growled at her. "I've always been Kevin Miller."

"Who is Tate Briggs?" Lissa asked.

"I don't know who the hell you're talking about."

"He's not lying," Zaria turned to blink at Lissa.

"No, he's not. He has no idea who he was before. Do you think this means he came from a mental hospital, maybe?"

"Could be. The drug could fix the ah, problems, I think," Zaria answered Lissa's question.

"Do you have locations you can give me?" I asked Ilya. "Of prisons, hospitals and such?"

"Are you thinking about searching them? I warn you, that will likely mean your death."

"Somebody has to do something," I hissed at him before flinging an arm toward Kevin Miller, part II. "That kid—the original, died in Kansas City in a firefight with the local police, after he killed two people at a hotel. They're reproducing our worst nightmares, and somebody needs to stop it."

"Nobody wants to eliminate this threat more than I do," Ilya growled back. "It would be wise to understand when you may be overmatched."

"We have two of the best with us right now," I lowered my voice.

"Lissa—I've seen her handle the impossible. With Zaria's help, I think we may be able to stand toe-to-toe with whatever your *Klyki* can throw at us."

"I know you think this may be simple to deal with," Ilya said. "This is only the beginning. I know them. I've seen them operate. They always start small, but trust me when I tell you that they want you to think it will be simple to eliminate them. You have seen the dangerous cub and desire to kill it, but the main threat remains hidden, waiting for you to try. Believe me—the tiger is preparing to attack."

"Then what do you suggest?" I said, not bothering to hide my anger.

"I have to consider this," Ilya said. "We must plan carefully, or they will keep distracting us with this sort of thing until it is too late and they have what they want anyway."

"Well, what they want is Winkler and Lissa," I said. "How the hell are they going to take them?"

"I do not know, since I don't have sufficient information from both sides. I believe it will come to this, though, that whatever threat they have devised, handing over two people will seem a bargain."

Lissa

"Those two don't have memories past two weeks ago," Zaria told me. We'd finally turned away from Kevin, to scrutinize his trucker-guards.

"So they could all come from a mental hospital?"

"It's possible, I suppose. I hope that's the explanation, anyway."

"They're basically useless to us—all three of them."

"Except as a distraction. We don't know that this Kevin is the same one who sat on the park bench with Zukov and Gorham's assistant."

"Well, that's comforting to know."

"We also don't know that there aren't more Gorhams out there. Or more of almost anyone. I can't see the meeting in this one." She turned back to Kevin.

"So there are more." I let my shoulders droop as that information soaked in. "Just as there could be more of Lester Briggs and Bart Orford."

"Afraid so."

"Do you think there are more Baikovs?"

"I sure hope not. I pray they're too egocentric to allow more of themselves."

"But we can't say that for certain."

"Nope." *And we don't know where Liron is in all of it.*

"Ah. The uh, tiger Ilya referred to a moment ago."

"Yes. He should get used to you hearing everything he says from half a mile away."

You think Liron has any help on this?

I sure as hell hope not.

That makes two of us.

"You overheard everything?" Bill and Ilya joined us. Bill was the one to ask, when he already knew the answer.

"Yep," I replied.

"What do you suggest we do with these three?" Bill nodded toward our captives.

"There's nothing useful in any of them," Zaria said. "They're clones, now, and have little in the way of memories. They have compulsion placed by a vampire, but I can see past that."

"Compulsion to do what?" Ilya asked.

"To distract us, just as Ilya said."

"You think that they're elsewhere, causing trouble?"

"Maybe. We'll probably find out soon enough. They gave us thirty-six hours. The clock is ticking."

"I haven't received any messages of trouble," I said.

"But what if you're not the first person they think to contact if something goes wrong?" Zaria pointed out.

"Fucking hell. I have to call Tony." Bill strode so fast toward the door and the hallway beyond it was almost a run.

I blinked at Zaria while terror froze my heart. If they contacted

Tony, then he'd abandon his search for me in England and we'd be fucked.

Royally.

~

Bill

"Tony, where are you right now?" I asked.

"Driving really fast in England and leading Hafer on a wild goose chase."

"Has anyone tried to contact you?"

"A few times, but I let it go to voicemail. I'm a little busy at the moment."

"Will you let me know when you pick up those messages?"

"I'll do my best."

"Thanks."

"Is that it?"

"For now." I ended the call while a forceful sigh exploded from my lips.

"We may have a solution," Lissa stepped into the hallway, followed by the others.

"What's that?" I demanded. Any way I looked at this, things could blow up in our faces in a hurry.

"Tony two-point-oh," Lissa said.

No, I didn't understand. Not then.

Not until I saw Bill four-point-oh, and a tall man with light-brown hair who grinned at me and punched my arm like he knew who I was.

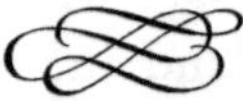

CHAPTER 9

Ilya

"I don't understand any of this," I said.

"Honey, you don't have to understand it. I just need you to work with me in this. It's what Lissa and I know to do to keep the timeline clean."

"What will you do with the other Bill—the new one?"

"Send him to England to work with the original Tony for a while. That way, there'll be one powerful person on that team in both places —to ensure that things run as smoothly as they can."

"They are powerful—these new ones?"

"Yes."

"More powerful than you?"

"Hmmph." Her snort was delicately derisive.

"Are you really a witch?"

"A part of me is—Karathian witch—in case you were wondering. Karathia is an alien world, Ilya. Someday, you'll understand that much better than you do now."

"So, these witches are quite powerful?"

"Some, as are many of the warlocks."

"I would like to see this one day."

"Hold that thought."

"For how long?"

"You'll know."

"You are too cryptic. I like this."

"Flatterer."

"Come here to me." I pulled her into my arms. I could tell she was worried. I wished to take those worries away, but they mirrored my own. Holding her was all I could do in this, and I was more than happy to have her pressed against me.

Lissa

"He's here," Bill announced from the doorway. We'd gone to his suite to wait for Tony two-point-oh to arrive.

He grinned at me when he walked through the door—this was the Tony I was married to in the future. The one who held the strength of one of the Powers That Be.

Tony, stop grinning, I complained in his direction.

Lissy, don't be that way.

This isn't fun and games, I snapped. *This is dead serious, and getting worse as we go along.*

Then maybe you should bring everybody up to speed. We can lay compulsion afterward, if we have to.

I sure as hell hope you remember everything you had in your head during this time, Tony, I grumped back. *We're gonna need information and locations in Russia. I have a feeling we'll end up there before this is over.*

Bree sent a message, he informed me as he walked farther into Bill's suite.

What's that?

She said to tell you that Winkler three-point-oh and Trajan six-point-oh are now at the beach house in Port A, disguised as plain werewolves to help Dalroy and Rhett protect Kellee and Winkler's pack.

"Oh, thank goodness," I slapped a hand over my face and spoke aloud.

"I've made arrangements for the right calls to go to the right Tony —in both places," Zaria came to place an arm around my shoulders.

"Thank you." I hugged her for doing what I'd have to do myself, otherwise.

"Don't thank me yet. I think we're about to get bad news."

"I think you're right." I pulled away from her as my skin began to itch furiously.

~

Bill

"Here's the message," Winkler handed his phone to me so I could read the note. Absently I took the device while staring at the Statue of Liberty—or what was left of it, from a NYPD harbor patrol boat.

Zaria had transported all of us straight to New York the moment Tony and I received the message that the statue had been destroyed.

More than a hundred tourists were unaccounted for, and that didn't include the bodies now being collected from the water by other patrol boats and the Coast Guard.

"This makes Fort Worth look like a kid's game," Winkler growled beside me. That's when I glanced at the note he'd received.

Come to us in forty-eight hours, and we'll hold off attacking our next target, the text read.

"Fuck," I breathed.

"Bill, Zaria and I have to fix this," Lissa joined Winkler beside me.

"How?" I shook my head at her. "This will take ten years to put together, with everybody and the cook working on it."

"Hmmph. We just need the cover of darkness, Bill."

"What then?"

"You have to wait and see. Oh, and arm yourself to the teeth—you and Ilya, both. Make sure all boats and the search and rescue teams are far away when we go in tonight."

"I'll have Tony relay that to the President, and hope he agrees."

"Do what you can. We'll work around small glitches if we have to."

"What the fuck is she talking about?" I growled at Winkler as Lissa walked away from us.

"No idea. Sounds pretty positive about whatever it is, though."

"Damn. I feel like I'm in the middle of the most frustrating science fiction story ever."

"That makes two of us. I've never seen her do some of the things she's doing, now. When those four vamps came after us at the bar in Fort Worth, I thought we had a nasty fight on our hands. Somehow, she put a shield around us, like I've seen Zaria do, and they didn't lay a claw on either of us."

"I'm still wondering about how I'm in two places at once, and Tony, too. Although I will admit, this one is nicer than the other one by a long shot."

"Smells the same, though," Winkler huffed.

"Thanks for that, it's somewhat comforting."

"Any time."

~

Lissa

We had dinner at the hotel, Tony was on the phone with the President most of the day and finally convinced him to order everybody away from the site come nightfall. Ilya had no idea what was coming, but he was ready to follow Zaria into the depths of hell if necessary.

"Get your weapons and gear; we're about to leave," Bill announced to everyone after dinner. He pulled out his nine-millimeter, checked the clip and slid it back into his shoulder holster. Then, lifting a rifle from beneath his bed, he proceeded to check it, too.

Ilya, dressed completely in black, was armed similarly. Tony, grinning, shoved a nine-millimeter into his shoulder holster. He didn't need anything else.

Winkler was prepared to turn if necessary; therefore, he didn't need an extra weapon. Charles refused anything else, although Bill asked if he wanted a rifle. Zaria and I, well, we were self-contained, weapons-wise.

"Time to go," I said. "I'll get us there. Zaria takes over after that."

"What are we doing, again?" Winkler turned dark eyes in my direction.

"Oh, we're about to meet this head-on, you might say."

~

Zaria

You will be shielded, I told Ilya in mindspeech. We'd gathered at the base of the destroyed statue, what was left of it, anyway. Just as Bill and Tony asked, all guards, patrol boats and helicopters had pulled back until they were half a mile away.

"Time to blur their binoculars and cameras," Lissa spoke grimly before acting.

"Huh?" Winkler gripped her hand as she stilled to concentrate.

"It's done," she opened her eyes and nodded in my direction.

"Now, what you don't know so far, is that the Kremlin has devised a way to reverse-engineer the alien drug—I know you know about it, Bill. Tony, too," I pursed my lips while looking from one to the other.

"But," Bill said.

"You guys need to stop pining after that filth," I said. "I destroyed your cache for a reason."

Bill's eyes became round—he didn't know what happened to it. Tony didn't either—the one from the current timeline. Future Tony knew from Lissa, so he didn't have a reaction like Bill did.

"But," Bill said again.

"They've found a way to reverse-engineer that shit," I stated flatly. "You'll be seeing all sorts of dead folks come back to life because of it, unless I miss my guess. Now, what we're about to do in retaliation, is reverse-engineer the timeline. This shouldn't have happened," I swept out a hand to encompass the destroyed statue. "We're going into a fight, so be prepared."

I bent time, then, to the previous evening, when six vampires who'd received a dose of Lissa's blood, along with eight werewolves, four of whom were Bart Orford clones and the rest looking like Lester Briggs, were busily placing charges while two other vampires held the night guards hostage by laying compulsion.

You're shielded from sight, but they'll know they're being attacked the moment you start firing or removing heads, I informed the others.

I'm on it, Lissa released her claws and prepared to turn to mist.

"How the hell is this still standing?" Winkler breathed, looking up at the still-intact statue.

"Honey, we bent time," Lissa informed him. "Now get to work; we have vamps and wolves to kill."

~

Ilya

The moment Zaria turned us loose against those who were laying hidden charges throughout the statue, I fired the rifle at the first one I saw. Unfortunately, that one was a vampire and not a werewolf.

I didn't have the nose to tell the difference, although I kept firing as he rushed me. Lissa half-materialized to remove his head before he could reach me.

Keep firing—it slows them down, she informed me mentally.

I kept firing, taking down the next one, who was werewolf. Had Zaria known there were others, waiting below the water line in scuba gear? They flung off masks and such to rush toward the statue's base and joined the fight.

Some of them were human—a single bullet brought one of them down. I kept firing until my magazine ran out, then shoved another clip in and started again.

Elsewhere, Winkler had become wolf to fight others who'd done the same; the werewolves had turned to attack us. I killed one who had difficulty coming out of his clothing. He lay in a tangle of black jeans, still caught up in them while bleeding out.

Charles was now down by the water, removing heads from anything I hadn't had time to fire at yet. That turned out to be a very good system—he knew the vampires from the others, and was going after them so I'd not target the wrong ones.

Bill and Anthony Hancock were running up the steps after the ones who'd gone higher to lay charges; I heard bullets flying and ricocheting inside the metal statue. I hadn't realized a boat had pulled up and emptied itself of twenty more until one of their bullets smacked against the shield Zaria built around me.

Had I recalled that, I'd never have worried about the first vampire. "Die, excrement," I hissed as the twenty came at Charles and me at a run, firing their weapons as they came.

Lissa

I'm here with you, I informed Bill. Tony, somewhere behind Bill, could take care of himself. Bill was first up the stairs, heading for the werewolves who'd gone to lay charges near the top of the statue. With all the bombs they'd planted, no wonder there wasn't a single, recognizable piece of Lady Liberty remaining afterward.

I'm removing the bombs, Zaria informed me.

What are you doing with them?

I thought I'd save them for a special occasion.

Good idea, I grunted, half-materializing to remove the head of a wolf who'd leapt down from the steps above to avoid Bill and his nine-millimeter.

Charles and Ilya have their hands full outside, Tony sent. *A bunch of new ones came out of the water, and then a boat landed, carrying about twenty more.*

Great, and here I thought we were making headway.

The harbor patrol is sending a boat and a helicopter—they've seen flashes of gunfire from a distance, Charles reported.

Will that be a problem?

It won't if you get Tony and Bill out here pretty quick, he replied.

I'll see to it, Zaria said. *I'll even give them some of my bomb stash as evidence.*

Good plan.

Are there any more inside the statue? Tony asked.

One more. Hang on, I'll get him.

Oh, lord.

Ohlordohlordohlord.

Phil.

Fucking-backstabbing-asshole-of-a-fucking-former-second-Phil. I didn't bother getting him. Still in human form, Phil held a detonator in his hand. He grinned as he prepared to push the button.

I didn't wait around to ask him how he'd been reincarnated; I took his head without a qualm while turning his hand to mist so he couldn't press the button. Then, releasing the hand and letting it drop (along with the rest of him) down the stairwell, I gripped the detonator close to my chest and shielded it—just in case.

Bill

"Here's the cache of bombs we recovered from the mission," I handed two crates of explosives to the harbor police, along with the detonator Lissa found on the last werewolf she destroyed.

From the look on her face, she'd recognized the werewolf, too. We'd have a talk after we cleared things with the NYPD and the Mayor, while Tony talked to the President on the phone.

"The intel we received didn't give us time to notify anyone," I told the lieutenant. "We had to put a team together and go before they blew the whole thing to kingdom come."

"I see that," Lieutenant Killebrew studied the crate of explosives warily. "We'll hand this over to our bomb squad," he said, nodding to a subordinate nearby, who pulled out a cell phone to make the call. "We owe you," he added. "This would have been a fiasco. Do you have identification on any of these?" He jerked his head toward a long line of covered bodies, many of them headless.

"Unconfirmed," I said. "We'll keep you updated if that changes."

"I'd appreciate that. I assume you'll keep the Mayor in the loop?"

"I'll have the President call him," I said. "Just to touch base and tell him he'll be informed of new developments."

"Who'd do this?" Killebrew shook his head.

"I can think of too many to count," I said. "The guards were overpowered here; this isn't their fault."

"We'll still question them, to see what they know."

"Understood."

Their compulsion has been removed and replaced, Lissa informed me. *It'll be just like you said—overpowered and taken hostage.*

I wanted to allow my shoulders to sag in relief. I didn't. "Let me know if you need assistance with any of this going forward," I told Killebrew. He nodded before turning to his men and barking orders.

"We're done, here," I turned to Lissa. "We'll have to get a boat here to take us back to shore."

"It's on the way," Tony walked back toward us, pocketing his cell phone. "The President's sending a Coast Guard cutter for us."

The eighty-seven-footer arrived in twenty minutes. We loaded in and were taken back to the harbor. Tony and I thanked the Captain before transferring into waiting SUVs. "The President wants a debriefing, so we'll be flying to D.C. Arrangements are already made," Tony said.

I wanted Zaria to take us, but that would give too much away. Besides, we had time to get our story straight during the flight. What I really wanted to know was this; how was Baikov going to take this? We'd pulled a victory out of his grasp, and now, the whole thing would look as if it never happened.

I'd checked the date on my phone and my watch; it showed the night before—and I hoped reliving this day would prevent the news being filled with deaths and destruction, as my first experience of the date had been.

$\sim$

Lissa

"We overheard some chatter at the last minute," Tony explained to the President, as we sat inside a White House meeting room later. It wasn't far from the one where we'd met to question the former Chief of Staff, and the scent of freshly-cut boards, paint and plaster was everywhere.

"I'm glad you overheard it," the President blew out a breath. "If you hadn't gone as quickly as you did, Lady Liberty would be blown to hell by now."

"I'm happy we arrived in time," Bill added. "We worried we wouldn't."

"I'd like to keep our names and the department out of this if possible," Tony said. "If you could put out a press release, saying the Harbor Patrol Division of NYPD took care of this, I'd be grateful."

"Reeling in an enemy?" One of the President's eyebrows lifted in speculation.

"Something like that."

"Good enough. I'll see to it and advise the Press Secretary. He's gearing up for a meeting in a few minutes anyway."

"Thank you, Mr. President," Tony nodded.

"Thank you, Director Hancock, Vice Director," he nodded at Tony and Bill.

Let's get out of here before he asks more questions, Tony sent.

I was all for that; I needed to tell Winkler I'd offed Phil a second time, and to put up his guard; I felt worse was coming.

~

Zaria

"We remember, although we've lived this day twice. Will they recall it, too?" Ilya asked me.

"You mean Baikov squared and their henchpersons?"

"Yes."

"They'll only remember that their plan was thwarted, and they won't know how. I'm aiming at the biggest fish in this—the one holding both Baikovs' strings. He'll know, and he'll be pissed."

"Won't that make us a target?"

"Honey, we're already a target."

"I suppose that's true. Will he be able to find us?"

"Nope. Not after tonight, anyway."

"How can you be sure of this?"

"I have something for all of us that'll make sure of it. I really want pancakes right now. Are you hungry?"

"And thirsty."

"Where do you want to eat?" Lissa turned in her seat in front of us to ask. The SUVs that delivered us to the White House were now driving us toward our hotel.

"A twenty-four-hour breakfast joint?" I asked.

"Sounds good. Bill," Lissa said.

"Lissa?" Bill sat in the front passenger seat and turned to look at Lissa in the dim interior of the vehicle.

"Know of a good, twenty-four-hour breakfast place?"

"Yep." He gave instructions to our driver and we were rerouted to *Oh, That's Waffle*, a twenty-four-hour place not far from our hotel.

"I love pancakes," I sighed. There was only a wedge left of a stack of three on my plate when I was too full to move.

Winkler had eaten a stack of six, with sides of bacon and sausage. He'd frowned while he ate as Lissa told him she'd killed Phil again before he could press the detonator.

"Who is Phil?" Ilya asked softly.

"Winkler's former Second, who tried to kill him for the software," I replied. "I think that's how he got reproduced—he had a buyer set up back then, and I figure they got his DNA or something—enough to recreate him for future use."

Winkler set his fork down; his plate was empty, but if it hadn't been, he'd still have stopped at this point.

"This—it's why they wanted parts of my father, isn't it?" He raised his eyes to meet Lissa's.

"We think so, yes. I'm sorry, honey. They're not holding anything back. They want to hit us every way they can, just to get whatever they want."

"I want them dead. Any way we can do it. I don't care what it takes or how much it costs."

"We have to find them, first," I cautioned. "They're not making it easy."

~

Refizan, Past

Breanne

Lissa was here—the past Lissa, before she became a member of the Hierarchy. The future Lissa was on Earth taking care of the wrinkles Liron was creating in that timeline. What she didn't know was that he'd also arranged to cause wrinkles here.

It wasn't hard for him to pinpoint her activities—her fight against the Ra'Ak had been recorded and distributed from one end of the universes to the other. Frankly, it was better that she handle the problems on Earth while I worked on the kinks Refizan was experiencing.

I'd brought help with me, too.

Zaria was helping Lissa, because I wanted someone who could *Change What Was* in both places, if Liron's plans proved successful in any way.

The General should have paid closer attention to Liron; he was the best strategist I'd ever seen, and was now attempting to reverse his own death in the future. Somehow, he'd planned for every contingency, including his death.

Randl even said he'd make his crew available, should they be needed in either place. I disliked pulling them away from their search for V'dar, but this past timeline balanced on the width of a single hair.

"What are we dealing with today?" Drake came to stand beside me. I held a copy of Lissa's old journal, given to me by Nefrigar. The original was held in the Larentii Archives and had a place of honor, there.

"This is supposed to be the day that Solar Red destroys the vampire caves beneath the city, in an attempt to kill the vampire population."

"How is Liron going to interfere with that?"

"Remember, the current Lissa doesn't have the power she does in the future. All a rogue god has to do is place a shield around the cave where they're gathering, and she won't be able to get herself or the other vampires out."

"What are we going to do to prevent that?" Drew now stood on my other side.

"I have an idea," Erland folded in, holding a tray of coffee and donuts. "Fresh from Le-Ath Veronis," he grinned.

"What's that?" I frowned at him.

"Quin loaned me some empty spheres." He let go of the tray of food and drinks, allowing it to float in midair while he *Pulled* in a wooden crate. It held more than two dozen spheres of varying sizes, most of which would fit easily in my palm.

"How did you come up with that?" I blinked at him.

"Quin. She told Ry that rogue gods had been inside spheres before. We can try stuffing more into spheres. She even placed the call in them, aimed specifically for rogue gods."

"Seriously?" I lifted one of the spheres out of the crate, which, like the tray, now floated in the air between us. The moment I touched it, I felt the tingle—and the pull it exerted.

"I'm going to add to her spell," I said, lifting the sphere to my lips and breathing ancient words against it.

Quin knew all those words. As did I.

"We'll have to get close enough to the rogues so they can't fight the call," I sighed, setting that sphere back and lifting another. "These aren't mindless, poisonous organisms. These are sentient, powerful beings and the farther away they are, the more capable they'll be of ignoring the call."

"So we have to trap them?" Drew asked.

"They'll have to understand that we're here to prevent whatever it is they're doing. We just have to hide behind Erland, here, because the

Ra'Ak believed that Lissa's deeds were those of Karathian warlocks or wizards, at first. They had no idea that a Vampire Queen could give them so much grief."

"We should have brought more warlocks," Drake teased Erland.

"I did," he grinned. "Ilya Ironsmith is on the way."

"You know the original Ilya is working with Zaria on Earth?" I smiled at Erland.

"He said he has memories that he didn't before," Erland chuckled. "He's ready to do whatever he can for you, Lissa and Zaria."

"We're here," Randl appeared with Ilya beside him. "Are you sure you don't need me to stay?"

"I think Zaria would like you to keep searching for V'dar. We know he is Liron's child, and Liron is causing all of this. We can't bring all our forces into one place or another—it makes us too convenient a target. I'll send a message if you and the others are needed."

"Good luck, then." Randl lifted a hand in a half-wave and disappeared, leaving Ilya behind.

"Whose ass are we kicking today?" Ilya asked.

"We need to lay a shield that will force other shields away," Erland replied. "Feel up to that?"

"Show me where," Ilya shrugged.

I know Lissa can see in the dark, but this is really dark, Drake sent as we set down outside the meeting chamber. Shielded heavily, we were invisible to the vampires filing in through the heavy doors.

Those same doors were set to collapse in less than half an hour, once most of the vampire population was inside. Since a part of me was also vampire, I could see as well as they could. Erland and Ilya had already taken measures to enhance their sight with a spell.

I'll cover for you, so the rogues building the shield won't know we're doing the same, I informed Erland and Ilya.

Are those spheres in your pocket?

I have four with me.

Good Let's hope we go home with trapped rogue gods after this is over, Erland said. I knew, although he'd never twitch a facial muscle to let on, that he was worried about *this* Lissa. The vid recordings of her fighting Ra'Ak had been his first vision of her, and he'd loved her from that moment on.

Erland would give his life to protect her in this timeline, he loved her so much. While Erland held the power of the En'nurifi, Ilya's power was that of a Sixth-level Karathian warlock, combined with the spirit of an entire planet. The representative gold coin lay on his chest as proof of it. I didn't ask the name of the planet—it was his information to divulge or not.

Those two, working on a sloughing spell together, probably didn't need to hide behind my shield because of Ilya's protective planetary spirit. Neither gods nor the Ra'Ak paid attention to elements of the natural worlds—it was like singling out a blade of grass from trillions of other blades of grass.

That was the power Ilya now wielded. Randl had joked that he and his crew were now one with the universe. His statement held more truth than most people suspected or understood.

As for the gold medallion around Ilya's neck—Zaria had provided additional protection for all of Randl's crew, including Ilya. I had yet to determine what it was or how it worked, exactly; I only knew that it was protection of the best kind.

Enhancing my sight with power, I watched the sloughing spell form and grow until it encompassed the entire rock chamber where the vampires gathered. Drake and Drew, at my back, guarded us while the spell formed and took hold.

It's done, Erland sent. *Are we watching this from a distance, so we'll know whether it worked or not?*

Of course. I have the spheres, remember? Wouldn't want to pass up the chance to catch a rogue god or two.

I hear you. Let's just hope they don't get suspicious, or discover that we're here.

There's a side cave not far behind us, Drew sent.

We'll go there, then.

~

Drake

When the first cave imploded not far away, it shook the cavern around us, bringing dust and rock raining onto the shield Breanne held around us.

Do they suspect we're here? Drew sent. It was the same thing I was wondering—if I wanted to destroy the chamber the vampires were in, I'd have gone to it, first thing.

I don't know, Ilya replied to our mindspeech. *Maybe they're just covering all the bases, in case there is someone else down here. Never hurts to be cautious.*

My shield will hold, and this cave hasn't collapsed yet, Bree pointed out. To punctuate her statement, another chamber, closer, this time, imploded, bringing more shaking and the subsequent deluge of rock and dust. My hands were against the inside of Bree's shield as I struggled to keep my balance. The shaking continued and worsened with another explosion.

The vampires are panicking inside the chamber, Bree reported. *Just as Lissa wrote.* Another explosion followed, crushing the doors to the chamber and cutting off the vampire's escape from inside.

Now we see if the sloughing shield works, Erland's sending sounded grim.

Lissa will be the only one to get through the sloughing shield—I tuned it to her mist, Erland said. *Anything she carries inside her mist will be safe with her.*

She should be making her selections of vampires to bring out, Bree noted.

I feel her bouncing against the rogue's shield, Ilya almost shouted. *Erland, link with me. We have to get her out of there!*

CHAPTER 10

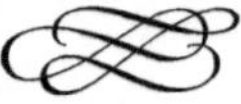

Breanne ended up adding her power to Ilya's and mine to allow Lissa passage. The sloughing shield had been only partially successful, and that spelled a powerful rogue to me.

What—or whom—had Liron allied himself with?

As for the spheres—we managed to capture one rogue who'd come our way to escape the chamber, but Breanne said he only held the strength comparable to the Powers That Be.

Small potatoes, she'd added, although she sent the sphere to Nefrigar in the Archives for safekeeping.

It was one less rogue for us to worry about on Refizan, but we all wondered how many rogues Liron had managed to recruit to his cause this time.

"Dad looks tired," Drew sighed.

We sat at a café across from Dragon and Karzac's apartment, discussing what had happened after Lissa finally escaped with her load of vampire refugees. Somewhere in Gabron's library, they were currently holding a meeting about Solar Red and the Ra'Ak, whom Solar Red believed to be their god.

Dragon arrived and walked wearily up the steps to the second-floor apartment while we watched. According to Lissa's journal, she'd begun cleaning the dojo for him, to obey the Refizani law of having employment.

Dragon knew about the implosion of the vampire caves, and also understood that Lissa had finally escaped. He still worried about her—I could see it in the set of his shoulders before he disappeared inside the apartment and shut the door.

"Doesn't look like a fun assignment, from any perspective," Drake shook his head.

"Most of them weren't." Karzac—the future version—arrived and pulled out an empty chair to sit with us. "Since this was my home world, I chose to come with Dragon rather than waiting at home for the final battle and aftermath. I'm glad I made that choice. We were both needed here, as was Lissa."

"Lissa almost didn't make it out of that cave," Drake said. "This time."

"I know. Breanne sent mindspeech. That's why I came."

"Do you think Liron knows now that Lissa is in both places at once?" Ilya asked.

"If he doesn't, he's a fool," Karzac huffed. "He knows she is pivotal to so much of the future. She falls, the rest of us fall—or mostly so."

"That may be why he's gone recruiting—beneath the General's notice, of course."

"There are many of the hidden—we know that," Karzac leveled his gaze on Breanne.

"Yes. We know that," her eyes dropped to her hands, which were folded in her lap. "Liron has searched them out, obviously."

"He's working really hard to prevent his death in the future," Ilya rumbled.

"I would, too, if I knew it was coming," Drake agreed. "This isn't just tied to Lissa, I think. It's tied to Zaria, too."

"Zaria did kill him," Breanne acknowledged.

"Most of us were there to see it," I offered. I'd stood beside Rylend while it happened.

"So. The future is built by Lissa, and held up and added to by Zaria, to bring about Liron's downfall," Ilya sorted through what he knew.

"That doesn't include the God Wars, which involve Breanne," Karzac pointed out. "Without those three, who knows what may have happened?"

"That's true," I dipped my chin in a nod to Karzac. The man could have been a philosopher rather than a physician, I think. He would have been a success at either.

"I hope this doesn't upset Lissa on Earth—she doesn't need the distraction," Breanne sighed. "And we have to get back to work—to make sure things go as they should. We have no idea how many rogues are here with us, working for the opposite to happen."

~

Washington, D.C.

Lissa

I wish I could call it a fucked-up dream, but I knew it wasn't. On Refizan, someone was attempting to change things there, too. Somehow, I figured Breanne or someone else was handling that part of it.

I'd dreamed I almost didn't get out of the vampire's cave before it collapsed on all of us. I'd gone to mist, but my mist had been bounced back inside the cave rather than allowing me through. I'd panicked as my mist bounced against that blockade, several times, in fact, before something changed and I was let through.

Zaria knew something had happened the moment I sat down opposite her in the hotel restaurant for breakfast. "I kept it warm for you," she said, pushing the Starbucks cup in my direction.

"I love you," I said, lifting the cup and sipping the caramel mocha as if it were ambrosia.

"I suppose you're wondering why I called this meeting," Breanne pulled out an empty chair adjacent to mine.

"Here's your vanilla latte," Zaria passed another cup to Bree.

"You knew she was coming?" I frowned at Zaria.

132

"I told her a few minutes ago," Bree admitted. "I said you might have had some new, not-so-nice memories crop up. I wanted to set your fears at ease."

"I have to tell you, my claustrophobia was sounding the alarm all over the place," I grumbled before sipping more coffee.

"I was afraid of that," Bree sighed.

"Ah, did you get something for me?" Charles arrived and took the last chair at our four-top.

"Yes." Zaria didn't sound pleased as she handed the last cup to him.

Breanne frowned deeply at Charles, who suddenly appeared flummoxed, although he didn't respond. "Don't make me sorry I invited you," Bree told him.

"I'll do my best," Charles held up a hand.

"As you've probably figured out, Liron is hitting us on two fronts," Bree began. "Here, and on Refizan. I think he wants both versions of you out of the way. He's just hiding behind the Russians' desire for Winkler and his security program to do it."

"You mean Winkler's not the primary target?"

"For the Russians, he is. Not for Liron. Winkler holds little importance to Liron."

"Fuck." I pinched the bridge of my nose with my free hand.

"Is someone helping you on Refizan?" Zaria pointed her question at Bree.

"Yes. Several someones, Ilya included."

"Good." I watched her mouth tighten as she considered what could happen to Ilya in both places. At least on Refizan, he wore a medallion that I'd bet my entire treasury on to keep him as safe as he could possibly be kept, given the circumstances.

"Are you all right—after your bout of claustrophobia?" Zaria now turned to me.

"I'll get past it—the dream was terrifying, and I figure the real me at the time was scared to death."

"We managed to capture one of Liron's rogue helpers, but he's low-level," Breanne went on. "Hardly strong enough to cause a stiff breeze, actually."

"Where is he now?" Zaria asked.

"Stuck inside a sphere in Nefrigar's keeping."

"Good." She visibly relaxed. "Whoever it is won't get away. I take it you had Quin's help in trapping him in the sphere?"

"Yes. Without her, it wouldn't have been possible."

"I like using Liron's own weapons against him."

"Me, too."

"You saw him creating those spheres, didn't you?" Charles asked Zaria.

"I did. I was terrified he'd find out I was stealing some of them."

"You stole some—from under his nose? That took, well," I hesitated, trying to find an appropriate word.

"A lot of stupidity?" Zaria smiled and shook her head. "I felt that way the whole time—that I was being stupid and he'd catch me."

"But you got away," Charles pointed out. "Thanks for this—I didn't realize caramel hazelnut lattes would be so good."

"It's my backup," Zaria said. "If I've had too many vanilla lattes."

"I hope we'll be exchanging information as things proceed," Charles then spoke to Breanne and me. "I warn you, too, you were gone three weeks during this period the first time around. You only have half that time left. Liron will up his game soon, unless I miss my guess."

I looked at Breanne, whose eyes had gone wide. I'd forgotten that. Griffin had bent time to get me back three weeks from the day I'd left. *Fuck. Fuck to the eighth power.*

"Don't underestimate what happened shortly after Lissa returned, either," Zaria pointed out. "Liron could be upping Jovana's game, and we'd never know it."

"Oh, dear God," I dropped my face into my hands.

"I suppose you've read all the records concerning Earth in the Larentii Archives?" I heard Charles ask while my mind buzzed with worry.

"I had plenty of time to do so, after Kal grabbed me and hauled me to the Larentii homeworld. I focused specifically on the Nineteenth, Twentieth and Twenty-first centuries."

"Wise of you to choose those records."

"I'll take that as a compliment."

"It was meant as one."

"What do you think he might do with Jovana, to up her game?" I forced myself away from my temporary stupor.

"Anything, including sending someone else in there with her," Charles shrugged. "I just don't have an idea who that might be, up to and including Liron himself."

"You're not making me feel any better, you know."

"I wasn't intending to. He could throw anything at us. Best to be prepared, no matter what or who."

"But the original you has to go in there," Breanne pointed out. "Those events can't change. Jovana has to be taken to Wlodek, and he has to pass sentence and hand her execution to Tony."

"I can go in with you—to take care of anyone else who might show up," Zaria volunteered. "The other you doesn't have to know. If you want, I'll make sure the other you is protected while you handle anybody else who thinks to cause trouble."

"That sounds great, except we don't have any idea who it will be."

"I know. The way I see it, we don't have much of a choice. I'd say we also need to be there when Tony gets hurt in the bombing. It could mean the difference between him being whole while bleeding out and being in pieces, which is far too late for a vampire's turning."

"You're not making me feel better about any of this," I sent Zaria a hopeless glance.

"I know. I'm sorry."

"It's not your fault," I sighed. "I appreciate your extrapolation, too, it's just—hard for me to hear it, that's all."

"What do you think we should do in the meantime?" Charles asked Zaria.

"I'd like to harass General Baikov some more. I just don't have a plan on how to do that at the moment."

"Well, Ilya knows somebody who knows somebody who watches the Baikov family in the Czech Republic; maybe we should start there," I suggested.

"Baikov has a family," Charles breathed as a light appeared in his eyes. "How fortunate for us."

"Fortunate for them that we're not assholes, like he is," Zaria interjected.

"Are you thinking what I'm thinking?" Breanne lifted an eyebrow as she gazed across the table at Charles.

"We can show them such a good time, they'll never want to go back," he grinned.

"While we're blackmailing the General, you mean? This sort of thing doesn't come without consequences," Zaria pointed out.

"People have already died who weren't supposed to," Charles turned to her. "Those kind of consequences?"

"What sort of leverage do we have against vampire Baikov?" Zaria locked eyes with Charles.

"I can inform the Honored One," he said, tapping a finger against his paper coffee cup.

"Do you have a way to do that so he won't send anyone else here to muck things up?" I asked. The last thing I needed was for the original Gavin to come gallivanting in to chase down Baikov and find me in the middle of it.

"I can tell him that Baikov has allied with rogue Russian werewolves, and then ask Weldon to have a conversation with him regarding what he knows. We can also say that Winkler is handling the werewolf end of the investigation and we're cooperating on the vampire side—Rhett, Dalroy and I."

"Make sure he thinks that you're enough to handle this," Breanne pointed a finger at Charles.

"Not to worry, my *Love*," he smiled at her.

"I'm not sure I like this," Zaria said, looking from Charles to Breanne, then meeting my gaze. I felt as if I were in the middle of it, and worried that this plan could go in several directions, most of them wrong.

In other words, I agreed with Zaria.

Besides, if Liron were involved in all this, we had no idea whether he'd planned for this contingency, and what he'd end up doing either way.

Plus, we had a Sirenali to contend with, and who knew how many reproductions from the reverse-engineered drug. Ghosts from our past were already popping up like mushrooms, seemingly overnight.

That spelled a devious, carefully crafted plan made by Liron, and if his past machinations were any indication, we might not be ready for what he'd unleash.

If we took people, well, he could take people, too, and that terrified me.

"I will not cooperate with this plan," I announced.

"Neither will I," Zaria nodded to me. "Not the part about the kidnapping, anyway. You can tell Wlodek whatever you want, but for me, Baikov's family is off the table. Liron will intervene, even if the Baikov's don't. All I will agree to is watching that family, to see if the human Baikov visits. Then we could take him and find out what he knows. He's just a large cog in this giant machine," she said.

A slow smile spread across Charles' face. "I was hoping you'd argue," he told her. "It's a stupid idea to kidnap the family."

"This was a test?" Zaria asked, her words stiff and angry.

"I should know better than to test you." He was still smiling. Zaria shook her head before scooting her chair back and walking out of the restaurant. Her latte disappeared a moment later.

She wasn't about to let Charles deprive her of her coffee.

"You really shouldn't bait her like that, and use me to help you do it," Breanne frowned at Charles.

"You, know, I'm kinda with Zaria on this. Have fun." My chair scooted back and I rose, taking my coffee cup with me. "Let me know when you're treating people like equals again."

I followed Zaria out the door.

~

Breanne

"She knows more about Liron than anyone else," I said, sipping my coffee. Zaria had placed a warming spell on it, so it stayed at the proper temperature until I finished it. "I'm not sure why you wanted to feel her out on this."

"She has some of me in her, remember?" Charles said softly. "Thankfully, she has something from her mothers, too."

"Ah. The secret you won't tell, huh?"

"I borrowed from three, you know," Charles sighed and sipped his coffee.

"Three?"

"Of the strongest and best I've ever known."

"Do they know?"

"Of course not."

"Are you going to tell them?"

"I want to tell them before I tell Zaria. This way, if I have to withdraw the information and go into hiding over it," he spread his hands. "On two of them, anyway."

"Why would you need to go into hiding? Any woman should be proud to have Zaria as a daughter."

"Even one they never knew about? Women generally don't like it if they're not included in things like that."

"Well, you owe them, I think," I insisted. "And why only two of them? What about the third—does she already know?"

"She's dead."

I went still. "I think you ought to tell me," I demanded. "At least about the dead one."

"Hmmph. I figure I'll hear from Wlodek in the future if he finds out," Charles stared at the white tablecloth beneath his cup.

"What the hell does Wlodek have to do with any of this?" I demanded.

"Because the dead one is Sarita."

"Sarita? The Vampire Queen who walked into the sun because she couldn't have children? That Sarita?"

"Yes. I'll likely hear from Merrill, too, because she was his turn."

"She has a child, and you fucking didn't say anything?"

"It's more complicated than that. She died before I was born humanoid. I had to bend time to get her blood—before she was turned."

"And then had plenty of time to bend time again and tell her she'd have a daughter."

"See, I knew you'd get upset over this."

"I'd get more upset if I were in Sarita's position and found out I had a daughter after it was too late."

"When you're dead, you usually don't get emotional like that."

"Are you calling me emotional?"

"Well, that's why I chose the women I did to be Zaria's mothers. I don't get emotional often, so I went looking for strong women who carried themselves—and their emotions—well."

"I really want to punch you, right now. Let me say again, any woman would be proud to know that Zaria is her daughter. I think you cheated Sarita, and now you're cheating two other women at the same time."

"Hypothetically speaking, what would you do if I told you that you were one of those women? How would you react? Tell me."

"I'd go straight to her and give her the biggest hug and the best *Love* I could, because she'd deserve it."

"See—that's why I haven't said anything. I think that sort of information would interrupt and distract her from the current mission. When it's over, I may consider letting all parties know."

"Charles, I never knew how cruel you can be at times."

"Bree, I," he dropped his gaze. I watched as he shifted in his chair before squaring his shoulders and looking at me again.

"You know who I was, once. You saved me from being that—by giving me *Love*. I can never repay that. You opened my eyes. Power isn't everything. I learned that on the day I tried to kill you, eons ago. I have a lot to answer for, and I feel that burden. Zaria is my gift to the universes, and a piece of my atonement. Bree, my *Love*, you *are* one of Zaria's mothers."

Lissa is the other.

~

What should I do with this information? Charles was right—I wanted to smother Zaria with *Love*, but things had gone dangerous here—and on Refizan. Distracting Zaria now could have consequences.

Damn.

And Lissa? She deserved to know, too, but there were the same reasons not to tell her. I was now at loose ends while this information turned over and over in my brain. Lissa and I, once this was over, needed to have a talk with our shared daughter.

After we came to terms with this ourselves. In the meantime, there was someone I wanted to speak with—one of Zaria's half-sisters—Conner.

Specifically, Conner as the Guardian, and also as the Shining One known as the *Mouth of the One.*

Call me if you need me, I sent to Karzac on Refizan. *I have an errand to run.*

~

"He sent mindspeech. He said you'd come," Conner told me. She and Kiarra, Zaria's other half-sister, waited for me in Conner's huge kitchen.

"He also said you'd ask about Sarita," Kiarra said. "Because Sarita was in love with Merrill, and he didn't reciprocate that feeling. He turned her to save her life rather than killing her when she didn't obey a vampire's compulsion."

"So he wasn't the one who drank from her?" I frowned.

"No. That was Wlodek," Conner answered my question.

"So. That explains a lot," I breathed a sigh and sat on a barstool, setting my paper coffee cup down in front of me.

"It does, but not all of it. Wlodek didn't make the attempt, because he knew what the odds were of her survival—females as a rule didn't make the turn on Earth. Already, I think he was falling in love with her and asked Merrill to either kill her for him or attempt the turn, which in most cases, would end up being the same thing."

"How do you feel—about learning you have a daughter?" Kiarra asked.

"I'm still working my way through that, and am caught between being pissed at Charles and wanting to hug the stuffing out of Zaria."

"Well, imagine our surprise when we learned we had another sister," Conner huffed. "We went through the whole gamut of emotions, but the main one was why didn't he tell us? We felt deprived of that bond of kinship. Now, Zaria just turns away when she sees us. She won't come and talk to us or anything."

"It may have to do with the fact that both of you recognized him eventually as your father. She still hasn't come to terms with that. Consequently, having sisters muddled all that up for her."

"And having mothers can do the same, if not make it worse," Kiarra nodded.

"For years, she had no idea who her birth parents were. No search on Earth could reveal that information, because humans couldn't reach it. She considered herself an orphan in every sense of the word, even with adoptive parents."

"And now you want to know what happened to Sarita after she walked into the sun, don't you?" Conner asked.

"If the Guardian knows," I shrugged.

"Her soul has been reborn, but we were commanded not to reveal that information. However, there is something else."

"What's that?"

"Zaria's surrogate mother—the one who carried her and then gave her away."

"Well, I hadn't thought about that kink until just now," I berated myself.

"This is where things get really interesting, because I think Charles wanted her to have a connection to all of the Three," Kiarra said. "Ashe's mother, Ashlynne, carried and delivered Harriett, who eventually became Zaria."

I stared at both Kiarra and Conner for several seconds, before I remembered to blink. "I know who Sarita is, now," I pointed a finger at Conner. "And, as far as I'm concerned, Zaria still has three living mothers." Surrogate or not, Ashlynne had played a part in Zaria's existence.

I disappeared the moment I saw confirmation of my guess in both their gazes. Avendor was my next stop; I intended to ask Ashlynne a few questions of my own.

～

"You're uncomfortable?" Ashe shook his head at me. "I'm uncomfortable every time I see her, and she's my mother."

"You didn't grow up calling her Mom, so that's understandable," I said. "You didn't know about her until you were sixteen, I think."

"I didn't know she was still alive for a long time. Now, Rabis, I have no trouble calling him Grandfather, so you figure this out." Ashe stood in the massive kitchen at SouthStar's big house, as they called it.

"Have you had a talk with Charles about Zaria?"

"No. Why?"

"Because Ashlynne was Zaria's surrogate mother."

I watched him go completely still. "You're joking," he said after a moment.

"I'm not—I just got confirmation from two of his three daughters."

"Conner and Kiarra?"

"Yep."

"So, he got her to carry his baby." Ashe shoved hands in both pockets and turned to look out the wall of windows lining one side of the kitchen. Those windows overlooked the gishi tree groves below the house—mile upon mile of them.

"That's not all. I also know who Zaria's actual mothers are."

"My mother wasn't enough?" He whirled to face me.

"Um, well, he took from three others to form the egg," I said.

"You'd better tell me before I go hunting him and choke him to death."

"Lissa, Sarita, and—me."

"You have a daughter?" His voice went soft.

"That I didn't know about, yes," I said. Frankly, I should have known before now, because Zaria was so much like Lissa and me. Since I didn't know Sarita, I couldn't say on that quarter.

"Want to help me strangle Charles?"

"I'll consider it."

"Damn," Ashe raked fingers through light-brown hair. "I have a sister—sort of."

"You don't think of Blackwing as your sister?"

"She won't even speak to me. What do you think?"

"I don't know," I shrugged. "I'm still trying to deal with this information. I can't tell Zaria right now, as much as I want to, because we're in the middle of a big mess on Earth and Refizan."

"Bring her here to tell her if you want. For now, let's go find my mother and have a conversation."

"Hmmph. You only show up if you want something," Ashlynne slammed a kettle on the stove to heat water for tea. She spoke to Ashe but leveled dark looks in my direction, too.

"I deserve that," Ashe said, taking a chair at the small kitchen table. "I keep telling you I'll build a bigger house for you and Grandfather, but you refuse. This street runs both ways, Mother."

"What do you want?" She sounded resigned while allowing her shoulders to droop. Her back was turned toward us as she lit the burner to heat water.

"We heard you acted as a surrogate for a child, once."

"He paid me."

"That's ah, unexpected," Ashe coughed.

"He paid me with a safe place to stay after that filth Friesianna took over. Thought she killed me, too, the bitch."

"Mother, you're not making this easy for anyone, including yourself."

"Why are you asking about the girl? Going looking for your long-lost almost-sister?"

"We don't have to look; we know where she is."

"I hope she doesn't want anything from me."

"I doubt that," I broke in. "She's powerful and important. You may want something from her. The trouble is, she'll see straight through you when you ask."

"If I could, I'd take this bitterness away from you," Ashe sighed. "I know you were in exile for centuries uncounted. Forced to live alone most of that time, too. I can only do something now, Mother. I can't change the past. I don't have that ability."

"No—you're not the Ka'Mirai. I know who she is, and she wouldn't change things, either, because we turned her away."

"That's a lot of prejudice to deal with," Ashe agreed. "The dilution of the race and such."

"The quarter bloods could gate—some of them. Father told me that I shouldn't turn them out—that I was Queen and could make that decision. I should have listened to him."

"A lot of people should have listened to him. They wouldn't, and that included Friesianna and Baltis. You know where they are, now."

"Dead, curse their souls," Ashlynne muttered angrily. "And another placed as Queen over my head, now. Not that I'd want it back," she held up a hand. "It's too much work and I feel old."

Tell me what to do to make peace with her, Ashe begged in mindspeech.

"I have something for you," I said, standing.

"What?" She sounded suspicious.

"What you've had precious little of," I said, and sent her *Love*.

CHAPTER 11

Lissa

"What is it they say about no rest for the wicked?" I asked.

Winkler and I sat at a table in *Deep Perkatory,* a coffee shop across from the hotel, talking. He'd gotten a report from Ace at the beach house, saying Kellee's doctor appointment went well and the babies were fine. Kellee, on the other hand, was pissed because she wanted to go shopping and Ace and the others wouldn't let her out of the house.

Poor thing.

Winkler had gotten off the phone with her, then proceeded to growl and snap at everyone afterward. I hauled his furry ass away from the hotel for a cup of coffee so he could calm down.

"I never thought we were the wicked," he said with a snort. "There I was, thinking we were the good guys. And girls."

"I was being sarcastic."

"And so was I."

I figured Zaria would see it in him plainly, but since I knew him so well, I could guess at his reference—he hadn't felt like a good guy since he'd taken down his own father.

"Get Weldon to change the law," I told him, making him blink at

145

my apparent shift in subject matter. "Tell him that a Packmaster should be able to step down and leave the job with someone else, and that the designated Packmaster will accept challenges—one at a time. Frankly, I'm kinda tired of seeing good wolves die just because they're getting a little long in the tooth."

"Hmmph," Winkler turned his head away to stare out the huge window next to our table.

"I'm serious, Winkler. What will Weldon do when the time comes for him? I know for a fact he wants his son Darryl to take over, and he also has a grandbaby now that I'm sure he'd like to see graduate from high school. Maybe college, too."

"I'll mention it to him."

"You do that."

"Ilya and Zaria are coming this way," Winkler announced, staring out the window once again.

"They like coffee too—we don't have the market cornered, you know. Winkler, I have a question for you. A serious question."

"What's that?" I had his full attention, now.

"What if you found out you had a child—that you didn't know about?"

"I don't. The only two I have are with Kellee." He didn't say her name with a shred of respect.

"No, I'm talking about me, here, not you."

"How the hell would you have kids? You couldn't before you were vampire, and you sure as hell can't now."

"Wow—thanks for putting it in such clear perspective," I grumped at him. "That's not what I meant, anyway. What if somebody manipulated your DNA or something, to reach that end?"

"Depends on what kind of person they turned out to be. Whether they'd accept they had a mother or father, and how well they'd fit in—how much like their mom or dad they were, I suppose."

"What if they were so much like you it hurt?"

"Damn, that's a no-brainer. I'd haul 'em in and start 'em in the family business."

"What if they're already in the business, so to speak, and did that all on their own?"

"So much the better."

"You make it sound so simple. What if they had no need for a mother or father?"

"Rejection?" Winkler was now getting to the base fear I held.

"Yeah."

"I'd have to try. Even if I walked away with nothing, that's what I had to start with, anyway."

"I see your point."

"What's this about, anyhow? That pile of grumpy vampires in England giving you fits?"

"In a manner of speaking." I didn't tell him that it was Charles, this time, and nobody else. I had a feeling about him—and Zaria—and me. Only time would tell whether my suppositions were correct.

"Want to invite them to sit with us?" Winkler asked, nodding toward Ilya and Zaria, who were now ordering at the counter.

"If you want to."

"I don't mind."

"All right." *Want to sit with us?* I sent to Zaria.

Sure. Be right there.

Damn, I hoped she was my daughter—at least partly, and I hoped she was okay with that.

～

Zaria

"I almost wish you could go tell Kellee to sit down, shut up and stop whining about going shopping," Winkler gave me a half-grin after Lissa moved to his side of the table, allowing Ilya and me to have the other.

"You mean granny Zaria?" I wrinkled my nose and made a face at Winkler.

"That's the one she'd listen to."

"I'll put it on my to-do list."

"It's a long list," Ilya joked.

"Don't we know it," Lissa agreed.

"To long lists," I held up my latte cup. Lissa tapped hers against it and smiled.

Later, we walked out of the coffee shop together. Lissa and I had shields around us, which meant that the snipers driving past failed to kill us, but several people crossing the street nearby weren't so lucky.

Our most recent clock had run out.

"I don't know how this is possible, but I am grateful it is," Bill walked around the three-dimensional image of the scene I displayed in a private meeting room at his headquarters.

The faces of the gunmen weren't covered, which meant they didn't care if they were recognized. Mostly, it meant their puppet master didn't care, therefore, they didn't either.

"That's Phil—again," Winkler growled at his former Second's image —the second one we'd found so far. Who knew how many of them existed, now?

Baikov was stepping up his game, and killing civilians in broad daylight.

"The other one is Aubrey—or Aubrey's clone. The actual Aubrey died recently," Lissa said. "And this one is walking in daylight, so that's a brand-new twist."

"That's Mick at the wheel," Winkler snarled, naming the former Second in the Austin Pack. At least he didn't have a gun; the other two were hanging out the passenger and back windows to do their shooting.

"There is technology that exists to allow Aubrey to operate in daylight—Liron will know of it, as do you," I said, weariness sounding in my voice.

"Yeah. I know about that, all right," Lissa grumbled. "He still should be asleep, somewhere, though. When I had one of those discs, I couldn't keep my eyes open in daylight. All it did was keep me from frying if I got caught in sunlight."

"That wouldn't be a problem if he carried one of those contraptions affixed to his spine and connected to his brain," I said. "Somebody else will be calling his shots if that's the case."

Lissa's eyes widened as she stared at me. "Please say there isn't more of that technology running around."

"Those things are outrageously expensive, so I'm hoping they pick and choose the recipients wisely," I replied. "Still, this is a setback for us—to know they're doing this with vampires to make them effective during the day. That technology means there's no witch involved, thank you."

"You don't think Ivan Baikov will have one installed, do you?"

"I doubt he wants anybody messing with his spine and brain; there's too much opportunity to turn him into a puppet. He's the one whose hand is up this clone's skirt, if you get my meaning."

"Xenides had Aubrey killed, so he's involved in this too. Ditto on the reasons he won't want one of those contraptions. I hope they don't try to trap René with this shit." Lissa was angry, on top of being worried.

René would still die, but that would come later. Other things should happen first, and that became my worry as well.

"And these got away," Bill sighed.

"No, they didn't. It just looks like they got away," I told him. "I released their particles on the fly, and let their image screech away. It disappeared two minutes later, so don't waste your time looking for something that doesn't exist—unless there's more of them out there, waiting to do the same thing."

"If that's the case, what should we do?" Bill stepped right up to the passenger-window image of the recreated car, where Phil held a rifle, prepared to fire indiscriminately.

"They're following us," I said. "I think we should take the game to them. We're running out of time, and we pretty much know where everything important happens after this. Did they send another demand?"

"Not yet," Winkler said.

"Then they've finally gotten the message that giving us a timeline only alerts us to when the next incident will happen," Lissa said. "We've been prepared for the last two; we may not get another demand—they'll just do something awful and hope it convinces us to come to them on our own."

Bill had listened intently to Lissa's words. He didn't comment, but his shoulders tightened. Bill wasn't stupid; he was beginning to suspect there was much more to this than met the mundane eye.

"I just got word from Bree," Lissa said, looking for a chair to sit down. "She says that there was an attack by Solar Red that didn't happen the first time around, and the Ra'Ak have released spawn in several parts of the city. Too many to keep them from infecting the population, unless she and the others take drastic measures." *The former me is having a conniption, as you can imagine, and Dragon isn't reacting well, either.*

"Fuck." I went to Lissa and hugged her. "I'm sorry this is happening to you," I whispered.

❧

Lissa

"I was in that meeting for two hours, and the whole time I just wanted to tell the President that those assholes were toast shortly after they started firing, but there could be an identical set out there, ready to do the same thing again." Tony paced and shook his head as he spoke.

Tony—future Tony—wasn't happy. He wasn't used to being raked over hot coals by a President who, to him, had been dead for centuries.

He'd gone to the White House shortly after the incident, while the rest of us, minus Charles and Trajan, had met with Bill at his headquarters.

"Look, I'm sorry you're having to listen to that, but things aren't going so well on Refizan, either."

"I'm almost sorry Gavin isn't here," Tony sighed.

"Which one?" I was busy hugging myself while I worried about the old me—and the old Winkler. In fact, I worried about the old versions of almost everybody I knew.

"The new one, obviously."

"Right. He should probably stay where he is, just in case."

"In case of what?"

"In case Liron decides to attack on three fronts instead of two. He can bend time if he has to, and take a bunch of people with him if he needs to defend Le-Ath Veronis."

"Who is this Liron guy? Why didn't we know more about him?" Tony demanded.

"One of the Hidden, I believe, and he took that status to a much higher level than any of the others. Plus, he pretended he was dead for a long time, until Zaria did him in sometime in the future."

"Then how the hell does he know to give us grief now?"

"We're back to the bending time thing, Tony."

"So he notified himself, somehow, that to prevent his dying in the future, he has to change the past?"

"Got it in one," I tapped my nose.

"Damn, this is complicated."

"Welcome to the Hierarchy," I muttered sarcastically.

~

Refizan, Past

Breanne

"Well, we got two more," I set the spheres on the table. "That may be a drop in the proverbial bucket."

"I will transport these to Nefrigar if you wish it," Kalenegar offered. He'd arrived to help with more than a thousand Ra'Ak spawn released in Refizan's capital city. He'd bent time for us, while past Lissa and Dragon had a difficult time getting to three separate locations to destroy spawn themselves.

Kal kept the presence of the others from Dragon's *Looking* skills, so they wouldn't be overwhelmed. They were almost overwhelmed anyway, because the old Lissa had to mist them from place to place to kill hungry monsters.

On top of that, Solar Red had massacred sixteen in the poorest quarter of town while Lissa was engaged with the spawn.

"Assholes," I mumbled aloud. "They're trying to throw us off, and who knows what they have planned next?"

"That I cannot say; I am no better at finding Sirenali—whether living or dust," Kal said. "Call if you need me again."

"I will." He disappeared while I wanted to tug my hair out by the roots. Liron's plot was carefully crafted to keep us confused and wary. Still, we had no idea where he was ultimately headed, or whom he wanted dead or out of the way at the end of it.

If I could have gotten my hands on Liron right then, I'd strangle him myself.

"You may have my assistance in this."

Someone new had arrived without an invite.

Kifirin.

~

Lissa

Which Kifirin? I demanded. *The one who put his teeth in my neck, or the updated version?*

The updated version, thank goodness. I don't know what I'd have done with the older one, Bree responded.

He's there, too, don't ever forget that. And he really doesn't need to know about you—who you are, what you are—you know who created him.

I understand that. It could destroy the entire history of the God Wars if that information gets out now.

Wait, Zaria says she has something to help, I reported when Zaria tapped me on the shoulder before handing several small boxes to me.

Send 'em—I'll accept any kind of help, Bree said.

Sent—do you have them?

I have several boxes with our names on them—including Kifirin's.

Zaria says to put them on and don't take them off.
Tell her thanks.
I will.

"Bree says thanks," I sighed, blinking at Zaria. "You don't happen to have some of those boxes for us, do you?"

"I do. Come on, let's go to Bill's suite and we'll hand them out. The thing is, though, we'll have to take Bill's, Trajan's and Winkler's back when we leave so things will go as they should."

I knew what those boxes contained, because three of my sons wore Zaria's medallions, too.

Zaria was hiding us from anybody who thought to *Look* for us or do us harm. Liron hid behind Sirenali bone dust; we now had Zaria's medallions. I wasn't about to ask her what they truly were—I had my suspicions and those were better kept to myself.

~

"Even if you're not shielded by Lissa or me, this should protect you," Zaria handed out boxes. "Put it on, don't take it off."

"What about us?"

Trajan walked in, followed closely by Charles. Night had fallen and I'd barely noticed. "Here," Zaria handed them the last two boxes. Charles' eyebrows lifted in surprise; he didn't expect anything from her.

He should know by now that Zaria wouldn't leave anyone out— even someone she felt confused or ambivalent about. From her perspective, I was completely familiar and sympathetic with *pop-up father disorder.*

"What's the plan?" Charles asked while slipping his medallion over his head and settling it beneath his shirt. He wore a polo and jeans, with loafers. He'd fit in almost anywhere like that.

"We'll be traveling to London first, I think," Bill said. "We'll pull them away from here, and I'm hoping they'll worry that we're heading their way. I figure they'll know you didn't die in this latest attack— especially when their hit men don't return."

"My jet's ready," Winkler suggested. He wasn't looking forward to a long flight across the Atlantic in a military transport.

"We'll table that—I have information that somebody got hit in California," Tony read a new message on his phone. "In Sacramento."

Winkler's phone began to ring and my skin itched furiously.

"We don't have time to talk," Zaria grabbed my arm and flung us to Sacramento.

~

Leigh Williams almost wept with joy the moment we dropped inside her oldest brother's home. It was nestled amid farmland outside Sacramento, with enough land for Thomas Williams Jr.'s pack to hunt on a full moon.

"Teddy's been hit," she hugged me. "Please tell me you can get him to a hospital."

"We have something better," I held her away from me.

"What?"

"Zaria." I jerked my head toward Zaria, who jumped as the outside of the house was sprayed with bullets. Well, I was a member of the Sacramento Pack—the original me was, anyway.

They were attacking me, now—through my pack.

"You have medical training?" Leigh looked hopefully at Zaria.

"In a manner of speaking," Zaria said. "Take me to him. Lissa, if you need help getting rid of the bastards outside, let me know."

"Oh, we're about to handle that, all right." I let my claws slide out before turning to mist.

~

Zaria

Theodore Williams, Thomas' younger twin brother, was dying when Leigh, his sister, led me into a back bedroom away from the bullets flying at the front.

"He got hit in the first round they fired at us—he was standing in front of a window." Leigh knelt beside the bed, which was covered in her brother's blood.

They'd hit him, all right—and almost cut him in half. A bullet wound or two to his torso and he'd recover easily. This was so much worse than that.

"Leigh, I know you don't know me, and you're about to see things you've never seen before, I think. It's nothing bad," I held up a hand when she shrank away. "It'll just get really bright in here for a while. As long as I'm glowing, I'm healing, all right?"

"Wh-where do you want me?"

"You can take that chair over there, okay. He won't feel any pain while I'm working."

"Okay." She stood and walked to the chair, settling on it and hugging herself tightly. Time was short and I almost blinded her, I turned the healing power up so bright. *Teddy*, I whispered into his mind, *I'm here, now. For you.*

◠

Lissa

More Bart Orford and Lester Briggs duplicates, at the head of a small army of werewolves, had attacked the Williams' sprawling farmhouse. Thomas and three of his pack were in wolf form, crawling along a large irrigation pipe in an attempt to get to one nest of attackers.

Authorities had set up a perimeter at the fence surrounding the property, but they were in a firefight with a separate set of attackers.

This was a carefully planned assault; at least fifty had come to keep both sides busy while attempting to destroy the Sacramento Packmaster and his family.

I'd had to *Look* to see where Thomas' mother was; thankfully she'd gone into Sacramento with an old friend to get her hair done. She was safe somewhere on the outside, and I asked Tony, who was now at the perimeter with Bill, Winkler and the others, to make sure she was guarded and kept away from this.

Thomas, I sent as I hovered over him and the other three wolves, *It's Lissa. I'm here to help.* He was expecting me the moment I materialized at his side.

～

Ilya

"Give both a rifle," Bill told the California Bureau agent, after he and Anthony Hancock showed their credentials. He was telling them to arm Winkler and me—to help in the standoff.

Charles had stayed behind, as it was still daylight in California. The sun was dropping in the west, but almost two hours of daylight remained.

In less than two minutes, Winkler and I were armed while Tony and Bill discussed the situation with the agent in charge.

"You know how to use that thing?" I asked Winkler, who flashed a grin in reply. "I'll take that as a yes," I told him. "What do you plan to do with it now?"

"Find a place to change, what else?" His words were soft as he and I began walking toward more farmland across a narrow, paved road. Fruit trees grew in neat rows in those fields—a perfect place for a man to become wolf, I think.

Two minutes later, we were far enough into an almond grove for him to transform. This was something I'd never seen, and was fascinated when he handed his rifle to me and began to disrobe.

"I wouldn't normally do this," he said, "but Lissa would say desperate times and all that." He allowed his jeans to fall to the ground after removing his western boots.

"Do what?"

"Stick a man and two rifles on my wolf's back and haul him into a firefight," Winkler growled. "Don't even think about arguing. If you do, I'll haul you in with my teeth if I have to."

"No argument from me," I said, taking a step back. Seconds later, an enormous black wolf, whose eyes gleamed in the dim light beneath almond trees, jerked his head toward his back.

"I'll lie low," I promised, slinging both rifles across my back and stepping to his side. As if he didn't trust me to leap onto his back, he gripped my belt in his huge teeth and flung me astride. I barely had time to grip handfuls of thick fur before we were racing through the grove.

The leap over the fence on the opposite side of the road almost unseated me, but my grip tightened, my knees clamped against heaving ribs and my teeth clenched to hold back a shout of momentary terror.

∾

Lissa

I'll drop you here, I told Thomas, as we hovered over a nest of four attackers. At least they were humanoid at the moment, and firing at the house. Four werewolves dropped into their midst could do a lot of damage in this situation; long rifles weren't so good for firing in close quarters. They'd just as likely hit one of their own rather than Thomas or one of his pack.

I lowered my mist until I was roughly two feet over the heads of the enemy. All four were on their stomachs in the sandy soil of a trench, using the raised edge as cover while firing at the house.

Dropping now, I informed my passengers, and released them.

As hoped, Thomas and his wolves went immediately into action, tearing and ripping into the four snipers. All four were so surprised by the attack from above, they didn't really have time to defend themselves before they died.

∾

Ilya

I'd trained to fire from horseback once upon a time; I was rusty at first, until I became used to riding a wolf rather than a horse. It came back to me, however, and Winkler's wolf knew where the sniper nests were.

After we'd taken out four nests, we became a target. Winkler yelped and almost went down when a bullet struck him in the hip, but he and I righted ourselves and I fired at the ones who'd hit him, killing all four with a spray of bullets to the head.

We've hit six nests, Lissa's mindspeech reached me and the werewolf whose back I covered. I wished I could tell her we'd just finished taking down our fifth.

They'd estimated fifty attackers or so—this meant that there were likely two more nests to destroy.

"Give yourselves up," someone with a bullhorn blared across the fields as Winkler continued to run toward the next nest.

Winkler went down with a yelp as another bullet tore into his shoulder and I went flying over his head, somersaulting across dry, loose soil and kicking up dust and grit as I hit hard and rolled.

Both rifles were torn from my grip by two men who appeared from beneath a covered trench; one that blended with its surroundings to hide their presence.

"Put those down or I'll kill you and make sure you're never reborn," Zaria appeared and stood over me.

I looked from the men to her and back again; I couldn't move more than that or both of us could die.

"Huh," one of them grinned—it was more an evil smirk than anything else, as he pointed the gun at her heart. He wanted to rest the barrel between her breasts, but he couldn't get the gun closer than six inches.

That confused him; he drew it back and attempted to shove it in again, with the same results.

"I'm warning you—put it down. Now."

He should have put it down. His companion, a somewhat wiser ass, lowered his weapon, at least. The first one laughed as he pulled the trigger.

The familiar click of a gun with no bullets echoed about us, as if we were trapped in a sound chamber.

That shouldn't have been—both rifles still had ammunition in them.

"I have these," Lissa arrived, dropping three more inside our sound chamber.

"Well, do they want to shoot me, too?" Zaria asked. "Ilya, you can stand up, now, if you want. Lissa, Winkler's hurt. He took two bullets. You may want to go take care of him for a bit until I can help you."

Lissa disappeared again, leaving Zaria and me with five attackers.

"Who wants to give up and go talk to Anthony Hancock and Bill Jennings?" She asked.

Two of the three Lissa brought, and the smarter of my two raised their hands. "Awesome. Now for you two," she turned to the ones who refused her offer, "Usually I make this painless. Is that what you want?"

"Hmmph," idiot with the empty rifle tried to fire it again. This time, it did—releasing a bullet with the accompanying sound that almost deafened everyone inside Zaria's chamber.

"Now see, that's a direct attack against me. Buh-bye, asshole." She held out a hand and turned him into winking sparks.

"I'll talk to Hancock," the last holdout dropped the rifle and raised his hands in surrender.

"That's what I'm talking about," Zaria smiled as I rose stiffly to my feet and stood beside her. "Ilya, a little help?"

"No trouble." I lifted the rifle and herded our four toward the road and the waiting authorities.

~

Lissa

Winkler was asleep after I removed the bullets and Zaria healed his wounds. Then, she'd put her hands on Ilya, who'd fallen hard and then rolled across the dirt, gathering serious bruises and cuts along the way.

He was now feeling much better and sat, drinking a glass of Scotch in Thomas Williams' kitchen while Zaria went to check on Teddy.

"Thomas and his three did most of the heavy lifting," I told Leigh, who smiled at me and poured a margarita for both of us from a pitcher. Thomas was talking with Bill while Tony and the CBI agents questioned our captives.

I'd removed heads from three, before they managed to fire their weapons at the wolves I'd dropped on their heads. The rest had died, casualties of werewolf justice. I was still trying to get my head around Winkler hauling Ilya on his back so Ilya could take out sniper nests as he ran past them.

"Teddy's going to be fine, he just needs a day or two of rest," Zaria informed us as she walked into the kitchen. "Have one of those for me?" She eyed the pitcher of margaritas.

"Anytime you want one," Leigh grinned and rose to grab another glass.

I figured Zaria might have a new pack membership before this was over. *How bad was it?* I sent to her in mindspeech.

He was nearly cut in half, and would have died without help, Zaria replied.

Then I can't say how glad I am that you're here.

That makes two of us.

We're taking the prisoners to holding cells in Sacramento, Tony sent. *How are Winkler and Ilya?*

Still in one piece and fixed up for the most part. Ilya's getting drunk; Winkler's asleep.

I'd be asleep too if I got shot twice. Damn, he's tough.

As tough as they come, I agreed. *And the Russian's no slouch, either.*

If he killed snipers while bouncing on Winkler's back, then he's damn good.

You know it.

It may be a while before we're done with these—are you comfortable where you are?

Getting that way. I poured myself another margarita.

CHAPTER 12

Zaria

"Have you heard anything from Breanne and the others on Refizan?" I covered a yawn as I asked Lissa the question. It was past three in the morning in D.C. when we limped back to our hotel rooms, after spending more time than anticipated in Sacramento.

"I figure she'll let me know if anything happens that shouldn't." Lissa stifled a yawn this time.

"I hope we don't have to get up again for a few hours," I said, reaching my door.

"Me, too." Lissa slid her key card into the slot next door and went inside.

"Zaria?" I heard Ilya call my name softly as he walked up.

"What, hon?" I turned toward him.

"I wish to stay with you this night."

"Honey, are you sure?"

"I am the one who should be saying that to you," he grinned and fell into his natural accent. "I do not wish to take advantage; just hold you."

"Well, that's about all I have strength for, anyway."

"Then this will be fine, eh?"

"As fine as we can get."

"Come, then." He lifted the key card from my fingers and opened the door. "We will turn the air conditioner to very cold and snuggle together like Siberian hares."

"Sounds awesome."

"Good." He shut the door behind us and kissed me.

∼

Lissa

At first, I didn't recall letting him in. And then I had to figure out which Winkler it was.

The old Winkler.

The one married to Kellee.

Fuck.

Well, we hadn't gone that far, thank goodness, but there he was, in wolf form, sleeping at the foot of my bed.

"Honey, you really need to get up and go back to your room," I reached down to run my fingers through the fur on his head.

"Grrrrrr."

"Your clothes are there. Breakfast is downstairs. They won't let a wolf in, or a naked man."

"Grrrrrr." He extended his growl while dropping off my bed and padding toward the door. I got to see his naked ass when he changed to unlock the door and let himself out. Yeah, I should have misted him to his room, but he didn't ask. Plus, I wasn't at my most coherent the morning after the day before, which was punctuated with at least three margaritas.

Trajan, you'd better let him in, he's naked, I sent before turning over and pulling covers over my head. Even through the duvet, I heard Winkler's door slam down the hall.

∼

Zaria

"Coffee?"

There is nothing sexier to me than that word, whispered against my ear in the morning.

"Hold on." I attempted to scoot off the bed, but Ilya's arms wrapped around me one last time for a hug and a kiss beneath an ear. Then he let me go.

We dressed and brushed teeth in record time, before heading toward the street. We had to find another coffee shop—*Deep Perkatory* was still closed after it was fired on by duplicate werewolves. Thick sheets of plywood covered shattered windows, and yellow crime scene tape was stretched across the door.

"There's a Starbucks two blocks down," I said. Ilya nodded, so we walked in that direction.

"Bill, Tony," we joined those two at their table; they'd arrived for coffee before we did. Bill was reading messages on his phone before showing them to Tony.

"The four we jailed yesterday were found dead in their cells early this morning," Bill grumped while Tony skimmed the texts.

"I'm glad you questioned them beforehand, then," I said.

"We didn't get a lot; there were holes in their memories."

"I think they rushed them to get them out there to attack. They didn't waste a lot of time training them, so they honestly didn't have information to give you," I said, tearing off one end of my heated croissant and stuffing it in my mouth.

"More duplicates?" Tony handed Bill's phone back and locked eyes with mine.

"Um-hmmm," I mumbled while chewing.

"Damn, this is frustrating," Bill grumped, lifting his cup and drinking. As usual, he'd asked for a flat white—a really big one. "It's like they're trying to wear us out, pulling us from one place to another, and attacking anybody we have ties to."

"Are there still plans to fly to London?" Ilya asked.

"There are; we'll accept Winkler's offer of a ride on his jet," Bill sighed. "I'm assuming we'll have quick transport back to the U.S. if it's needed."

"You will," I told him. "Whatever is needed. Not only am I more worried than I was, I'm angrier than I was."

"The Williams family will have guards watching their farm until the next full moon," Bill shook his head before drinking more coffee. "Thomas Williams says he'll be happy to provide assistance to us in the future, in exchange for our help in this."

"Doesn't sound like a bad idea," I observed. "There are plenty of things he and his pack can do for you."

"I think you're right."

"I uh, had to tell POTUS that Lissa was here to help Bill, because she ah, wouldn't lift a finger to help me under the current circumstances, and that this is off the books for her," Tony told us. "POTUS was quite relieved to have her on the case, as you can imagine."

"I've sent full reports for his eyes only," Bill added to Tony's admission. "He's given me point on this as a result."

"Well done, you," I told Bill, giving him a smile.

"Save that for when this is over," he said, although a smile tugged at a corner of his mouth.

"I'd like breakfast somewhere," Ilya said after emptying his coffee cup.

"There's a place not far away that's good, and the morning rush is just about over," Bill said. "Come on, follow me."

Lissa, we're headed to The Breakfast Nook if you want something to eat, I sent.

We'll be there shortly.

~

Lissa

"We're coming with you," Charles announced as he and Trajan exited their hotel rooms.

"Up during the day, Charles? What have we come to?" I teased.

"Nothing good after yesterday," he said.

"What do you mean?"

"I mean that they know now that they can crook their finger—by attacking anyone we know—and we'll come running to take care of it."

I almost stumbled over my own feet when he put everything in such blunt perspective. "Do you want to talk while we walk, or mist to the restaurant and save it for a breakfast meeting?"

"Mist first, then talk."

"Right. On it." Thirty seconds later, we materialized in a shadowed corner near the restaurant and walked toward The Breakfast Nook's entrance. Zaria already had a table waiting that would hold all of us.

"Ilya, can you get information from your friend on Baikov's family— we don't want to threaten his family in reality, but we can let him know that we know where they are." Tony pointed his fork in Ilya's direction.

"Hmmph. I worry about this tactic."

"So do I," Zaria voiced my own opinion on the matter.

"Right now, it's what we have," Tony frowned. "Just a few photographs sent to the right place, and maybe he'll back off on these attacks."

"Charles?" I turned toward him—he was eating what the others thought to be the obligatory vampire meal with others. They still thought Zaria was protecting him from sunlight, too.

Frankly, he wouldn't have ordered such a large meal if he wouldn't enjoy any of it. Eggs and coffee would have done the trick, but he'd ordered eggs, sausage, toast and a small stack of pancakes. And he was eating all of it, too.

The schmuck.

As if he knew what I was thinking, he pointed a smile in my direction. "I think," he sipped coffee for a moment before continuing, "that whatever will come of this will come anyway, whether now or in the future."

"Yes, but," Zaria pointed her fork at him.

"But what?" He lowered his eyes and concentrated on his plate.

"This may determine where the blame will fall," she said.

"Bad with the good," Charles shrugged.

She was her father's daughter—and her mothers'. His logic, tempered with empathy and understanding.

Bree, I sent, *I think I'm one of Zaria's mothers.*

You are. As am I. I figured this out.

What about the uh, I began.

That's a story for later. Don't worry, it's nothing bad, just—unusual.

All right. How are you feeling about this?

I just want to hug her.

Yeah. Me, too.

I guess that'll have to wait until we all have time to talk. Gotta go—things are getting a little heated around here.

Heated?

They've set half the city on fire, I think, hoping to burn out any remaining vampires.

Fucking hell.

You got that right. We're helping as much as we can; Dragon's hands are tied on the power thing because of the Ra'Ak's presence. One bad move and the entire planet will be toast. How are things on your end?

Not nearly that bad, I don't think. Go back to what you were doing. Let us know if you need help.

Will do. She cut off our conversation.

"Will you contact your friend at Frederica's?" Tony asked Ilya.

"Only if there is no other choice."

"I think we're to that point, now," Tony said.

"They live in a very fine manor home, built three centuries ago in Ostrova. Tales have grown through the years that the family was once poor until a lost relative appeared and lavished them with money and a new home. The family has been there ever since," Ilya explained later, after speaking with his friend over a secure line.

"I'd bet most of what I have it was vampire Baikov," I snorted. "Who broke the vampire laws to do it. Then, no doubt, he fixed his many-times great-nephew up with the folks at the Kremlin, and the rest is history."

"Vampire laws?" Ilya frowned deeply at me.

"It's against the rules for any vampire to contact his former family. Not that I should be telling you that, but you'd probably figure it out for yourself."

"What is the penalty for this?" he asked.

"Well, that depends. Even if Wlodek decided that Baikov deserved to die for his infractions, he'd take a back seat to what Xenides is doing right now."

"Xenides?"

"A vampire worse than Baikov, if you can believe that."

"I find it hard to believe, this is true."

"Does General Baikov hold dual citizenship in the Czech Republic and Russia?" Zaria asked Ilya.

"He does. I believe some manipulation of the records was done to achieve this. The government desires that you report a dual citizenship, of course, but as they manufactured Baikov's, I'm sure he isn't expected to do so."

"What about you, Ilya?" Zaria asked quietly. "Ukraine doesn't recognize dual citizenship."

"I know this." He looked away for a moment. "My family are citizens of Ukraine. I am officially a citizen of Russia, as they refused to allow me to leave them when Ukraine did."

"In other words," I began.

"In other words, Baikov threatened my life, and the lives of my family if I refused to continue my work for them. I kissed my wife and children good-bye. Three years later, before I could get back to her, my wife passed. I was forced to leave my children in the care of a family friend. Still, I manage to see them now and then; Andrei has moved away from Ukraine and now lives in another country."

Ireland, Zaria sent to me. *Dublin, actually.*

I don't blame him, I returned.

"Are we still scheduled to fly to London tomorrow?" Trajan asked. He and Charles were still with us, while our meeting continued inside Bill's suite.

"We are. Pack your things, Second of mine," Winkler ordered.

"I need lunch," I said. "Who's buying and where?"

~

Bill

"I have to take a call," I said shortly after my cell phone rang. I walked into the bathroom and shut the door—the President was on the line.

"We have a snag," he told me the moment I answered.

"What's that?"

"Someone at the FBI ran some images through the software, without authorization," he told me.

"And?" I went cold—whatever he said next I wasn't going to like—I was sure of it.

"You're aware of who the Blacksmith is, I assume?"

"Yes, and he's helping us with this mess."

"I understand that, and trust you not to spill any sensitive information to him. What concerns me is this—that information was passed to an outside, unknown party. Now, you probably know better than I do who that could be."

"The Kremlin," I hissed. "No doubt in my mind."

"I'll admit, that disguise is damn good—nobody would recognize him like that. Some of the mannerisms, however, are what helped nail him. You ought to tell him he's been compromised."

"I'll let him know," I said. The President ended the call. I stood inside the brightly-lit hotel bathroom, holding the phone in nerveless fingers while I stared at my image in the mirror in alarm.

~

Lissa

"Winkler, have I ever told you that your software is too damn good, sometimes?" I glared at him. Ilya hadn't taken well to the news that he'd been identified, and that the information had probably been sold to the Kremlin.

Baikov knew already where Ilya was, unless I missed my guess.

"Outing allies wasn't in my realm of thinking when I built it," Winkler mumbled. "Catching criminals when they walked into banks was my top priority. You were the one who convinced me to sell it to the government."

"I did, didn't I?"

"It's worked out, for the most part. Until now."

"The vamps still don't know, and they still don't need to know," I shook a finger at him.

"What about Charles?"

"He knows how to keep his mouth shut."

"We have pictures taken by an agent in the Czech Republic," Tony said as he and Bill walked through the door. They'd left half an hour earlier to make a run to Bill's office.

"And?"

"No Baikov, but surveillance has been set up in strategic spots around the house. Ilya wasn't kidding—that house is a whopper," Bill said.

"I'm telling you, vampire Baikov did that for them."

"Are all vamps filthy rich?" Winkler asked.

"Most of them," I shrugged. "I have all the holdings from my now-deceased sire, and they'll come to me once my ah, training period is over."

"How much?"

"Too much—most of it ill-gotten, I think."

"If I had a dollar for every time I've heard that story," Bill sighed. "Makes me wish for law-breaking vampire forebears."

"You really don't need any," I patted his arm. "Honest."

"You need to decide who else you want to look like," Zaria took Ilya's hand and led him toward the door.

"Sean Connery?"

"Do you have a Scottish accent?"

"Of course."

~

Later, when we met for dinner, Ilya resembled Sean Connery, although he couldn't be accused of copying the actor, and he didn't have the beard that the actor sometimes wore. His dark hair was liberally salted with strands of gray, but still I saw servers and customers staring now and then.

I'd say Ilya wasn't displeased at all with Zaria's work.

"A grilled cheese and tomato sandwich?" Zaria handed the menu back to our server. "With a side of asparagus, please."

"If you'll get the pot roast, I'll get the chicken fry and we can split," Winkler nuzzled my ear.

"Let's do it," I said firmly, folding my menu. Winkler would end up eating two-thirds of everything, but I wasn't very hungry anyway.

~

The Kremlin

Kornel Baikov

"What do you mean, the images of that treasonous bastard disappeared?" Uncle Ivan demanded over the phone. "If someone erased them, show them what happens to those who make terrible mistakes."

"They weren't erased—they disappeared while we were looking at them."

"Our system was hacked?"

"Our experts say no. Absolutely no evidence. Nothing else was disturbed."

"Were copies made?"

"Those have also gone blank."

"How is that possible?"

"I don't know. Perhaps it is this Zaria person—the one who placed a decapitated vampire into my bed. Nobody came or went from my bedroom that night. When I awoke, dead eyes were staring into mine and I was freezing from being next to—that."

"Kornel, are you becoming squeamish now? I though I taught you better than that."

"The only thing we can rely on is our memory, now—we know what he looks like," I pointed out.

"What if he disguises himself again?"

"We'll keep searching. We know Kuznetzov is somewhere near William Winkler—he has gone straight to our target—to protect him, no doubt."

"We know how to stop that from happening, don't we?"

"His daughter or his son?"

"Let us target the son—we know where he is, do we not?"

"We do."

"Besides, we take one down, he will do whatever he can to protect the other, including turning himself in or handing us the target willingly."

"As always, you are a master strategist, Uncle."

"Yes. You should learn this from me, you know."

"As you say, Uncle." I ended the call before he could aggrandize himself further.

~

Zaria

I'd asked to be alone for an hour. Ilya nodded and went to his room to pack for the trip.

Then I began sifting through everything, including the Metal Library.

Nothing.

I found nothing that would be affected if Andrei Kuznetzov lived to a ripe old age—on Revalus in the future, alongside shapeshifters and Pod'l-morphs.

If Andrei stayed here, he'd die by Baikov's command—it wouldn't matter which of them gave the order. Ilya would seek revenge for his son's death, like before, but now, even Katya's life was in danger. Before, it hadn't been and when she was grown, she'd take up her brother's cause—she and her husband.

Not this time—they'd kill her, too.

Andrei had been assassinated because of his struggle to keep Ukraine out of Russian control the first time around. This time, it would be because his father thought to help us. I hoped Ilya was done with his packing; we had a trip to Ireland scheduled in our very near future.

And there were several things to do once we arrived.

~

Ilya

"How do you know about my son?" My voice was harsher than I intended, but Zaria frightened me by saying Andrei was in danger and we had to go to him.

"Ilya, you can waste time by getting all huffy, or you can come with me to save his life. Decide now, okay?"

I wanted to ask if she was sure. Andrei was well-hidden and moved often, to stay hidden. How could they find him so quickly?

"Fine. We will not waste time. Take us there," I tossed out a hand in resignation. What followed may have been one of the most difficult things to witness I would ever recall, because Zaria landed us inside Andrei's small apartment, just in time to see him shot and watch him die.

I had my pistol out to kill his attacker in less than a blink.

~

Lissa

"We'll be staying here, at a hotel near Wembley Stadium," Bill tapped the screen on his laptop, which displayed a map of London.

"There are rooms for all of us, up to two weeks. I'm hoping we won't need that long, actually."

"I'm glad their football season doesn't start until next month," I said.

"We'll still run into a couple of concerts, so look for crowds coming in. We have rooms on the top floor, so there could be a lot of foot traffic in and out."

"Are you planning to blend in?" I frowned at Bill.

"I'm planning to employ the software—a lot," Bill replied. "And Zaria's shields, too. We got an update on the agent who sold Ilya's images to Baikov."

"He's dead, huh?"

"As a doornail. Stabbed in the heart, just like the ones in California."

"Baikov has another mister, I'll bet money on it."

"Can a mister get through Zaria's shields?"

"Not unless she allows it."

"Thank God."

∾

Dublin, Ireland

Ilya

After killing Andrei's murderer, and while I ranted at Zaria's tardiness by shouting and gesturing wildly while tears ran down my face, Zaria began to glow. I called her names and wept for my son as she ignored me.

Reaching out a hand that shone like the sun, she held it over Andrei's body.

I continued to shout.

Until the miracle happened.

Andrei sat up, his hands going immediately to his chest where he'd taken two bullets. All evidence of that, blood included, had disappeared.

"How?" He looked from me to Zaria, who still stood over him.

"How, indeed," Zaria turned to me. Her eyes looked like molten gold.

"Andrei?" I'd stopped shouting the moment he sat up. He'd been dead, and now he wasn't.

"Papa?"

Zaria stepped back. I went to my son and lifted him to his feet, then wrapped him in the tightest hug while both of us trembled with shock and joy.

"We have to take you to a safe place, Andrei," Zaria said, interrupting our reunion. "Decide now—come with me to Revalus or stay here and remain a target."

"Revalus?"

"Honey, it's a few hundred thousand light years from here. You have to trust me. Please."

"I don't wish to leave," Andrei said.

"Fuck." Zaria's shoulders drooped as she turned her back to me. "Ilya, this is the only opportunity you'll get to save your son's life. Andrei, if you die again, I can't save you. Do you understand?" She whirled to face both of us.

"Are you planning to go elsewhere?" I demanded. "Why couldn't you save him again?"

"Because I shouldn't have saved him this time," Zaria snapped. "I don't belong here on Earth. Please understand that. Both of you. All right?"

"I don't understand any of this," Andrei said. I agreed with his assessment, but didn't say it aloud.

"You see this," Zaria pointed to her face. "This is a temporary thing. This is what I look like when I'm myself."

She changed.

Grew taller. Much taller.

Her skin became the blue of a summer sky and black hair turned blonde.

And then the wings, white as snow sparkling with gold, spread away from her back.

Andrei said something about angels and almost fell. I gripped his elbow to hold him up.

"Decide now whether you wish to live, Andrei Kuznetzov. I can't save you a second time."

I gaped, I know I did. She was this? How? Why? I didn't understand who or what she was any longer.

"Guard your thoughts, Ilya; I can see all of them if I want."

"Are you an angel?" Andrei breathed.

"I am the Vhanaraszh, beloved of the Larentii race, capable of *Changing What Was*. If you no longer want me, Ilya, I will understand. Choose your path now. Time grows short."

"I will stay here with Andrei," I said flatly. "Let them come back. We will take care of further attempts."

"Good-bye, Ilya."

She disappeared, leaving me staring at an empty space in Andrei's apartment.

What had I just done?

Wait, had my disguise been removed?

"Andrei, what do I look like to you?" I asked.

"Like you always do."

"Gather your things; we have to go. Take that filth's weapon, you may need it." We stepped over the body of the KGB assassin on our way out the door.

CHAPTER 13

*L*issa

"He's with his son. They made a choice," Zaria said. She sat at the breakfast table, looking like she hadn't slept in a week.

"What happened?"

"I saved the life of his son, Andrei. Andrei refused to go to a safer place. He and Ilya think they can handle this on their own."

"That's fucked up," I mumbled while lifting my coffee cup. I didn't say that it was a no-brainer that it hurt her—what he'd done.

What they'd both done.

It wasn't the first time Ilya had done a double back flip with a twist into the deep end of the idiot pool, either, where Zaria was concerned. Maybe getting saved by a woman just didn't seem macho enough to him—or his kid. Vampire Baikov would eat them alive and spit out their bones.

"So, the Russian deserted, eh?" Bill took a seat at our table, as did Tony.

"He did."

"I hope you know what he knows, then."

"I do." Zaria's words were flat. "Probably more than he does."

"Good. We're scheduled to leave at eleven hundred. Are you packed?"

"Yes," I answered for both of us. Zaria could move her things in less than a blink if she wanted, as could I.

"What about Ilya's things?" I asked gently.

"Sent them to him when I got back."

"Good. No loose ends," Tony said while studying the breakfast menu.

Tony, shut the hell up, I sent.

"Huh?" His head jerked up and he looked from me to Zaria and back again. "Sorry," he mumbled and hid behind the menu.

Bill's phone rang. "Gotta take this," he was out of his chair quickly. Five minutes later, he was back, talking about Admiral Hafer, who'd been making unusual moves from London to Las Vegas and was now back in D.C. One of Bill's agents had reported the unusual activity.

He's spying for the Russians and for Rahim Alif, Zaria informed me in mindspeech.

He doesn't need to be caught now, I sent back. *The other me has to be involved in all that. Hey, the Russian President was at Camp David when I did capture Hafer,* I recalled.

And then that President was replaced by another in the future, remember?

Yeah. Maybe he showed up to see what he could find out.

Or maybe he was running scared from some of his own people—the Klyki, for instance.

You think they threatened him?

It makes sense. We know who's really in charge of Russia right now, don't we?

The Baikovs, I admitted with a mental snarl. Ilya understood all that; too many others were afraid to speak their mind on the matter. People ended up dead for less than that, and often in the strangest of circumstances.

I didn't mention Ilya's name to Zaria—I figured she didn't want to hear it right then. Why on Earth would he and his son refuse her help? That confused me more than anything.

"We have bigger fish to fry than Hafer," I told Bill. "He can wait a few weeks, I think."

"Good. I need to make a few more calls. Meet us in the lobby at ten-hundred."

❧

Manchester, England

Ilya

"Katya's fine," Andrei pocketed his cell phone after talking with her.

"We can't go to her, you know that. They'll be watching for me and it will put her in more danger."

"I know, Papa."

"What's wrong?" I asked him. His words were curt and he sounded out of sorts.

"She said she couldn't save me next time. Does that mean there will be a next time?"

"I think you worry too much. I have made a call to our friend, B," I went on. "He will do what he can to make sure Katya is safe if the worst happens."

"Maybe we should have asked her to take us with her."

"Perhaps," I drew out the word. Yes, I was missing her, but when she'd shown us what she was—I was shocked and disoriented for several moments. She'd spoken of aliens before, but I'd never considered that she was so very alien, or that her appearance would be, too.

"Papa, she had wings. Did you look at them? They were dusted with gold, like her blue skin."

"I saw."

"She said she could *Change What Was*. What does that mean?"

"I do not have a degree in alien matters," I growled, letting Andrei know to stop the questions.

She brought him back from the dead, my guilty conscience informed me.

From the dead.

Change What Was. Those bullets—both of them—had gone straight through his heart and he was dead by the time he hit the floor.

How could anyone, no matter what their race or planet of origin, accomplish something like that—as if it never happened?

Only Zaria could answer that question, I think, and I'd refused her help.

And her help for Andrei, too.

Fear gripped my heart like a cruel hand. She said she couldn't save him next time. So far, she'd never lied to me.

There *would* be a next time, and it terrified me.

"We are in England, my son," I turned to Andrei. "I suggest we travel to London—she and those with her are coming and will arrive in a matter of hours."

"Zaria is coming here?"

"To London, yes."

"Good." He sounded relieved. "We can take the train or hire a car."

"I have my bags—we'll take the train."

~

The Kremlin

Kornel Baikov

"Sir, they've been seen in Manchester. We expected them to travel to Liverpool by ferry, but they flew to Manchester instead."

"I still don't understand how they were able to kill our agent," I complained to my first assistant.

"He must have gotten careless," my assistant shrugged. "Perhaps he wasn't expecting Ilya to be there, and they caught him by surprise. Nevertheless, the body was removed and all evidence cleared away."

"Good. Watch them in Manchester, then."

"We've received word that they've gone to the train station, to travel to London," another assistant walked in to hand a communication to my first assistant.

"Have someone get on the train with them. If we can't take them down during the trip, then we'll have others waiting for them in London," I waved a hand. "Make sure they both die, this time."

"I'll see to it." My first assistant walked smartly out of my office, shadowed by the second.

~

London

Ivan Baikov

"I am sending in the female," I told Kornel. "She will be mist aboard the plane and will wait until they are over the ocean to kill the occupants. I am already in London, and will wait here for the news of their demise."

"I'm glad she was ready to send," he replied. "Much ahead of the others, that one."

"She may not survive the fight with the others," I pointed out.

"This means little to us; we have more coming."

"I will place orders to ditch the jet in the ocean, if she is successful."

"To hide the evidence?"

"In a manner of speaking."

"Good. At least she takes your orders, Uncle. I had a bit of trouble with her until Fedor commanded her."

"It only takes a vampire, nephew. Xenides told me of this quirk in the original."

"Then I will drink to quirks. Make sure she is prepared to do everything you tell her."

"You do not order me, remember?"

"Yes, Uncle."

~

Lissa

We were walking toward Winkler's jet when Zaria gripped my arm. She sent what she sensed—someone was aboard the jet.

Someone invisible and in sleep mode.

We can toss her out of her misting state, I sent to Zaria. *She'll fry in daylight, too, because she has no protection from it.*

We could do that. Or we can shield everybody and wait to see what she does when we hit darkness.

She wants to kill us—that's a no-brainer.

Then I have a suggestion. Let's play this close to the chest for a while. I think we can hold the jet together if she gets too crazy.

I think we can, too. This is a duplicate of vamp Lissa one-point-oh, after all.

Agreed. I figure vamp Baikov ordered her onto this jet, and we'll let him think he has the upper hand—at least until we're over international waters and hitting darkness.

Sounds like a good idea. Let's do it.

Want to tell the others?

I'll handle it.

Thanks. I'm not in an explaining mood right now.

Understood. Been there, done that.

I know.

～

Ilya

Andrei had left his seat to go to the toilet. He knew to be careful—to be watchful. His face was pale when he returned, although he didn't say anything for several moments. I saw the source of the trouble, then—he walked past our seats carrying a magazine and a briefcase.

Our tail had arrived. I had no idea how they'd found us so quickly, but they had. No doubt they knew of the agent I'd killed in Dublin, too, and were trying to piece together what had gone wrong with their plan to kill Andrei.

I wanted to laugh bitterly; nothing had gone wrong with their plan to kill Andrei. Zaria had intervened on his behalf, and now he lived again.

How quickly would they kill him next time?

Zaria, I wish you could hear me, I thought in her direction. *I wish I could change my mind and send Andrei to a safe place. We are being stalked on a train from Manchester to London, and our lives may not last much longer. Please know that I care for you—I wish I'd had sense enough to say that before.*

As expected, there was no reply. I'd wasted an opportunity, and the sharp pain of that foolishness pierced my heart.

~

Lissa

Zaria and I took seats across the aisle from one another on the jet, toward the middle so we'd be prepared for whatever our invisible guest thought to do.

Winkler growled low when he learned we had someone else aboard, but neither he, Bill nor Tony said anything. Charles lifted an eyebrow and also remained quiet.

Trajan sat beside Winkler, in case he was needed to protect his boss. Bill, on the other hand, sat in a row between Charles and me, hoping, no doubt, that two vampires could provide some protection.

You're all shielded, as is the jet and the cockpit, I informed them as the jet began to taxi in preparation for take-off. *She won't get to the pilot and copilot for sure.*

"Can she hear us?" Bill ventured to ask.

"Not right now—she's in the rejuvenating sleep, although she's mist."

"Convenient, I suppose," Winkler shook his head. The jet lifted off the ground and we were airborne.

"We'll hit sufficient darkness when we're roughly three hours away from Heathrow," Charles said. "With no land in sight. You know what Wlodek would do in this case."

"We're not Wlodek," Zaria snapped at him.

Charles, why the fuck did you bring that up? I sent to him.

I'll remove her head if it's necessary.

Good. You're plan C. Let's try plans A and B first, okay?

I'll hold back until there's no other option.

Thank you.

~

Ilya

We switched trains in Stafford, choosing to go a longer route through Birmingham. Our tail wasn't fast enough to catch us, but I didn't think for a moment we were in the clear.

Especially if they put assassins on every train out of Manchester in case we attempted a switch; it's something I would have done.

"Now we wait to see who else shows up to watch us," I said under my breath, once we'd taken our seats on the other train to Birmingham.

I spotted him as he walked through our car later. A member of the *Klyki*, no less—a werewolf.

Say nothing you don't wish to be overheard, I sent a message to Andrei's phone.

One of them? Andrei replied.

Yes. Be wary. Stay together.

Of course.

The werewolf was already sending a message on a cell phone he pulled from a pocket when he exited the car. Someone could be waiting for us in Birmingham. I wondered if they'd wait to see if we got off the train, or board somehow and kill us while we traveled.

"Papa, please say you have her phone number."

He meant Zaria.

"She is in the air, I think," I mumbled.

"Papa, it's worth a try. At least leave a message. Tell her I am sorry and wish to reconsider."

~

Lissa

With two other vampires on board, there was no doubt as to when it was dark enough for our ghost to manifest. What surprised most of us was the way it happened.

Charles had claws at the ready, in case she materialized fighting—after all, she'd be helpless against the shields Zaria had built around everything.

Zaria, on the other hand, didn't act surprised at all when the duplicate of me appeared, crying and begging for asylum.

~

Zaria

It took a while to stop her from crying. Like Lissa in her original version, this one hadn't wanted to be a vampire and hated everything about it.

She'd been a political prisoner who happened to have the same blood type as Lissa, and they'd reverse-engineered her, just as I thought they would, to create another Lissa.

I worried that there could be many others, and that those wouldn't be so morally-minded as this one. She was smart, though, and figured out quickly what they wanted from her—and obeyed vampire commands to make it look as if she were fully cooperative with their plans.

"Do you know if there are others like you?" Bill asked gently, kneeling next to the seat where she sat.

"I saw them working with six others," she sniffled and accepted more tissues from Lissa. "There could be more—I don't know."

"Six," Winkler growled and stalked toward the back of the jet, his shoulders set in an angry square.

"Please, I didn't want to be this. They forced me," she repeated for perhaps the fourth time.

"We know," I said. "What would you do if we could give you your life back and put you in a safer place to live?"

"I would bless you for it," she dabbed her eyes again.

"Do it," Lissa dipped her head in a nod.

"It will be very bright in a moment; don't let that frighten you," I told her. "It's part of the process."

"They told me it was irreversible," she admitted. "It is no surprise they lied."

"Oh, they were right about that part," I told her. "They just don't know about me."

"Who are you?"

"Zaria," I said and released the light I held to *Change What Was*.

Ilya

Get off the train, the voice entered my mind. Not Zaria's. A male voice—a gruff one. We were pulling into the Birmingham station, and had no plans to leave the train. I felt we were safer there, although the Klyki was now sitting near the door at one end of our car, watching us while pretending to read.

Get off the train. Trust me. Zaria asked us to come.

Us? There was more than one?

"Zaria asked someone to come. We must leave the train," I told Andrei softly. Yes, he'd left a message on Zaria's phone, but she likely wouldn't read it until after we were dead once we reached London.

"Are you sure about this?"

"Not sure at all. Come."

"But," he argued.

"Andrei, it matters not if we die in Birmingham or London. We get off here."

"All right." He stood and looked about him, while others gathered belongings, ready to depart.

We followed them out, through the door opposite the one guarded by the *Klyki*. He rose when we did to follow us, but there were several passengers in between. Therefore, we stepped off the train first.

And then everything stopped—noise, conversation, scents, motion —all of it.

"You're not in danger," two men walked toward us. One had broad shoulders, light-brown hair and eyes that were surely blind.

The other—the one who'd spoken, was of Asian descent and wore a long braid down his back. His hair was black as midnight, except for the white streak that ran through it.

"What is happening?" Andrei's head swiveled as he took in the scene about us. I turned to look behind; sure enough, the *Klyki* had closed most of the distance between us, and had removed a weapon from a pocket.

Yes, it looked like an ordinary pen, but it likely held two doses of poison that would take us down in minutes.

I whirled back to the two who'd met us—and presumably saved us, too.

"Zaria sent you?" I asked, forcing my voice to remain normal. I thought Zaria's talents amazing. This was amazing, too, in its own right.

"We owe our lives to her," the blind man grinned. "When she asks for a favor, we're all over it, like ducks on June-bugs, or that's what a friend of mine says."

"He has no idea what a June bug actually is," the Asian man said. "I'm Travis. This is Randl. We need to get out of *split-time* quick."

"First, I'll take this," the blind man—Randl—stepped around me and deftly removed the pen from the *Klyki's* fingers. "He won't need it, now."

"Ready for London? We got you a room with two beds next to Zaria's, and she can take things from here," Randl said. "If I were you, I'd practice my apologies before you see her again."

"May I have that?" I asked, meaning the pen.

"As long as you put it to good use." The pen was handed to me.

"You may depend upon it."

"Good. Let's go; Travis and I have one more stop to make before we go back."

I wanted to ask them where that was, but didn't. The way he'd stopped time around us, I worried it could be a when as much as a where.

Two minutes later, we and our luggage had been delivered to our room at the hotel near Wembley Stadium, and our rescuers disappeared.

"Well, Papa, she did tell us she couldn't save me again; looks like she asked somebody else to do it instead," Andrei sighed and dropped onto the side of his bed, his hands hanging loosely between his knees.

He was trying to relax after our recent experience, because the werewolf would have killed us had our rescuers not arrived.

~

Lissa

"That's Randl and ah, Travis," I explained to Winkler. I'd almost introduced Travis as my son, but Winkler might not be able to wrap his head around that information. He'd already seen me do things he shouldn't have.

"What are they doing here?" Winkler frowned as both spoke softly with Zaria at the front of the jet.

"They're taking Elena to a safe place so the Baikovs can't get to her again."

"Good. I think we're fortunate that this one was more like you. I don't think we'll get lucky like that again."

"I'm thinking the same thing," I admitted. "Six others. Can you imagine what that fight could look like?"

"I don't want to. It scares the hell out of me."

We watched as Elena stood and nodded to Travis before they disappeared. Sirena would gain a new citizen; Randl would decree it. He wouldn't have taken her with him if he hadn't approved.

There was no way in hell that the Baikovs could ever touch her again, unless all the universes fell.

"Well, that's done," Zaria sighed as she took a seat in front of us. "They had to rescue Ilya and Andrei first, but there's no way I was going to let them die on a train to Birmingham."

"Alabama or England?" Winkler's words were dry.

"The latter, I assure you."

"Where are they now?" I asked.

"In a hotel room next to the one I'll get in London," she said. "I'm really tired. Will you miss me if I go soak up sunlight somewhere and take a nap?"

"Go," I waved a hand. "Just be back when we land. I'll send mindspeech if we need anything in between."

"Soak up sunlight?" Winkler asked after Zaria disappeared.

"It's good for her," I shrugged.

"Things just keep getting weirder," Winkler huffed and took his seat. He patted the one next to him, inviting me to sit with him. I didn't turn down the invitation.

~

The Kremlin

Kornel Baikov

"What do you mean, they disappeared?"

"Our agent was right behind them. One moment they were there, and the next, they were gone. According to his report, sir."

"What about surveillance video?"

"His lapel camera verifies his account. They were right in front of him, getting off the train, and then they weren't there. Those outside the train were recording images, too. We've run their videos back many times; they show the same thing, with no interruption in the time stamps on either."

"This is impossible," I shouted at my first and second assistants, sweeping out a hand and knocking a brass pencil cup off my desk. It clanked across the Persian rug underfoot, scattering pens in its wake before rolling to a stop next to my credenza. "My uncle will have heads over this," I continued the rant while ignoring my clumsiness.

"We must add this to the puzzle of how they made their way from the East Coast to the West in very little time," my second assistant cowered as he spoke. "Kuznetsov was seen in both places, with very little time in between."

"This was not brought to my attention because?" I hissed through clenched teeth. I understood that the female vampire could carry others quickly within her mist, but to travel that far as such, and reach the destination while it was still in daylight?

That was unheard of.

"Get me the trainer on the line. I wish to speak with him immediately."

"Right away, sir."

~

London

Ivan Baikov

Night had fallen; I hadn't been awake long when I received the call from Kornel's assistant.

"The General wishes to inform you that two of the females are dead," he said hurriedly before I could chastise him for having the temerity to speak to me.

"And how is that possible?" I demanded. I was needed at Heathrow, where I would wait for the news to come of the destruction of the jet over the Atlantic. I had no time for this or for Kornel's assistant.

"We ah, had news that it might be possible for the original female to mist while in daylight. That could prove to be a miraculous event for us if it were true."

"Stop babbling and get to the point."

"We attempted it with two of our females—forcing them to change to mist in darkness, before releasing them in simulated sunlight. The ah, results were not satisfactory. The General only wishes you to know."

Before I could shout at the worm on the other end of the call, he had already hung up.

~

Lissa

"The arrangements are made—the media will be informed shortly,"

Bill ended a call on his phone. Soon enough, on both sides of the pond, word would spread that our jet crashed into the ocean.

There was other news, too. With everything that had happened, it had slipped my mind. In Paris, a hotel had been bombed while the original Tony was inside it. I was forced to go *Looking* to make sure everything happened as it should; so far, it had gone as it had the first time.

For now, too, Baikov would believe us dead while we landed at a private airport in France. Zaria would transport us from there, while the werewolf pilot and copilot would be guests of a local pack in the French countryside until the jet was needed again.

"An associate has sent copies of the photos taken of Kornel Baikov's family in Ostrava, to one of the General's associates. We'll see how he handles the information," Tony said. He'd been talking with Bill after receiving the news on the bombing, and keeping himself busy after he learned of it.

Strange, I know, to think that René had already carried Tony to his home in France, after performing the turn before Tony died.

Time was indeed growing short, and I worried over Liron's absence. Not once had he poked his head in to interfere with anything we'd done so far, to weigh the scales in the Baikovs' favor.

Perhaps Ilya was more than correct on all of it—that this was only their opening salvo, and much, much worse was planned the deeper we fell into the rabbit hole.

Would he fall for our fake deaths, as Baikov likely would—at least at first? I had no idea how much time we had before that lie floated to the surface, only to be disproved.

We'd already dealt with spies and double agents—were others waiting? In addition to that, we were still no closer to the drug, the Sirenali or the Sirenali bone dust. I had a feeling that only a trip to Russia would eliminate any of those threats.

"We'll have a talk with Ilya when we get to London," Zaria waved an arm, causing her two bags to float and follow wherever she walked.

"About where to go, once we get to Russia?"

"Yes."

"Is everyone ready to go?" We'd deplaned and were herded into a small office inside a nearby hangar, where airport employees had been warned away. As it was nighttime, it wasn't difficult to achieve.

I glanced in Tony's direction; it wasn't the light—he looked almost green. He knew what was happening to him and René at this very moment, and it brought up bad memories—of almost dying after the explosion, and being in terrible pain while René frantically searched for him.

Winkler shut the office door with as little noise as possible, but it still made me jump. Then, Bill nodded to Zaria, so she'd transport us to London. She dropped us behind a hardware store not far from the hotel, and we walked toward the entrance, which took roughly five minutes.

"There's a tube station near here," Charles stepped to my side as we carried or pulled our bags to the hotel.

He'd know—this was his stomping grounds, after all. Wlodek's mansion was an hour's ride away, if traffic cooperated. If I misted there, I could arrive in minutes. I had no desire to face *that* Wlodek again, and pitied my former self for having to deal with what was coming after her return from Refizan.

"All here?" The desk clerk began checking us in. I looked around at the huge lobby, where a few guests, some of them dressed for dinner or an outing, wandering in and out. There was a lot of marble and glass around us, which raised my worry to level two.

They also weren't kidding about it being close to Wembley Stadium. I could almost reach out and touch the stadium from the front desk.

"It just looks close," Charles whispered in my ear beside me.

"Lissy," Tony walked up to me. Something in the tone of his voice made me jerk my head up.

"Tony?" I asked. I saw the pain in his eyes, and that wasn't something I'd seen often.

"I think I should tap out," he said aloud.

"But," I began.

"No," he held up a hand. "The other me is ah, becoming vampire, and not that far away. As is René."

We'd all heard it—it was all over the news. The present Tony had supposedly died in a hotel bombing in Paris. While he was presently disguised, he'd felt the pull of it—and the fear of it—the moment we landed in Paris.

On top of that, he wanted to see René. Talk to him. That would be a huge mistake and he realized that. After all, René would die himself in less than two months, and that pain was waiting to happen again.

"Who will come to take your place?" I asked Tony. Gavin shouldn't come for perhaps the same reasons—he was too close to this and he was related to René, rather than René's last turn, as Tony was.

"Rigo volunteered." Tony's head was down, his hands in both pockets as he whispered his reply. "Actually, Aryn and Aurelius offered, too, but I think they'd call too much attention. Rigo is a spy's spy. I think he'll be better at this than I ever was."

"Then go now. Tell Rigo to," I began.

"I am here, Tiessa," Rigo took my arm and steered me away from Charles and Tony. "Let them deal with getting Tony away unseen."

I let my head droop against Rigo's chest for a moment when we stopped, and his hands rubbed my arms as I rested against him. Tony was right to leave, but things felt out of control from such a sudden change.

Lissa, we have a problem, Zaria informed me.

Huh? My head jerked up and I turned quickly in her direction.

Over there, standing behind the man checking her in? The scents reached me the moment my eyes widened. They were here, fresh off a bombing in Paris.

Oh, my God, I breathed in reply. *It's Jovana and Rahim Alif.*

CHAPTER 14

*L*ondon
Lissa

"They're on the second floor," Zaria told Bill as we rode the elevator to the top of the hotel.

"Fuck. Right here under our noses and we can't do a damn thing," Bill growled. "I can alert the local authorities because I have no jurisdiction, but people will die if they attempt to capture both."

"People may die anyway. We have no idea why they're here," I pointed out. "Did you get anything from either?" I asked Zaria.

"They're both waiting for instructions from Xenides," she said. "They don't know why they're here, either."

"Xenides sent them here. He's best buds with vamp Baikov this time around, so they could be here on Kremlin business," I said.

"You think they showed up in case we didn't officially die earlier?" Winkler asked.

"It's possible—that they're backup for vamp Baikov. Baikov must have Xenides over a barrel, or Xenides doesn't know that Baikov wants me dead," I mused. "Xenides really, really, wants me, you know."

"I'd say Baikov has him in the dark about that," Zaria suggested. "Since I haven't laid eyes on him I can't say for sure, but that's my guess. By the way, we're all disguised as of now, and your passports will change whenever your disguise does while we're here."

"That's handy," Winkler said.

"A necessity," Rigo said. "I would do it myself if Zaria hadn't. She has also arranged for our scents to be changed, too. Jovana will not be able to tell us from any other human."

"That's something, at least," Charles agreed.

"This elevator is so polite," Trajan broke in as the door opened and our floor was announced.

I smothered a snicker as we walked toward our rooms.

Zaria

I hesitated outside the hotel door before knocking. Ilya and Andrei were both inside, waiting for my arrival. I didn't know how this would go, but Andrei was sincere when he'd left the message begging me to help them.

I had information for him, too, after speaking with Randl, but the final choice would be his to make.

Ilya's reaction was the one that worried me. Had he known of Andrei's call, or had he allowed it after considering his options, once his life and that of his son looked to be over? I'd heard Ilya's thoughts, and he sounded a desperate. I wanted him to trust me, and I was about to find out if that were the case.

The *Klyki* had caught up with both of them, as I'd known they would. Without Randl's arrival, they'd have died of an unknown poison, a preferred weapon in the Kremlin's arsenal to get rid of inconveniences.

Raising my hand, I rapped lightly on the door. Andrei was the one to open it. "I am so sorry I did not believe you," he began.

"I am the biggest fool," Ilya said, stepping in to stand beside Andrei.

"I'll give you that," I nodded before walking in and allowing Andrei to close the door behind me.

~

London

   Ivan Baikov

Xenides didn't like open spaces. He failed to understand that we were as anonymous inside the hotel bar as we would be anywhere else. We would pay in cash, as always, and those who served us wouldn't recall our presence.

Nevertheless, Xenides wore a deep frown as he toyed with his wineglass. Jovana smiled and laughed at something Alif was saying. I didn't care what they talked about; I'd only been asked to arrange this meeting, after all, by the one who'd created the master program and the drug, before offering it to us. Of all the world's leaders, he'd approached us first, and the initial experiments were too good to refuse.

He'd been paid very well for what he offered, but he required that we leave ultimate control in his hands.

We were happy to do so, as our scientists needed training from him in how everything worked. He also asked for research space outside Moscow. Again, that was given readily.

Then, when he brought in his assistant, D'slay, things went even smoother than before. D'slay would carry this one's orders to his minions, and they responded well and quickly to all demands.

Or they died.

Not our problem; they learned swiftly or we had no use for them.

"When will he get here?" Xenides wasn't used to waiting on anyone or anything, and frankly, as he was older than I, he would have the upper hand in a battle of compulsion.

Xenides wanted what he wanted, however, and the female vampire princess was at the top of his list. Too bad he didn't know that she was already dead.

"You're wrong. She's still alive."

He slid onto the empty edge of the circular booth where we sat, all pretending to drink except Alif, who was enjoying his martini.

Xenides had never seen our scientific benefactor, Liron, before.

Something about him appealed greatly, no matter who or what you were. I'd seen scientists staring at him with worship in their eyes at the top-secret facility where our experiments were performed, and our new agents were created.

The news of my failure to destroy Xenides' princess was disheartening, but Liron did not appear angry over the matter. In fact, he sounded as if he expected it to be as it was.

I didn't argue—one didn't argue with Liron; I'd learned that early on. Whatever his talent was, it wasn't because he was vampire, werewolf or any other creature I'd heard of. I imagine I should have been more curious, but oddly, I wasn't.

"Who is alive?" Xenides asked.

"Your princess, who else?" Liron said, taking his napkin from the table and setting it across his lap. A server appeared at his elbow moments later; Liron ordered a full meal and a drink.

I glanced at Alif; he had the worship in his eyes that so many others did when they gazed upon Liron. As if he were a god or some such. I dismissed it; he was merely a very powerful man.

"General Baikov," Liron turned his gaze upon me, "I wish to move two prisoners from the facility in Siberia. They will be brought to Vladimirsky Central, then transferred to the research facility for reassignment."

"I only need the names and I will see to it," I shrugged. If Liron wanted them, there was a good reason.

"Here," he drew a piece of paper from a pocket and handed it to me. I had the fleeting thought that the pocket had been empty until he reached inside it, but dismissed that thought immediately.

"These two—I do not think they will make good candidates," I began after reading the names.

"It's already done, Ivan. They're on their way to Vladimirsky now."

I wanted to argue, but the words caught in my throat and nothing I could do would force them from my mouth.

Liron didn't wish to hear my arguments. I must accept that.

What did it matter that they were dissidents, or Ilya Kuznetzov's cousins? We'd kept them to keep Kuznetzov under our control and fully cooperative. We had eyes on his daughter, too, and he knew it.

We still didn't know where he and his son were, but wherever they'd gone, we'd find them soon enough. Kuznetsov would go back to his old work or he and all his kin would be eliminated.

"Exactly," Liron nodded as if he could read my mind. That should have troubled me. It didn't. "The trap for the werewolf is now here at the hotel. You will have him very soon, I think. These two," Liron tapped the paper I still held beneath my fingers, "are part of a larger plan. You may be surprised by how well it will work."

~

Ilya

Two for transfer—chanson—B.

"That's not a song, is it?" Zaria's eyes met mine after I allowed her to read Bespalov's message.

"No. Mikhail Krug's most famous song is about Vladimirsky Central, a prison," Andrei answered for me. He'd known exactly what the message meant, as had I. "In Russia, *chanson* has a deeper meaning than the French assign to it. It specifically is used to describe songs about criminals, or romanticizes organized crime and such—like Robin Hood or whatever. Our only cousins were being held as political prisoners in a Siberian prison camp. Bespalov is saying they're going to Vladimirsky."

"And from there, who knows. They may be marked for those unholy experiments, to get back at us," I sighed.

"Does he know how long your cousins will be there?" Zaria asked.

"I can ask. I cannot guarantee he can get the information."

"Will you? Ask, that is?"

I wanted to say I was willing to do anything for her. I held back. Stupid, I know. "I will send a message," I said, rising to walk into the bathroom.

~

Zaria

I watched him shut the bathroom door behind him. Andrei's shoulders drooped; he didn't see the necessity for the privacy, but Ilya wanted it for some reason.

"I have a different place for you, if you want to go," I told Andrei. "Randl says you can come work for him if you want."

"The blind one? What does he do—besides stop time?" Andrei asked.

"He and those around him are hunting down the biggest threat to the known universes," I said. "He told me he has a place for you—if you want it. Have you ever wanted to be a pirate?" I added.

"I played a pirate when I was young," Andrei admitted. "But," he gestured with a hand, indicating he was now an adult.

"They are an entity for justice, hiding behind the façade of piracy. They're not really pirates," I smiled at Andrei. "They call themselves the BlackWing Pirates, and they have a fleet of starships and cruisers at their disposal."

Andrei went still. "You mean like in the movies?"

"There's very little similarity between them and the movies. Movies are fantasy, no matter what planet or culture you're from. There is real danger involved, but the work is rewarding."

"What if I don't fit in? It sounds as if I need to learn many things."

"Talk to Randl. I believe he'll let you take a trial run at it, then decide for yourself."

"Then I accept, but I have to tell Papa."

"Of course. Let me know when that happens; I'll either take you myself or have Randl come for you."

"Papa won't accept the offer; he'll stay to protect Katya."

"I know. They both have things to do here, anyway. I couldn't take them, even if I wanted to."

"Do you know how strange that sounds?"

"More than you know."

"They'll be held at Vladimirsky for three days, once they arrive. The location for transfer has not been revealed to Bespalov's contact inside the facility." Ilya was back after having a conversation with his ally.

"I need to speak with Lissa," I said. "If you're hungry, order room service and call if you need me."

$$\backsim$$

Ordinandis, Refizan

Breanne

Pieces of the puzzle were falling into place, with cracks and vital differences between this and the first time. Fifteen spheres filled with rogue gods now resided inside Nefrigar's vault at the Larentii Archives; we'd accomplished that much, at least.

The days were winding down, too, with the huge battle at the end already forming, and no doubt Liron was padding the original ranks with who knew what or whom.

Somehow, somewhere, Liron had set up a warning to his past-self, in case his future-self died. I had no idea what that warning was, or what form it took, but it had been more than effective.

After all, if he were able to stop Lissa somewhere in the timeline, his future-self was less likely to die. And, if he were able to eliminate other major players, then his job of staying alive would become easier, still.

Liron.

Creator and father of *the god who always comes at the end*. Randl had passed that information along, and frankly, it made all of us afraid.

Had we fought so hard to win the God Wars, only to have everything collapse afterward? I was beginning to think if there were an actual devil, as so many believed, his name would be Liron.

I'd seen him, as had Lissa, in all his falsely-radiant, winged beauty. Zaria and I had seen past that, however, to the corruption beneath his façade.

"Why couldn't you just stay dead?" I whispered aloud.

"Did you say something?" Erland now stood beside me as I gazed out the window of our large apartment in Refizan's capital city.

"Nothing that makes any difference," I hugged myself. I was worried, as was everyone around me. One slip and we could all go down.

"There are Ra'Ak attacking the Solar Red temple up the river," Drake and Drew arrived, breathing hard. "Lissa is there, trying to get those children away. We have to go help."

I didn't bother with a reply; instead, I gathered everyone and folded space to help my sister.

~

London

Lissa

"I think we could get in and replace his cousins with no difficulty. After all, if they're being delivered to Experiment Central, then that's the easiest way to get there," I pointed out. "Right now, we're held back by Sirenali or Sirenali bone dust, and can't find anything."

"It's a decent idea," Charles agreed. He, Bill and Winkler were all in this impromptu meeting, after Zaria told me about Ilya's cousins—both women—who were political guests of the Kremlin.

"But we still don't know what Liron has up his sleeve," Zaria cautioned.

"True, but let's face it, I'm stronger than he is," I said. "The old me isn't, but this me is. If he thinks to coerce us, somehow—he tried that last time, and you showed him how useless that was."

"What did he do?" Bill asked.

"He had my daughter, and threatened to kill her," Zaria shrugged.

"How did that turn out?" Bill's forehead wrinkled as he gazed at me.

"Zaria killed her before Liron could."

"What?" Winkler shouted.

"Relax, she's fine," I held up a hand. "It's just something Zaria can do—changing things that happened. It took Liron by surprise."

"You know he's plotting something we won't expect," Zaria said. "We need an ace up our sleeves, too."

"Then good luck finding one," I told her. "I don't know what might affect him anymore."

"I'll think about this. We have three days," Zaria said before disappearing.

～

Zaria

"I can take you to Sirena now," I told Andrei. "Ilya can come, too, to see where you'll be and understand that you'll be taken care of. I think I want to talk with Randl again in private, so you can get to know some of the others at the palace."

"Palace?"

"Well, there's no king or queen," I replied to Ilya's worried question. "Just a few people in charge, you know, and it's nothing like you've ever seen or experienced before."

"Then take us; I wish to see this—Sirena." Ilya now wore a frown. He didn't trust any government, and with his past experiences, I couldn't blame him.

"I'll introduce you to Tamp," I told him. "He used to be one of the biggest criminals ever."

"What?" Andrei's speech was cut off as I bent time and folded space.

～

Sirena

Randl Gage

"You'll have a place—and work if you want it," I explained to Andrei, who walked through the great hall, his eyes on the high ceilings once decorated by Sirenali royalty.

That was before the original planet was destroyed by the Larentii long ago. Sirena was currently rebuilt from the dust of the first; Zaria had done that for us. Those of us living at the palace belonged to the *Formidables*, a special, self-governed division of the BlackWing Pirates.

I chose those who could come here to live and work. Andrei would fit in if he wanted to fit in. We had need of someone with his talents, I think.

"This is Phrinnis Tampirus," I introduced Tamp as he walked toward us. "He will show you where your quarters will be, should you choose to stay. And he'll give you a tour of the rest of the palace, and answer questions."

"They haven't eaten," Zaria told Tamp. "Will you take them through the kitchens first?"

"It will be my pleasure," Tamp smiled at her. "Andrei, Ilya, if you will come this way," he led them toward an exit that would eventually take them to the kitchens and food.

"You wanted to talk to me?" I turned to Zaria.

"Yeah. Something worries me, and I think you're the only one who might understand. Plus, if you'll agree to it, I may need to borrow a couple of things."

"Whatever you need," I told her.

"Wait until you know what it is, first."

Lissa

Winkler wanted a drink, so I followed him to the bar inside the hotel. We were shown to a booth, large enough for two-and-a-half people.

Larger booths were occupied against the opposite wall, with the bar in between, but Winkler and I had the best view out the window. That's how things usually went for him—even disguised, he looked wealthy and important wherever he went, so of course he was given the best.

I was dressed in nice jeans and a top, but my appearance didn't scream money like Winkler's. He was the peacock; I was the peahen. Go figure.

The hostess who led us to the booth wasn't eyeing him either. Uh-uh. Nope. Winkler grinned after sitting across from me and lazily draping an arm across the low back of the booth, as if he owned the place.

"Someone will be here shortly to take your drink order." She kept smiling at Winkler and didn't bother to look my way.

"She smells like she had sex ten minutes ago," Winkler's mouth turned downward as he frowned.

"Honey, I didn't want to say anything," I said, toying with the napkin on my side of the small, round table. "I had to cut off the scent after a second or two because it was so strong."

"May I take your drink order?" The waiter arrived. He was all business and wasn't the one the hostess had sex with, thank goodness.

"I'll have a Scotch on the rocks," Winkler ordered, "And some of those chips I saw walking past when we got here."

"Which part of the U.S. do you come from?" Our waiter smiled.

"Texas," Winkler grinned.

"I knew it," the waiter chuckled. "You have a bit of that drawl I heard earlier today. Someone else was here, who said he was from Texas and he sounded like you."

"We do get around, now and then," Winkler agreed. "Lissa, what do you want?" He turned the waiter's attention away from himself.

"I want a glass of Riesling," I said. "And I'll help him with his chips," I added, indicating Winkler.

"We'll have your drinks out soon, and the chips after that," the waiter promised and walked away.

"I was gonna say fries," I told Winkler with a grin. "Just so he could correct me."

"Beat you to the punch, eh?" He winked at me.

I hadn't even had a sip of wine, yet, and still I wanted to mist him to his bedroom and tear his clothes off. I figured it was remembered frustration from centuries ago, and I could fold space and have sex with the Winkler who was all mine, but there was still that bit of bad girl in me that I wanted this one, too.

This one is married to a very pregnant Kellee, I reminded myself and resolved to mind my manners. That meant looking out the window at the behemoth that Wembley Stadium was, until I caught the reflection behind us from inside the bar.

I didn't understand at first how Winkler and I were suspended in midair and pulled away from our booth, but we watched in horrified fascination as Winkler's father—or his duplicate, anyway, in werewolf form, leapt at us in slow motion while we were held away from his onslaught.

The subsequent crash through the plate glass window sent guests flying toward the exit, some of them screaming and shouting as they fled.

Outside and below, the wolf hit the walkway with a sharp yelp, and then everything reversed itself.

The wolf rushed backward through the window, while shattered glass repaired itself as he was pulled through it in reverse. Suddenly, Winkler and I were in our seats again, while I watched the werewolf's image recede in the reflective glass.

The crowd was back, normal sounds were back, the werewolf disappeared somehow, and a shout of anger sounded from the other side of the bar.

"We have to go," Charles said when he and Zaria appeared beside our table. "Liron and his bunch don't need to see any of us."

"What happened to my ah—the werewolf?" Winkler growled once we were inside Bill's suite. Like a caged wolf, he was pacing the length of Bill's windows.

"His particles are separated," Zaria said. "I'm sorry if that upsets you, but he'd been programmed to kill Lissa and take you," she answered Winkler's question.

"Do you think there are more of them?" Bill asked. He'd raked fingers through his hair at least a dozen times after we got to his room and Charles explained what we'd seen.

"It's possible—they took enough to create more than one from the body," Zaria replied.

"I hate this," Bill shook his head. Rigo, leaning against a wall, listened to everything with quiet interest. It was the spy in him, analyzing what he knew and building a picture from who knew how many puzzle pieces.

"We can't take Liron on here," Charles explained what Winkler wanted to know but hadn't voiced, yet. "Too many things could go wrong, and the entire city of London could be destroyed if he sees fit. Zaria pulled us back until just before Liron and your father's duplicate became aware of your presence. She destroyed the wolf as he was on his way to join Liron's group."

"So, where is he now—this Liron guy?" Trajan demanded.

"Gone, thank goodness, to whatever hole he crawled out of," Charles growled. "He took Jovana, Alif and the others with him."

"So he was here to have a meeting with them?" I turned toward Charles.

"I believe so," he dipped his head in a curt nod. He didn't like letting Liron go any more than I did, but he was right—London was in danger every moment Liron spent there. If destroying it meant destroying me, then he'd be all for it.

He could have taken Winkler, too; that was probably his goal—to hand Winkler to Baikov to placate the Kremlin and destroy me at the same time.

He'd have to destroy me if he took Winkler; I wasn't about to settle for that. Maybe he understood how much Winkler meant to me, and how determined I'd be to get him back if Liron did succeed in taking my wolf.

Or, maybe he didn't know those things. Frankly, I had no idea what Liron knew or didn't know.

The only one who'd actually faced off against him was Zaria, and she'd beaten him back both times, the first by outsmarting him, the last by killing him—in the future, of course.

That left this middle-Liron to deal with, who'd waited until his future-self alerted him somehow of an impending demise. I had no idea how he'd accomplished that, but he had and here we were.

"I have a question," Ilya said. He'd been brought in by Zaria; I understood that Andrei, his son, was now on Sirena with three of my sons to look after him—and Randl, of course.

"What's that?"

"We are disguised, are we not? How were you and Winkler targeted?"

"Texas," Zaria sighed.

"Texas?" Winkler's frown was deep.

"The waiter asked you where you were from. When your duplicate father walked in and sat down with Liron and company, he was recognized and told by the waiter that he'd met another man from Texas across the bar. The rest is history."

"Fuck me," Winkler mumbled and shook his head. "Fuck me royal."

"What do we do now?" Bill asked.

"Lissa and I are going to replace Ilya's cousins in a Russian prison —in three days," Zaria replied. "I'm hoping we'll be taken to the facility where Baikov's experiments are done afterward, so we can destroy the entire thing. If Liron shows up, because he's behind all this, you know, then I hope we have what it takes to get rid of him, too."

"That's roughly the time when your original self will return from being off-planet," Charles pointed out quietly.

"I know," I sighed. "It worries me, too, that these things are coming together like that, as if we're being funneled into a specific container, for a specific purpose."

"I'll have to go back to Wlodek by then—you know why," Charles said.

"Yes, I know why." Not only had the original me returned from Refizan, but there was Wlodek to deal with, Jovana to deal with, and a shitload of Xenides' vampires to deal with, too. Xenides has sent an army to attack Wlodek's mansion, in an attempt to destroy the Council and take over the entirety of Earth's vampire population.

With my help in the past, they'd failed in their mission. Had I not been there, Griffin wouldn't have come to help and neither would Dragon. Everything hinged on my being there.

Everything.

"It just keeps getting more complicated," Zaria said.

"You got that right," I told her. "I really need that drink I didn't get earlier."

~

"Macallan is cheaper in Scotland," Zaria lifted her glass to me. We'd gone to Edinburgh to get our drink, after everybody else agreed that a drink sounded good. We got pub grub to go with it; Zaria ordered the broccoli-stilton soup with fresh bread while Winkler and the rest of us had fish and chips.

"To the best booze, and cheaper, too," I held up my wineglass to clink with hers. She and I needed to make our plans for replacing Ilya's cousins, but that would have to wait until we were sober enough to do it.

Bill ordered two bottles of wine for the table, and he and I were making our way through the Riesling and a pinot noir, while the others had mixed drinks or straight Scotch.

"Should we go back to London?" Bill asked, pouring another glass of wine for himself.

"I vote we stay here," Winkler said. He'd had four drinks and he didn't even slur his words. He didn't want to run into another version of his father, either, and I fully understood that.

It would be like meeting an evil version of my mother, which would scar my soul. Winkler had enough scars; I knew that much, and he didn't deserve more.

"Can we accomplish everything from here?" Bill asked the obvious question.

"As long as Zaria and Lissa are here," Ilya pointed out. "Without them, the rest of us are tied to mundane travel."

"I'll go back to Wlodek," Charles said. "That will put me closer to London, and better able to get in touch with the rest of you if needed. Zaria, I'd still like to speak with you privately, sometime soon."

"Sure." Zaria emptied her glass of Scotch. I knew, as did Charles, that she wasn't looking forward to having a private conversation with him, no matter when it was.

CHAPTER 15

*E*dinburgh, Scotland
    Ilya

He'd asked us to call him Tamp, and led us through most of the massive palace. Many of Randl's associates lived there, and there was a hum of power about all of it, but nothing I could identify.

"Papa, I would be a fool to refuse this," Andrei told me after two others had sat down to eat with us. One called himself Vik, the other, a dwarf, was named David. David told us that he was originally from Australia, and through Zaria's good graces, had been given a new life and citizenship on a planet solely inhabited by others like him.

"I can verify that," Vik, who was nearly seven feet tall, told us. He and David both spoke English to us, and it made Andrei feel comfortable as we shared a meal of finely-cooked fish and vegetables.

"We can train you on weapons and any fighting disciplines you don't already have," David told us. "And, if you want, Travis and his brother will teach you to fight with blades."

"For when a pistol or rifle just won't do," Vik grinned.

"Of course. Why wouldn't that be so?" I said, only half sarcastically.

"You'd be surprised," Tamp said. He wasn't eating, although he was having a drink while the rest of us ate. "If you're Falchani-trained, almost anyone will welcome you into their employ."

"It takes discipline to master the art of the blade," Vik said. "If you're not interested, there are other things to specialize in."

Following the meal, Vik and David walked with us, and helped Tamp tell us about the people who lived at the palace, and what they did in their normal duties aboard a BlackWing Pirate ship.

"What about health care and such?" Andrei asked.

"Well, we have healers on call; if Zaria can't help, then Quin or someone else will help out if needed."

"Healers? But what if surgery is required?" Andrei asked.

I hadn't told him how Zaria had healed werewolves of bullet wounds, or reminded him that she'd brought him back from the dead.

That realization reached him almost as quickly as it did me.

"Never mind, I think I understand," Andrei sighed.

"I thought that might be the case," David chuckled.

Once our tour was over, Zaria came to find me. I almost didn't want to leave, but I had Katya to think about.

Therefore, I was now standing at a window in a hotel in Edinburgh, while the sun rose for the day. *I hope you will be safe and happy, Andrei,* I thought, and wished I had Zaria's talent to speak mind-to-mind.

$\sim$

Lissa

"I can scent the kinship, so they can't hide them from us once we're there," I said. "They may be covered in Sirenali bone dust, and I'll still sniff them out."

Zaria and I were having a meeting without our human or werewolf counterparts over breakfast and coffee in Del City, Oklahoma—in the past. Charles had gone back to Wlodek's the night before, or he may have wanted to be in this meeting with us.

"On the off-chance that they've managed to cover their scents and we can't find them, we pull back and regroup," Zaria said.

"My hope is that they're keeping them together, to make it easier to move them."

"That's my hope, too, but we can't count on it."

Zaria was wary of our plan. I was worried, too, but felt that ultimately, if Liron and I squared off against each other, he'd lose. My biggest concern was that the Earth would lose, too. Wielding so much power anywhere near a solar system would tear it apart, and Zaria surely wasn't prepared to hold the entire thing together while Liron and I fought.

"I hoped I'd find you here," Bree sat beside me in our booth. "You're thinking about taking Liron on, aren't you?" Her brows drew together and she frowned at me.

"Well, what else should I do? He needs to be taken down."

"It's not so easy to kill a god, remember?"

"But," I held up a hand.

"Only a few are actually strong enough to destroy a god."

I went still. *Only a few.*

As in Three.

"Not even three," Zaria shook her head. "One. Or two."

"Huh?"

"The best you can hope for is to banish him where the others from the God Wars are," Bree pointed out. "After you overpower him. Then, you have to make a connection to the closed universe where the others are imprisoned, and while holding that connection open, pray that nobody trapped there finds out and uses that conduit to escape."

"You mean open a door and toss him in before anybody else can get out?"

"That's pretty much it."

"Would you like to order?" Our waitress arrived to see if Bree wanted breakfast.

"I'll take scrambled eggs, toast and coffee, please."

"I'll have your coffee right out." I watched as she walked away, her footsteps making the familiar squeak of soft-soled shoes on tiled flooring, while Bree's words slowly sunk into my brain.

Not so easy to kill a god. Only one or two could do it.

I wasn't one of those two.

Yeah, it pissed me off more than a little.

Zaria sat on the other side of our booth, picking at her biscuit and strawberry jam while Bree and I talked. "Are you saying we shouldn't go to Vladimirsky Central?" I asked Bree.

"No, I think it's the best way to get where you need to go to destroy Liron's Sirenali and find the source of the bone dust. Without those things, he'll be forced to rethink his plans, especially after we deal with the mess he's making on Refizan."

"How is that going?" Zaria asked.

"We're worried they'll throw everything they have at us during the temple battle, and everything they have could turn out to be a lot. Even Ashe has offered to come if we need help."

My head jerked up when she said that—if Strength, also known as the Mighty Hand, offered to get involved in a battle, then he thought it was truly serious.

Was he one of the two who could kill a god? It would make sense that Strength would be one of those.

Breanne—she hadn't actually killed one, had she? If so, it was only their physical body. Their eternal spirit was—*damn.*

Eternal.

Just as I'd be an eternal spirit if my corporeal body died. I could take another body, but it wouldn't be the one I was born with—it would be someone else's.

"I got rid of a lot of rogue gods by taking them into the past, long before they actually existed. Once they passed that point, they winked out of being, because they hadn't been," Bree shrugged. She was reading my thoughts and had gotten ahead of me on some of them.

"What do you want me to do?" I asked her.

"I hope I'm able to get to you when the time comes, so I can build the conduit between this universe and the one where the other rogues are trapped. You can toss Liron through; I'll shut down the conduit immediately after, so nobody can escape."

"That makes it sound too easy," I said.

"I'd like easy, to be honest. This mess with Refizan, and what you're dealing with here, has been anything but."

~

Vladimirsky Central, Vladimir, Russia
Charles

I'd sent the original me back to Wlodek, with selected topics to add to the official record. Wlodek only needed to know the bare bones of things, and Lissa, Zaria and a few others were conveniently left out.

He'd believe that Dalroy and Rhett were guarding the original Winkler and his wife in Port Aransas, Texas, while we dealt with the events concerning Xenides and his unholy alliance with the Baikovs.

I'd been sending regular reports, letting him know that Ivan Baikov had gone rogue and had allied with our enemies; Ivan was now on the list to be hunted and destroyed. My last report was to be directly to Wlodek when he awoke for the evening, and he'd learn that Ivan had been seen in London.

With Xenides and Rahim Alif.

Heavily shielded, I walked along the narrow catwalk on the third floor of the prison, the empty, central space above the first floor beyond the railing I walked beside.

A prisoner transport had arrived moments earlier, and word from the prison lieutenant was to check the two men in and take them to the third floor, where an empty cell awaited.

There were no other empty cells at Vladimirsky; it was filled to capacity and beyond, with four to six to a single cell. Tuberculosis was a spreading concern in any Russian prison, and its proliferation had gone unchecked, due to lack of proper medical care, shortages of food for the prisoners and the availability of illegal drugs and such, all combined with the lack of light and proper ventilation.

This one, like the others, was heavily shuttered. Built in 1783, the building was old and little had been done to keep it in good repair. A prisoner's comfort was of no concern, after all, and humane treatment was certainly considered a comfort.

A door clanged shut below; the men were on their way. Invisible to the guards and prisoners, I waited outside the open cell door for the new arrivals.

Heads down, lips tightly pressed together, the men shuffled up the steps to the third level, prodded by two guards armed with rifles.

Hands and feet were chained, preventing them from walking fast or far. This was the fate of those who thought to argue with or oppose the Kremlin's policies.

They imagined they'd die an early death at a prison camp in Siberia. Instead, they were brought here, on their way to an even worse death.

Except Zaria and Lissa were going to intervene.

I wanted to see both men first, to ensure they were worthy of such a benevolent rescue. It wasn't hard for most to pity these—or any other prisoners held within these centuries-old walls, but I was Wisdom, and understood when I should allow my heart to be involved.

The chains were removed while I watched, and then the cell door was closed and locked. The guards walked away.

I folded inside the cell to watch and listen.

"We are dead," Leonid Kuznetsov told his brother, Maxim.

"I know. Is it too much to hope it will be easy?"

"Probably."

"What do you think Ilya has done to displease them?"

"Would it matter?"

"Not anymore."

"At least it's warmer here. If we're lucky, we'll die in our sleep tonight."

They're in cell three-twenty-one, I sent to Zaria. *On the third level of Vladimirsky Central.*

Thank you.

Taking one last look at the prisoners, I folded away.

~

Zaria

"I had a breakfast meeting with Lissa. The food didn't settle well," I told Ilya as we sat in a nearby restaurant, so he could have breakfast in Edinburgh. "I'll just have tea, this time."

"Something worries you?" His mouth drew into a straight line after he spoke.

"Lots of things worry me. I know where your cousins are—or at least where they were as of early this morning."

"Where?" He was suddenly searching my face for clues.

"They arrived at Vladimirsky Central, and are in a cell on the third level."

"Warmer there than where they were before, at least. That prison camp in Siberia is generally for those who will die in prison."

"Not known for leniency, eh?"

"That word has been stricken from all records. Where will you send them—Leo and Max?" he asked. "Can they go to Sirena, too?"

"I'll have to ask Randl. If not there, somewhere else will be found. They have a say in this, too, you know."

"Ah. You may end up having to send them to Ukraine, then. That's where they were going when they were arrested."

"Want to tell me about that?"

"I thought to retire. That decision was changed for me. I speak and read too many languages, all fluently, and can fit in anywhere. Baikov didn't want his source of information to go home to family."

"You must be sick to death of all this," I sighed.

"And I am. I went to work every day because Andrei and Katya would become targets to ensure my cooperation. They're not above using any source of leverage they can find to get what they want."

"Except you're off the reservation right now. They tried to kill you and Andrei over it."

"I know. I will be sent to prison for a short while after I report in, but then they'll send me out again; they always do. You've seen that running is foolish; they have eyes everywhere."

"Sometimes our lives get fucked up, and we're left wondering about the final turns we made to bring us to that point," I said.

"I have gone over that road many times," Ilya confessed as his food was placed in front of him.

"I'll take more tea," I nodded to our server's question. She went to fetch it.

"I suppose if there were an afterlife," Ilya cut into his eggs, "I would ask whomever was there waiting, why it is that people get knocked around so much during their mortal existence."

"Some people say it's to see what you're made of," I offered. "But even steel and concrete get battered after a while. Concrete will go back to dust, while an object made of steel will often be so damaged you can't tell what it was in the beginning. I think what is left, that we have to hold together, is our will—and our love. Those two things can go through the roughest beatings imaginable, and still remain intact."

"Yes. It is my love for my children that keeps me going, when I would have stopped long ago, no matter the consequences, had it just been me."

"And that is what makes you worthy," I told him.

"Worthy for what?"

"Someday, you'll know."

"Will you tell me what that is? Someday? You, yourself?"

"I'll be sure to do that."

"Good." He gathered eggs and a bite of ham onto his fork and ate while nodding.

"What are you planning to do when Lissa and I leave to replace your cousins?" I asked him after a while.

"Make my way back to Moscow, what else? I'll check in before entering the country, so there will be someone waiting to escort me off the plane. Then the questioning and the time spent in a cell come after that."

I wanted to take that from him—make sure he didn't suffer more than he had already, but I couldn't—not if I wanted the timeline to remain intact. I breathed a sigh into my fresh cup of tea and drank.

Muscovy Research Facility

Kornel Baikov

I glared at the piles of bones waiting to be ground up and then turned my gaze upon the supervisor. "These should have been processed already," I hissed at him. He cowered, which was my aim.

"Three of the prisoners we had working the machines are dying of tuberculosis and cannot move from their beds," he quavered. "I have requested more, but they are slow in coming."

"Tell them to send healthy prisoners," I snapped at him. "You should have had sense enough to do that to begin with."

"I cannot control what gets sent, even if I do make the requests," he whined.

"You say those three are sick in their beds?"

"Yes, sir."

"Kill them and destroy their remains. I have no use for them now. They are a drain upon the country anyway."

"I'll see to it."

I walked away from him; I had no more patience for such. I didn't understand why Liron wanted so much of the bone dust—I had a good supply of it already.

"I am taking what you have," Liron turned a corner of the facility ahead of me and began walking in my direction.

"What about the clothing production here?" I asked. "We have enough for the uniforms I ordered, but more will come in the next few days."

I caught sight of his stormy expression and stopped talking. "Be happy that I find what you have sufficient—barely." He now stood in front of me, so close I could feel breath upon my face. "I have need of it. You are the one who can wait for more."

What did he want with it? I couldn't fathom his reasons, but they had to be enough. My words of rebuttal were clenched behind my teeth and my anger fizzled.

I would wait to have uniforms protected with bone dust. It did not matter that I had to do so. Liron had need of our current supply.

"I can have it loaded for you," I managed to offer as he stalked away from me—in the direction he'd came.

An angry gesture of denial was all I received as he disappeared around the corner.

~

Ordinandis, Refizan

Breanne

Ever since half the city had burned, there was debate among politicians regarding Solar Red and whether Alliance troops should be requested to keep the peace and force the temple to account for their involvement.

Too many of Refizan's leaders had been bought by the renegade religion, however, and they refused to cooperate in asking for help.

Whether that would end up being a good or bad thing was irrelevant. Time was winding down and the final battle was gearing up.

A hush had fallen over the city, too, as if it were holding its breath, waiting for the blow to fall. People everywhere were afraid, and looked suspiciously at anyone they didn't know well.

Solar Red, backed by an actual, revenge-seeking rogue god, had spread terrorism across a peaceful planet. Liron deserved the worst anyone could throw at him because of that.

As for finding him or the Ra'Ak or some of the priests—that had become an impossibility. More Sirenali were involved, no doubt.

Or Sirenali bone dust.

Lissa, I sent to her, *I think I know the whole reason why they're making so much bone dust in Russia. It isn't just to hide the Baikovs.*

You just scared the snot out of me.

You and Zaria have to go shut that operation down, I told her. *When you get there, bend time backward.*

I see what you're getting at, she said. *I'll do my best.*

Erland, get everybody together, I sent to him. *We need to have a meeting.*

~

Edinburgh, Scotland

Lissa

"I think we need to push things up," I told Zaria. I'd sent mindspeech to find out where she was; she and Ilya had gone to a restaurant outside the hotel, so he could have breakfast.

"You mean trade places sooner than tomorrow?"

"We need to get into the country sooner, and that's the only way I know how to do it," I said.

"There is a faster way," Ilya set his coffee cup down.

"What's that?"

"Come with me. I can call General Baikov and tell him I am turning myself in. You can set me down at the checkpoint in Ukraine that is closest to Moscow. If you remain unseen, as I know you can, you may follow when they take me to Baikov for questioning."

"He'll do this himself?" My eyes widened.

"He won't be able to help himself—or stop himself from landing a few blows. Do not protest," he held up a hand when Zaria thought to do so. "I am used to this. It means nothing."

"Where is this checkpoint?" I asked.

"On the Russia side, just past the border," Ilya explained, pulling out his cell phone. He had a map displayed quickly, and showed us where it was.

"If we set down just inside the border," I said, "We can skip going past the Ukraine checkpoint."

"True. We need a car," Ilya said. "People walking in tend to upset the guards."

"We can get a car, no problem," Zaria mumbled, staring at the map. "What do you want to drive, Ilya?" Her eyes met his.

"I always wanted a Hummer."

"Okay."

"The time in Moscow is three hours later than it is here," Ilya added.

"When would you like to get there?" I asked him.

"If I call Baikov now, and tell him I can arrive just before sunset, you understand that his uncle may take an interest in my appearance as well."

My head jerked up and I stared into Zaria's eyes. *Two for one*, I sent to her. Her reply was the barest nod.

"Good enough. Make the call," I tapped Ilya's phone. "We'll be right behind you the whole way."

~

Zaria

"Winkler, you and Bill need to be on the first plane back to the States," Lissa told them. She'd called a meeting the moment we returned to our hotel.

"What about me, Tiessa?" Rigo asked.

"Rigo, if you wouldn't mind guarding them on their journey, that would take a big load off my shoulders," Lissa explained.

"We should be fine—I'll find a military transport to take us to France, and from there, we'll take Winkler's jet to D.C.," Bill said.

"We don't know what they have planned, and somebody may have to get you off that plane in a hurry," she told him. "Rigo can do that, and he's not susceptible to any vampire's compulsion."

"Not even one that's older?" Winkler's eyebrow lifted.

"There are no vampires older than I on this planet," Rigo sniffed.

"Damn," Bill whispered. "I'll get it set up, then." He nodded to Winkler and Trajan.

I take it things are changing? Charles sent.

Things just got speeded up. We're sending Bill and the werewolves home. The rest of us are taking the scenic tour into Russia.

I heard that from Bree already, he returned. *Have fun. Be careful. Don't forget to write.*

I'll be sure to send a postcard, I retorted.

Good enough.

"General Baikov is expecting me at the checkpoint," Ilya walked in after having a phone conversation in the bathroom. "I believe he intends to come himself; he says a helicopter will be waiting to take me to Moscow. Even with a helicopter, the trip will take around two hours."

"Can't be helped," Lissa said. "Get packed up. Bill, will you handle checkouts later?"

"Sure."

"What are you going to do between now and time to go?" Winkler frowned at Lissa.

"We have to find Ilya a Hummer."

~

"I was very disappointed when they stopped making them," Ilya walked around the used black Hummer sitting on a car lot in Little Rock, Arkansas. "This one looks in good shape."

"We'll only need it for a little while," Lissa agreed. "Although this price is outrageous." She stared at the priced scrawled on the windshield while frowning deeply.

"Lookin' for a Hummer?" A used car salesman sidled up to us. As if all three of us standing around the only Hummer in his parking lot wasn't a good enough indication.

"We'll take this one," I said, to quell further discussion. I had no desire to watch the overly-large digits appear in his mind as he added up his commission.

The car wasn't worth ninety-seven thousand, but Ilya wanted to drive it into Russia. Therefore, we would drive the damn thing into Russia.

"It better work," Lissa glared at the man.

"Come on in and we'll talk financing," the man waved us toward the nearby showroom.

"No need. I have a credit card," Lissa whipped out a black American Express.

"Oooh—fancy," I teased her.

"You know it. Come on Elmer, let's get this show on the road."

"Elmer?" Ilya hissed as Lissa started to follow the salesman, who was almost running toward the showroom.

"That's his name. Didn't you read his name tag?"

"Elmer. Fine. Let us spend money like we have good sense," Ilya gestured with a hand. "I could have gotten him down to seventy-five, I think."

"Men. Always wanting to haggle," I teased and bumped his shoulder with mine. He laughed, and that was the reason I did it.

Ordinandis, Refizan

Breanne

Somewhere, across the city, the original Lissa sat on the rooftop of a building with Dragon, waiting for the sun to set. Once darkness fell, the city's vampires would stream from their hiding places to join the fight against Solar Red.

I worried they'd be slaughtered completely, this time; that all of us could go down, in one way or another.

I, too, sat on a rooftop, waiting for the final shoe to drop, as the old saying went.

"Bree?" I heard Ashe's voice before he appeared—he'd flown in as the bumblebee bat, only to materialize at my side.

"Ashe," I acknowledged his presence, while never taking my eyes off the Solar Red temple not far away.

"I ah, got word from Randl."

"What did he say?"

"He said you might need this."

This turned out to be a gold coin. Heavy, too, as I took it from his hand.

"But why?" We were about to engage in battle. Why would I need money? I stared at the coin in my hand. Yes, it was beautifully made, as if it had been minted in a long bygone era. There was no date on the coin itself, and I found that odd.

"Did Randl tell you anything else? Such as why I might need a gold coin? I mean it looks really nice and all, but how will it help? We're about to go to war here, I think."

"You need it because I hide myself in it."

I jerked back as a man with an odd smell—like flowers and rivers and freshly tilled earth—appeared on the rooftop before me.

"Who the hell are you?" I demanded, scooting and scraping backward on the roof tiles at his sudden appearance.

"I am Refizan. Who did you expect?" he asked.

CHAPTER 16

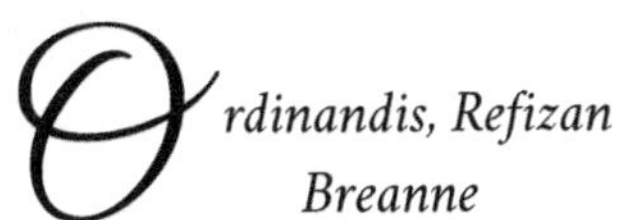

rdinandis, Refizan
    Breanne

"I am mother and father nature, but more than that," he explained. "I warn you, I will not participate in the battle itself, but I will help you however I can."

"How's that?" I asked, wondering how father nature could help anyone in this situation.

"I can feel them upon the planet. You may not see unless they become visible, or drop their cloak of Sirenali dust. If they touch my lands, however, I will know what they are, and how many."

I stared, open-mouthed. I know I did. "They can't hide that from you?"

"It is something I can do, yes." His gesture could have been a shrug. "We do not fight this battle. The war we will fight is in the future, alongside the *Reviendus Ar'pexi.*

Reviendus. It meant Soul of the Universe. *Ar'Pexi*—it meant holder of many souls, and worked both ways; they held him, he held them.

"Honey, I don't think I have time to ask all the questions I have," I told Refizan. "Right now, I need you to give me numbers and kinds, if you can."

"Shall we start with the Ra'Ak, then?" he asked.

"Please."

On the Border Between Russia and Ukraine

Lissa

"I'm glad we don't have to drive the whole way to Moscow in this thing," I said as we bounced along.

"I can fix it, if you want," Zaria offered. Ilya, who was driving, appeared to be having a good time—or as much of a good time as he could, considering what he was facing only a short distance into Russia.

The checkpoint—and General Baikov—were no doubt waiting for him.

"The original owners took this thing up and down rocky cliffs, I just know it, and now it rides rougher than a buckboard filled with splinters," I complained.

"There, all fixed," Zaria waved a hand.

The difference was like night and day. We now traveled smoothly along E101, and I could see the checkpoint ahead of us.

At least six armed guards stood at the crossbar, and on either side lay black-and-white painted concrete barriers.

"Any last words of advice?" Ilya asked before I turned Zaria and me to mist.

"Don't take your medallion off unless I tell you to," Zaria said.

"Right. I love you, by the way," he announced to a seemingly empty vehicle, before slowing to a stop in front of the guards.

With a sigh, he put the vehicle in park and shut off the engine. Then, he slowly opened the door and slid to the concrete surface of the road, his hands held high. Earlier, he'd handed all his weapons to Bill, so they'd find nothing in the Hummer or on his person.

Still, they weren't gentle when they cuffed him. When General Baikov came walking out of the small guard house wearing a huge frown, Zaria's mental gasp frightened me.

He's obsessed, she sent to me. *I can't see the location of the experiments in him.*

Damn, I replied. *Well, here's to a two-hour helicopter ride to the Kremlin, then.*

That's always been one of my dreams, Zaria's sending dripped with sarcasm.

We followed Ilya's forced path to a waiting helicopter, and misted inside once he was seated and buckled in.

We'll have to mute the noise, I told Zaria, as a headset was placed over Ilya's ears.

On it.

The trip took a little more than two hours, and we landed atop a building on the outskirts of Moscow.

A quick mental search told me it was an office building, with some holding cells in the basement. Ilya would be taken to one of those, unless I was badly mistaken.

~

Ilya

I'd been here before.

Twice.

Both times I was questioned—and beaten—before I was sent to a prison cell for a few months.

Third time is the charm—the old English saying sighed through my memory. Upon leaving the helicopter on the rooftop, I was led to the doorway that opened onto stairs, leading down to a small landing where an elevator and more stairs waited.

Baikov wouldn't take the stairs—we'd ride the elevator to the basement. I found myself hoping that my guardian angel—if she were such—was invisible beside me. It gave me comfort to imagine it, even if she weren't there.

Seven floors downward, the elevator stopped on the lowest level. There were no windows here, and little hope. Most understood, once they were brought here for questioning, they would not walk out as free men or women.

If they survived their questioning, they would be hustled out in chains and loaded into a prisoner transport, bound for one prison facility or another.

When the doors opened, we were met by two others. One was the usual, armed guard, the other, thanks to the images supplied by Lissa and Zaria, I recognized as Ivan Baikov, Kornel's many-times great-uncle.

"Follow me," the armed guard led us toward a hallway. I'd gone this way before. Bright lights and an uncomfortable, steel chair, bolted to the sanitized, concrete floor, waited there for me.

A door into an interrogation room opened; the strong scent of bleach reached my nostrils. Someone had died here not long ago, and they'd used the substance to disinfect and clean the floor and the chair.

"Sit," I was half-thrown onto the chair in question—at least it was dry after its most recent cleaning.

More chains appeared as I was connected to the chair itself, hands, arms, body and legs.

"So," Ivan Baikov began. "My nephew tells me that you have cooperated with the enemy against us."

"In what way? Is he sure of my cooperation?" I responded with a question of my own. "Perhaps they also held me—as you are holding me now—in only the highest regard."

"You will answer truthfully from now on."

If I hadn't seen the light in his eyes as he gave the command, I might not have understood that he was laying compulsion. I think I should have been helpless against him after that, but I wasn't.

"I didn't cooperate with anyone," I said, working to keep my voice even.

"But you were seen with them."

"Because I wished to learn why they had such an interest in killing General Baikov."

"They wished to kill me? You know this how?" Kornel asked.

"I intercepted a communication sent by the werewolf in Dallas. You told me to watch for such things, did you not?" I blinked at Kornel, feigning innocence. "He attempted to learn who had broken into a safe deposit box at a bank in Austin. Somehow, General, your name had surfaced and he considered you a person of interest in this theft."

"Did it mention me by name?" Kornel demanded.

"It only said Baikov. What else was I supposed to think?"

Kornel and Ivan exchanged a look. "Perhaps it was the scent that tipped them off?" Ivan said quietly. Kornel nodded, in an attempt to convince his great-uncle of his understanding.

I knew Kornel. He understood nothing.

"Tell me about the vampire princess. Lissa. I was engaged to her once," Ivan barked.

"I had no knowledge of her engagement to anyone—that was never revealed to me. I'm sorry I can't report on any of her movements—she told me not to."

"You were under her control?"

"I did what she asked. I don't recall much of it."

"Do you know where she is now?"

"No. Once I managed to escape and meet Andrei in Dublin, I don't know anything of her movements."

"How did you kill the guard we sent to keep your son safe?"

I wanted to laugh at Kornel's description. Only he would call a KGB assassin a guard.

"I shot him. I feared Andrei was in danger. Was he not in danger?"

"We will revisit that. How did you escape at the train station in Birmingham?"

"Our follower dropped a pen. When he bent down to retrieve it, Andrei and I disappeared in the crowd."

"He knows nothing," Ivan flung out a hand in anger. "Kornel, he is all yours."

"Very well," Kornel said. "Shoot him," he ordered the armed guard.

The guard's pistol was removed from his side holster, and the gun aimed at my forehead from perhaps fifteen centimeters away.

I refused to close my eyes.

Therefore, I watched as the pistol was fired. Instead of killing me instantly, the bullet ricocheted backward and hit the guard in the forehead instead. Kornel shouted; the guard dropped to his knees and fell face-first toward me, spreading blood down my pants leg as he slid against the fabric. Ivan began to curse.

~

Lissa

After the guard committed suicide by shooting at Ilya, who wore one of Zaria's medallions, Ilya was moved by Ivan's orders. Zaria and I followed.

I hoped we were headed to the proper facility this time; Ilya was forced into a van, still wearing heavy chains. I misted Zaria and me into the van and hovered over Ilya's left shoulder while two more guards glared at him from seats across from his, their hands on the grips of their pistols.

I wanted to laugh and tell them what happened to the last guy who pulled a gun on Ilya, but I didn't. I had no idea how Zaria had built those medallions, but they worked like a charm.

A really, really, special charm. *Vampire Baikov is obsessed, too, isn't he?* I asked Zaria, once we'd settled in for the ride.

Yeah. Nobody I've seen so far knows where the facility is, or they're obsessed and can't reveal the knowledge of it.

I sure hope we're going there now.

Me, too.

~

Refizan

Breanne

Somewhere behind us, and unknowing, Lissa was fighting a battle inside the Solar Red temple.

Here, on the outskirts of the city, amid farmland where they'd gathered to storm the temple and put a stop to so many things happening in the future, lay the bulk of Liron's army.

Ashe had built a shield around the temple area, so strong that nobody could get past it unless he allowed it.

Only those Ra'Ak originally involved in the slaughter were there; these that we faced had come to join the fight. More than a thousand Ra'Ak, in addition to other creatures Liron found to support his cause, now faced off against us. Except for the temple battle, the only thing that stood between the city of Ordinandis and Liron's approaching army was us.

To me, it looked like a smaller version of the final God Wars battle, there were so many set against our small battalion. If the nature spirit of Refizan hadn't come to our aid, these would have hidden themselves from us until they attacked the Solar Red temple, and by that time it would be far too late to do anything about it. That thought terrified me.

"Ready to dance with these devils?"

My eyes widened at Hank's appearance, and what followed him—an army of High Demons, in full Thifilathi.

Except for two, who were Thifilatha. Reah, the Queen of Kifirin, and Lexsi, her Crown Princess, had come to fight beside us.

We needed them—they were more dangerous to the Ra'Ak than the males were.

"How did you know we needed you?" I blinked at Hank, who was still grinning at me.

"God of War, remember?" He tapped his chest. "Now, time to get down to business. He became Thifilathi, then, to lead his troops against the army of Ra'Ak, who'd caught his scent and were now bellowing their challenges.

"Shall we give them what they want—a real war?" Ashe took Hank's place, as Hank's twenty-foot Thifilathi roared and stalked toward the Ra'Ak. Behind Hank, his High Demon army lifted their voices in a thunderous growl of their own.

"Oh, sure," I said, as Edward, one of Reah's mates who was also the Elemaiyan War Eagle, swooped overhead with a piercing cry.

~

Russia

Lissa

You think this is it? I sent to Zaria as the transport rumbled over several speed bumps after turning into a large parking lot.

Adjoining that parking lot was a large building, newly-built in my estimation.

This hasn't been here long, Zaria replied. *If they constructed a new facility, it could be the right age for the experimentation they've done.*

While Zaria and I floated as mist over Ilya's head, he was ordered out of the transport, his chains clinking as he walked toward a steel door in the side of the building. The door opened, allowing vampire Baikov inside first, followed by human Baikov, a guard, Ilya, and then the driver and the last guard.

The door was shut and locked behind us, but that wouldn't keep Zaria or me inside. I was more worried about Ilya, to be honest.

A long hallway, built of painted cinderblocks, led into another room, and the scent of death and burning reached my non-corporeal nostrils.

People had certainly died here, and then they'd been cremated.

Along one side of the large room were huge doors with metal bars to lock them in place, and temperature gauges affixed to the wall beside them. It was a no-brainer what those were, especially since the word *Krematoriy,* written in large, Russian letters, was posted above them.

They needed the bones for bone dust. This is where the flesh of those poor souls was burned away and their bones harvested and ground to dust.

"Shall I show you what you will become?" Vampire Baikov turned to grin at Ilya. "I was told you might be able to resist us in some way, but once we have you in our oven, you can scream all you want. See if your help will come after you there."

"Let us show him around, first, to see what it is we do here," human Baikov said. "Shall we show him the bone room, Uncle?"

"Of course. That should make him wish for a bullet to the head, rather than what is now planned for him."

How well will that medallion work? I sent to Zaria.

Well enough, but that's not what worries me. I think we should grab Ilya now and get the hell away from here.

I didn't feel itchy, and that was my standard sign that something was wrong or that I was in danger. Instead, I felt nothing, even with a forced tour of Experiment Central.

Stay with me, here—we need to find the Sirenali and the bones, first, I cautioned. *To get rid of them. Besides, Ilya is as cool as a cucumber. He's not even sweating,* I observed.

Ilya sweating is also not my greatest concern. Something isn't right, here. I feel it.

I think there's something of concern here, too, but my proverbial skin isn't itching right now, and that's the best barometer I have.

Then I hope you're right—let's go—they're heading for the door at the far end of the room.

~

Ilya

"Oh, one more thing," Ivan Baikov had his hand on the doorknob, but stopped before turning it.

"Yes, one last experiment," Kornel agreed. "Shoot him," he barked at the closest guard, pointing in my direction.

His pistol was out quickly, and the bullet fired in my direction faster than that. Just as before, the bullet ricocheted and hit the guard squarely in the forehead, killing him before he slumped to the floor.

"What is it that gives you this protection?" Ivan Baikov approached me. "Is it someone? Tell me immediately."

Again, the compulsion rang out in his voice, and like the last time, it affected me not at all.

Tell him it is the medallion, Zaria's voice entered my mind. *If he wishes to take it, allow him to do so.*

"It is a medallion that I wear that protects me," I spoke aloud, lowering my eyes.

"Where?" Ivan demanded.

"Around my neck."

"Then I will have this, and you will die the next time I order it, eh?" He stepped closer and fumbled for the chain around my neck. I was grateful it was long enough to pull over my head, else he would have strangled me with it.

"This small thing? It kept you from dying?" Ivan dangled the medallion in midair as he scrutinized it. "Well, I will have it for myself, then, and be invulnerable in your place."

I watched, both angry and helpless as he draped the chain around his neck.

What happened next I will never forget.

I'd never seen anyone die like this. Ivan Baikov exploded in a blast of black ash and torn clothing, while everyone around us, except for the dead guard on the floor, ducked or ran.

~

Lissa

Well, hell. Nothing like an exploding vampire to force our hand. I materialized from my mist, as did Zaria. The guard who attempted to shoot me regretted it—for the full half-second he remained alive.

Ilya's chains disappeared immediately, and he punched Kornel Baikov so hard he fell with the first blow.

That's when Baikov's army showed up—or Liron's, actually, and there were suddenly six more of me to contend with, in addition to eight of Winkler's father, more Phils, Lester Briggs, Bart Orfords and Kevin Millers. They must have taken every cell from the bodies of those last three, because there were too many to count in the time I had to try.

Our shields were up, but they were climbing over one another to cover the invisible bubble above our heads. Zaria and I were backing into the next room, stepping over what remained of Ivan Baikov. Ilya had already gone inside the room and was searching for a weapon of some sort to help us fend off our attackers.

Two had already died; he'd wielded a pen from a pants pocket and poisoned them, first thing. Yes, we could have grabbed Ilya and folded away, but we still hadn't destroyed the bones or found the Sirenali.

Shut the door, I shouted to Zaria, who was following me inside the bone room. With power she slammed it closed, then employed more power to thicken the door and the walls around it.

I was grateful; more vampires had arrived to join the army outside, and they were pounding into the door and the walls with all their strength.

"I have a shield around this room," Zaria told me. I didn't remark on the worried expression she wore; rather, I chose to study the piles of bones against the far wall, next to a machine that was surely a grinder of some sort.

"There should be more, I think," Zaria whispered, as the pounding on the door became louder and more insistent.

"More of what?" I didn't understand.

"More bones. I've *Looked*—they're emptying some of the remote prison camps for this." She swept out a hand.

"They're in trouble on Refizan," I turned to stare at her.

"You're in trouble here," a voice called out. That's when the floor caved and disappeared beneath our feet.

Refizan

Breanne

In the midst of the battle, I heard mindspeech from Refizan himself, but the message made no sense. Ashe had an impenetrable shield over our portion of the battle, and another over the Solar Red temple, so the original timeline could be preserved as well as possible.

They are coming, Refizan reported to me. *I cannot prevent it.*

They? I sent back to him as the ground began to crumble beneath our feet and the whirling vortex that appeared sucked all of us, friend and foe, into its midst, no matter how much power we employed to stop or fold away from it.

~

Wlodek's Mansion, Kent, England
Charles

Zaria's medallion sent a shock through me. Something had happened to her and Lissa, that was obvious.

When I reached out to Breanne and Ashe, there was no response.

This wasn't the time to panic, although I wanted to. Had Liron managed to outwit us all? That thought raced through my brain, and I was more than grateful that I'd placed the original Charles in stasis again and hidden him away.

Frankly, I needed to know where they were and what happened—to all of them. First, though, I needed to visit Refizan, to ensure that the original Lissa still lived.

~

Lissa

Trapped in a vortex. Zaria and I passed one another as we traveled at different speeds at different levels. I didn't know what had happened to Ilya at the last—he wasn't here with us—at least not that I could see. I worried that he'd been killed, but that wasn't my primary worry.

No, my primary worry was that no matter how much power I expended, I couldn't break away from this mass of whirling, grinding, grayish-brown air.

Zaria? I sent to her. *Can you get away?*

I haven't tried—I'm trying to make sure Ilya is all right, she replied. *I think he's still in the bone room, but I can't be sure of it. I'm looking for him here, just in case he fell in anyway.*

At least mindspeech still worked, but I was beginning to feel dizzy, and that wasn't a good thing.

Who did this to us? I asked. Who told us we were in trouble?

That was Liron's voice. Did you not recognize it?

Of course it was. Please tell me this is a dream after eating bad bananas or something. Or, better yet, tell me how to get out of this place.

I'm not sure we can do much to get out of it—we have to wait until we reach the next level.

There's a next level?

We're at a stoplight, I think. When it turns, we'll be sucked farther in.

Farther in where? I don't even know where the hell we could be.

Well, unless I'm wrong, we're headed to the universe that holds the rogue gods. Somehow, Liron managed to build a bridge between us and them—in two places. Here, and on Refizan.

Oh, dear lord. Liron was taking all of us down, and making it look easy.

～

Solar Red Temple, Refizan

Charles

I found Dragon and Lissa fighting Ra'Ak and spawn, while Solar Red priests attempted to flee the carnage. At least the innocent civilians were able to run past Ashe's shield, which remained intact.

Yes, I could get past it, because he'd given me permission long ago. So far, nothing felt amiss, here. I folded to the last known place where Breanne and Ashe had stood, not far outside Ordinandis.

The gaping hole was the first clue of what had happened.

Liron, somehow, had managed to pool enough power to build a bridge, and my suspicion was that the bridge in question led to the rogue gods' universe.

Where they waited to kill anyone who arrived.

Standing so close to this hole, I attempted mindspeech with Ashe.

Nothing came back. This chasm, like a black hole, was sucking everything into it, and had Ashe not built his shield around it, the entire planet would have followed them in.

That left me with the final question—*where was Liron now?*

he Vortex
    Lissa

A stoplight.

Zaria was correct. After what seemed like hours, and was likely only minutes, we were sucked farther into the vortex, only this time, she and I were left dangling in a near-vacuum at the center while the gray winds whirled faster around us.

It's like being inside a tornado, Zaria observed.

No cows or trees flying by, I pointed out, attempting to quell growing fear with humor.

Not a tornado, then.

Guess not. You think we're at another stoplight?

We haven't gotten there, yet, so yes.

How the hell did Liron do this? How did he put enough power together to create it? It had taken the Three last time to send the rogues to a closed universe and seal them inside.

I'm trying to figure this out myself, Zaria answered my first question. *It may have something to do with this thing he did to send a past-self a message about his future-self's demise.*

That doesn't make much sense, I admitted.

Nothing about any of this makes any sense, she replied.

Lissa?

I heard Breanne's mindspeech.

Bree? Bree, can you hear me?

I can hear you, but we're trapped inside a whirlwind and we can't get out. Ashe and I together couldn't put enough power into an escape. Even the High Demons are here with us, and with the Ra'Ak and the others, it's not pretty.

Same here, I responded. *Nothing works. Zaria and I are trapped.*

You expended power? Zaria broke into our conversation.

Yes, but what does that have to do with anything?

I'm thinking about that, okay?

How are the Ra'Ak reacting? I asked after Zaria went silent again.

Trying to snap and bite at everything they're whirling past, but what looks close can be far away—it's like we're trapped in a funhouse with the worst mirrors imaginable, and they're all swirling around us like they're angry, drunk and going way too fast.

So they haven't bitten or eaten anything? The Ra'Ak?

Not yet, but they're still trying. I figure they're putting every ounce of their power into it, too, but it's not having any effect.

Who else is there with you—on our side?

Reah, Lexsi, Edward, Hank and the High Demon army, Erland, Drake, Drew—several others who came to help. I only catch glimpses of them now and then when they fly past me.

I cursed then, long and loud, although the winds around us carried my spoken words away before they could become anything besides my breath.

We're falling again, Bree's words were nearly cut off.

They'd gone ahead to the next stoplight, no doubt, while Zaria and I still hung suspended at our last one. *Bree?* I attempted to reach her again, with no response.

We have to be at the same level, I think, Zaria said.

Yeah. I get that. How long will it be before we follow?

I don't know.

I wanted to shout at Zaria then, because her relative calm in this situation was beginning to frustrate me a great deal. Absurd ideas formed in my brain—of going to mist and blowing it outward, to destroy this massive tornado that tore its way around us.

Please don't, Zaria sent.

I was only thinking about it, I replied.

Thinking really, really, hard about it, actually. I had no idea what Zaria was thinking, but she'd gone into a lotus position as if she wanted to meditate. *What the hell was that about?*

∾

Ilya

For whatever reason, I hadn't fallen into the chasm with Zaria and Lissa. Instead, I'd been left standing on a narrow ledge near the reinforced door, while my medallion settled itself around my neck again.

Yes, I wasted foolish minutes afterward shouting into that bottomless pit for Zaria, but there was no reply. I worried that she and Lissa had met their end, and the one who'd spoken at the last—a shining man with wings in the far corner—had murdered them after he disappeared.

He wasn't concerned for me or for anyone else inside this facility —he'd achieved his goals, I think. My goal, however, was becoming obvious. The unnatural army was still outside the bone room door, and they continued to pound on it, as if getting through meant they could march right in and kill me at their leisure.

"As good an idea as any," I told myself aloud. Inching along the ledge, which was uneven and barely the length of my feet, I worked my way toward the door—to open it and allow my attackers inside.

∾

Charles

I'd tried using Zaria's medallion to locate her, but there was no sign. Now, I held it in my fist and asked it to locate Ilya—the human version.

They'd gone with him, after all, and I hoped I'd find information through that source.

My eyes widened as the vision of him darted into my mind—he was stepping along a narrow ledge above a chasm, and nearby was a door, outside of which many waited to kill him.

Yes, the chasm was no surprise—it echoed the one on Refizan. The other things Ilya faced, however, had come as a surprise. No doubt Liron intended them to fall into the pit with Zaria and Lissa, but they'd been held back by a reinforced door and wall.

Score one for Lissa and Zaria, I thought grimly and folded space to Russia.

~

Kornel Baikov

"Knock the door down," I yelled at the vampires. What good were they if they couldn't knock down a single door?

My lip still bled and my nose throbbed from the unexpected punch Kuznetzov landed, but that wouldn't happen again. Once this door was down, I'd make sure he never did another thing in his life.

I wanted my vampires to make him bleed before he died. I didn't care that he'd killed my uncle—I was tired of living in Uncle Ivan's shadow anyway. For the blow Kuznetzov struck against me, however, he would die.

He no longer had the medallion to protect him—it had killed my uncle, instead. Somewhere, beneath all the feet smudging Uncle Ivan's ashes, it had probably been crushed to dust.

"Hit harder," I shouted, as the door still would not yield.

Suddenly, as if by an unseen hand, the door swung open and my vampires—six of them who were poised to strike more blows against the door, fell through the open gap, screaming and flailing as they dropped into an inky, deep pit.

I cursed as others rushed forward, only to fall into the pit as well. "Stop where you are," I bellowed.

Most of the others heard and obeyed—shortly after they realized they were hearing the screams of those preceding them into what was once the bone room.

Then, as I began to step my way backward from the door and the gaping hole beyond it, the screams began anew—this time at the back of my army. The surge forward came shortly after, and more passed through the door and fell into the pit.

Cursing and shoving those around me out of my way, I worked through the crowd to see what was causing this new panic.

Only to be met by a strange sight.

Three vampires stood there, claws out, eyes red. I had no idea who they were, but they were not my *Klyki*.

Already, they had killed many of my werewolves. Where were my princesses? Had they deserted me? They'd been instructed to stay and protect me. So far, they'd done a very poor job of it.

As I stared down these newcomers, I heard two more screams behind me—more had fallen into the pit.

"This is not your concern," I barked at them. "You are trespassing."

"I disagree," the shortest vampire replied.

"Misters, to me," I barked to the empty air about me.

This time, they appeared, three on my left, three on my right. Good. All were still alive.

"You will not set them against me."

Someone new had arrived. He was more than nine feet tall, with blue skin and long, red hair.

What was this? "Kill him, first," I pointed my princesses toward the tall, blue one. I watched him smile as he raised his right hand. Then, when my six attempted to attack him, they dissolved into sparks in mid-leap.

"Never threaten a Larentii," the tallest vampire spoke, now.

"Tell us where Lissa and Zaria are," the third one demanded.

"Probably down that hole inside the bone room," I chuckled. "Liron's work, no doubt. He is quite talented, I think."

"You really did make a deal with the devil," the shortest one spoke again. "Too bad you won't live to recall it."

"Kill me and you start a war with Russia," I snapped at him. I recognized his accent—he was British. The middle one was American or close enough. The third vampire had the faintest hint of a Greek accent, but one I wasn't familiar with—where exactly did he come from?

The tall blue one spoke to the others in a language I didn't understand, although all three were now nodding at him.

"What are you saying?" I demanded.

"Kalenegar just pointed out that there are natural gas pipes into this place, to run the crematory and to supply heat and power. I doubt Russia will get into a war over a gas leak and subsequent explosion, do you?"

"You cannot," I sputtered.

"But we can," the British vampire spoke again.

~

Ilya

Still holding onto the doorframe with one hand, I did my best to pull any who came too close through the door and into the pit. Baikov remained outside, having a conversation with someone. I had no idea who it was.

I was grateful nobody was shooting, actually.

Get ready, a voice sounded in my head.

I recognized that voice. Charles was outside. How had he gotten here? *Ready for what?* I wondered.

I wasn't curious long; the entire facility exploded into an enormous fireball, fueled, no doubt, by the natural gas funneled into it. Somehow, I was pulled away before any of the blast touched me.

~

"Where am I?" I asked.

"You are in the future, at my home," the tallest vampire explained. "I am Merrill. This is Wlodek, and Charles you already know."

"The future?"

"You've already been to the future—it's where Zaria took Andrei," Charles explained. "If you're hungry, we have food here. What we want from you is whatever you saw at the last, before Zaria and Lissa disappeared."

"A shining man appeared, who had wings—similar to those Zaria has."

"Liron," Charles growled. "What else?"

"Before he arrived, Zaria said that the pile of bones in the room wasn't enough—that Baikov and his cronies were emptying the prison camps to get more. Lissa said that someone was in trouble on—Ref, ah," I wasn't sure of the pronunciation.

"Refizan," Charles prompted.

"Yes. That's it. She said they were in trouble, and then Liron appeared and said we were in trouble, too, and that's when the floor collapsed into the pit. I think Zaria must have saved me somehow, because my medallion returned, and then I was shoved backward instead of falling into the pit."

"She may not know for sure that you were safe," Charles said. "And that would be a grave concern."

I wanted to ask why, but didn't. I wished for the answer, and was afraid of it at the same time. "Where is she? Do you know?" I asked instead.

"On her way to the worst place possible," the one named Wlodek growled.

"Where is that?" I couldn't keep the fear from my voice.

"The universe holding the rogue gods," Charles supplied. "And that is most certainly the worst possible place."

"There are rogue gods?" If there were, that meant there were gods to begin with. That was a terrifying thought.

"Don't let it worry you right now—we have to figure out how to get them back." Charles turned away, a hand at his chin as if deep in thought.

"It would help if we knew how Liron built the bridges to begin with. He knew where we'd show up, and that provided the place for the connection between this world and the other. Now we need to know how he did it," Merrill shook his head.

"He'd need more power than he holds to do it, so how was that accomplished?" Charles asked.

"If he could get through to the rogue universe, he could combine power with some of theirs," Wlodek observed.

"But he'd need the power to get there to begin with," Charles argued. "Somebody here either gave it to him, or he stole it somehow, or managed to create it himself."

"He may have grown, but I can't see anyone giving anything to him from the light side," Merrill said.

"There's something we're not seeing, here," Charles went back to his thinking pose and paced away.

"What do we know so far? Can we start from the beginning?" I asked.

Charles turned. "You may be hearing things that don't make any sense to you, or you find impossible to believe."

"I just learned my son is in the future. What can top that?"

"Liron is a rogue god," Merrill began. "And he dies in the future—Zaria kills him with a loan of power from Charles. Somehow, Liron has notified his past-self, and here we are in the past, dealing with things that didn't happen the first time around."

I had to consider that for several moments. *This time around? I was in a second incarnation of a life I'd already lived?*

"Actually, it's your third time, but you'll have to talk to Zaria about it if you want an explanation," Charles informed me, after pulling my thoughts straight from my head.

"If I ask Zaria those questions, we have to get her back, first," I pointed out. "Pretend I understand everything. What do we know so far—of what and how he has changed things in this time period?"

"He has made allies of those who didn't associate with one another," Wlodek began. "In particular, Xenides and Ivan Baikov, two old vampires, with Xenides being the elder of the two. Ivan did not perish the way he did the first time, either, due, no doubt, to his alliance this time with Xenides and his association with Liron himself."

"He believed Liron to be an especially talented scientist," I said. "These experiments with creating more of Lissa, and Winkler's dead father and such—of course, both Baikovs would see the usefulness in that. They could recreate anyone they wanted, if they could do that."

"Including themselves?" Merrill turned to Wlodek.

"We discussed that, and believed that both of them were too vain and egocentric to have a duplicate made," I said.

Charles' head was down as he considered our conversation, until now. Slowly he raised his eyes to mine and blinked at me.

"Oh, no," he breathed. "I think I know what happened, and if I'm right, we are in a universe of trouble."

Without bothering to tell us, he transported us away, and I found myself landing in what could only be called a massive museum, with collections of books, artifacts and other strange creations that I didn't recognize.

A tall, blue man, who must surely be of the same race as Zaria, walked toward us after appearing from nothing.

"Nefrigar, we need your counsel," Charles spoke to him.

"Nefrigar is the Chief Archivist of the Larentii Archives," Merrill told me softly.

"Is that where we are?" I asked.

"Yes. You are one of only a few humans who have been here. It is a great honor to be allowed to come."

Nefrigar wore no shirt and only loose-fitting trousers, with no shoes. I watched as he and Charles held a silent conversation with one another. Nefrigar, more than eight feet tall, was joined by the taller, red-haired blue man who'd come to the research facility before it was destroyed. Now he was back and listening intently to what Charles and Nefrigar discussed.

"It is possible, I think," Nefrigar spoke aloud. "In that particular time, it is pre-God Wars, and minor rogues abounded. How difficult would it be?"

"Not difficult at all, in my way of thinking, and he had more than enough empty spheres," Charles agreed.

"This isn't good," Merrill breathed.

"What are they saying?" I begged. I didn't understand any of this, while Merrill appeared to understand and believe it.

"I think we may know how Liron was able to increase his power to a sufficient level, and make sure he could be in several places and times at once."

"We may know the how, and the why," Charles said, "but how do we reverse it, or neutralize what he's done and bring them back?"

"He may not have taken everything into consideration," Nefrigar spoke cryptically. More mental conversation ensued.

"True," Charles nodded. "Do you think that will have any bearing?"

"I don't know," Nefrigar admitted. "We can hope. I think if we attempted to go down the chasm after them, we run the risk of being pulled in with the others, and that may be his ultimate goal in destroying everything."

"I think that if there is any way to escape Liron's grip," Kalenegar spoke for the first time, "then Zaria, Lissa, Breanne and Ashe will surely come up with something."

"Except they are likely not together—not until they reach that cursed universe," Nefrigar pointed out. "And by then, it could be far too late."

"Archivist, do not squeeze my heart," Kalenegar pleaded.

"Do you think that my own is not involved? Reah is also there, with her daughter."

"My apologies, Archivist," Kalenegar dipped his head to Nefrigar.

"How many did Liron abduct?" I turned to Merrill in alarm.

"Too many. If Liron succeeds in this endeavor in our past, then the God Wars are all but won—by the wrong side."

～

Lissa

Lissa? I heard Bree's mindspeech again—after we'd dropped much farther into the tornado's vortex.

Thank goodness, I sent to her. *Are you all right?*

Other than being trapped, we're fine—even the Ra'Ak, who appear to be resigned to the fact that they could be whirling around for eternity, are still intact. The winds are stronger here, and we can barely move a finger.

Same here. Zaria is still twirling past me, stuck in a lotus position, I reported.

I hope Charles is figuring this out, Bree said.

Well, he is the Mighty Mind. If anybody can figure it out, then he'd be the one. I didn't add that in this, Liron had outmaneuvered us every step of the way. Was he smarter than Wisdom? That thought terrified me.

We're fall-, Bree's mindspeech was cut off again. Damn. There wasn't enough time to attempt to reason this out while we could communicate.

Are they gone again? Zaria sent.

Yes. I still felt grumpy over the fact that she didn't appear to be doing anything at all. *Lissa?* she said after several moments passed.

What is it? I didn't sound happy, and I knew it.

Can you reach your medallion?

I don't know that I can move anything, I admitted.

Will you try? If you reach it, then concentrate on Charles, all right?

Why?

I'm trying to get you out of here.

What about you?

I don't wear a medallion.

You made these things and didn't create one for yourself?

It wasn't necessary—until now. I know when others are in danger—yours hasn't stopped squealing in my brain since we got here. We'll see if you can reach Charles through his medallion—if you can get your hand to yours to start with.

And none of the folks with Bree have a medallion, do they?

They do, but I don't think Charles can handle getting more than one out at a time, and even one may turn out to be impossible to rescue. They're all going off in my head, and I've had to mute most of it, so I can think. Try to reach your medallion, okay?

All right. Trying to move a hand now. I couldn't imagine anything that had ever been harder to do in my life. After what felt like forever, I may have moved my left hand an inch up my torso.

We dropped again, and when we stopped this time, I could hear Bree shouting my name.

I hear them, she sounded frantic, once I replied to her mindspeech. *They're roaring and cheering. We've almost reached the rogue gods, and they're waiting for us.*

When she stopped her mindspeech, I heard it, too. We were so close, now, I felt I could reach out and touch some of the louder voices.

I heard the intent in those voices, too. They all waited to destroy us.

Liron had done what they couldn't accomplish; he'd won the God Wars.

CHAPTER 18

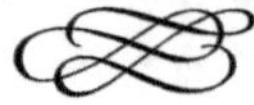

*C*harles

Charles? Lissa's voice sounded desperate—and exhausted.

Lissa? I practically shouted her name in mindspeech. *Where are you? How can we get to you?*

We're so close to the rogue gods' universe I can see it though the whirling winds at times, and hear them shouting their victory, she replied. *I can only reach you through Zaria's medallion, and it's taking all my strength to hold onto it in this violent tornado around us.*

We have the where, now, we just don't know how to get you out of there, I said quickly.

Can you pull me back—through Zaria's medallion? She says it may be the only way, and might not work. At this point, anything is worth a try.

What about Zaria?

She doesn't wear a medallion. Said it wasn't needed until now—that she's tuned into them and never expected to need help—not like this. How did this happen?

We think Liron used the drug to create more of himself—out of lesser rogues, I reported.

Oh, lord. That's how he has the power to trap us.

We think so. I will connect with my medallion, and then ask Wlodek,

Merrill, Nefrigar and Kalenegar to add their power to mine. If it's possible to pull you away, it will be done.

Do whatever you have to do, Lissa said. *The rogues are waiting, otherwise. I'd rather die trying to escape than be at their mercy when we fall through this vortex the last time.*

Mercy? There will be none, I replied grimly. *Hold on, we're connecting now.*

~

Breanne

I'm not at full strength, but I'll lay a shield around us the moment we land, Ashe told me. *I can arrange to cover everyone except the enemy Liron pulled in here with us. I hope the rogues will be occupied momentarily with Ra'Ak and the others, while I gather strength and we attempt to get away.*

If we can just be still for a moment, and I can get rid of this dizziness and headache, I can build a connection between the rogue universe and ours. You'll have to stay behind the rest of us—to keep any of them from following us back.

I'll do it, Ashe agreed, his sending grim. I knew what that tone of voice meant—he was willing to send the rest of us through if I could create a conduit between the two universes. If he was left behind, so be it.

He'd make as many rogues pay as he could, before they tore him down and destroyed his corporeal body.

It isn't so easy to destroy a god—rogue or otherwise. I'd learned that the hard way. In the rogue gods' universe—there were no corporeal bodies for them to steal and inhabit. Ashe, if he couldn't get back, would be spirit only, and forced to hide from the rogues who would hunt him until the end of time, in an attempt to destroy him once and for all.

Fuck.

~

Lissa

We have more coming to help, Charles sounded desperate after the first two attempts to pull me out of Liron's vortex failed.

I'd felt the power wielded to make those attempts; it was staggering and still couldn't drag me more than a few feet away from my previous position.

Liron was determined to have me, one way or another, and I worried that there wasn't enough strength left in the light universe to counteract the dark one, with which Liron had allied.

He isn't only allied with it, Zaria's voice entered my mind. *He wants control of it. He's setting himself up as the General, times who knows how many. If he and all his duplicates think with a single mind, then the other rogues will never make another decision for themselves.*

We have more—making another attempt, Charles sent. I may have screamed when I was jerked away from Zaria and into the empty, previous chamber we'd occupied.

How many more? Charles sounded weary.

We fell at least four times.

Three more? Fuck Liron from beginning to end, Charles cursed. *We'll need more to pull you away. I'm calling for anyone who can to help.*

Call Randl.

I can't say why that name popped into my head, but it did.

Sending a call now, Charles said. *We're trying to renew our energy. Don't give up hope; we're working on this.*

Charles

Randl must have emptied Sirena of anyone who held power. They'd come, following behind him as he appeared in the Archives.

Then, he said something all of us should have known. "We need to go to the pit Lissa fell through," Randl said. "With all of us working, and with Tamp here doing what only a Pod'l-morph can do, I think we can reach Lissa."

If I'd had more than a few seconds to consider what he said, I might have reasoned it out. I didn't bother. Instead, at a nod from Nefrigar and a multitude of other Larentii who'd arrived to help, I transported all of us to the gaping hole in Russia, which was still surrounded by the debris of the experimental facility, in addition to first responders and armed guards.

Nefrigar placed the area in stasis first, then moved all the people we found at the location far away. We didn't need the hole widening and swallowing more up while we attempted to get one person out.

"What are you going to do?" I asked Randl, as he stepped up beside me and gazed into the black pit.

"Tamp is going to get me to the first stopping point, where I'll split time," he said. "We'll attempt to do that twice more—or until we reach Lissa."

"How is Tamp going to get you anywhere in that mess?" Merrill demanded.

"Like this," Tamp walked up and changed, as only a Pod'l-morph could. He became a thick, twisted, steel-and-titanium vine of thorns. Pod'l-morphs could become anything—animal, vegetable or mineral —or in this case, metal.

Dangerous metal.

"Once we get to Lissa," Randl said, "I'll send a message," he tapped the medallion around his own neck. "Send your power down this vine and pull us all out, if you can."

Tamp's metal vine grew, reaching far into the sky before bending and diving into the pit before us. At one point, Randl leapt, grabbing onto a dangerous, gleaming spike and allowing himself to be propelled into the darkness.

"Is this going to work?" Merrill sounded too afraid to hope.

"I have no idea," I admitted. "We'll wait and find out."

Liron

I was once of the *Al'Riyu*—in the Hierarchy. I had my desires and ambitions, however, and they were my own—no other's. The

General's desires were nothing to me. I knew he'd be defeated and hid myself to prevent him from commanding me. Even my maker couldn't find me, as hard as he tried, once I decided to conceal myself.

As for the General, who commanded the other rogues, he thought power would carry him through.

He was only half right.

Power and cunning had carried me through, and soon enough, I and my son would rule all universes. I was only a single step away from destroying enough of the gods of light to win the God Wars.

The timeline in which they won would disappear, in favor of another, solely of my making. All would bow before me and my son.

I imagined storming the Larentii homeworld after that, and forcing them to my will—as it should be.

They would pay for destroying Sirena long ago. The Sirenali were my people. I'd planned for them to create the drug, but when they were destroyed, I had the idea of introducing it to a world of light instead.

The Lyristolyi never knew I was behind all of it—that my virus had been introduced through them. By the time they determined how dangerous it was, it had already leaked into other parts of the universes, and did my work for me.

I would mark this day in the timeline, as the day in which I came to full power and the gods of light and darkness fell under my rule. Yes. I would think of a name for it, and command that all celebrate it from this moment on.

My goal had been to destroy the Queen of Le-Ath Veronis. The moment I learned that the bitch Zaria was also involved, I set my sights on her as well. Then, when even the Mighty became involved, it turned even sweeter, as I plotted their fall.

Now, to arrive in my power before the rogues waiting, and force them back while I bring their quarry the final distance to them.

Things had fallen into place so perfectly, I'd surprised even myself. A celebration was certainly in order afterward. I'd command it.

❦

Randl

We'd dropped until we stopped, and Tamp pulled his metal vine up short while winds whirled around us.

Let's hope this works, I sent to Tamp, who also had mindspeech.

If it doesn't, I think it may be more than difficult to pull back from this—I feel the power dragging us farther in, he replied.

I don't think I've ever had a conversation with a piece of metal before, I told him. He'd sounded worried—I wanted to calm his fears until they were justified.

Hmmph, was his reply.

Reaching out, I attempted split-time, and everything stopped.

We have success at the first level, I sent back to Charles, before urging Tamp's vine farther into the pit.

≈

Lissa

Zaria? I sent. I didn't think she could hear me, but I had to try.

I can hear you, she returned.

How?

I left a marker behind us at every level, she replied. *I hear you through that marker.*

Thank God, I mumbled back. I imagined she hadn't been doing anything, and she had all along. *Are you still at the last level? Charles is sending Randl in to try to help me get out.*

Good. If anybody can do anything in this mess, it will be him. Is Tamp or any of the others with him?

No idea. Why?

It would be better if those two came in together.

I'll trust you on that. What is Liron waiting for? I went on. I worried that he'd have her and the others by now.

If I know him at all, he's gloating somewhere and planning a parade to celebrate his victory.

Lissa? Randl's voice reached me.

Randl? I wanted to ask if he were real and not just my imagination.

We're past the second level and heading into the third. Each one is getting worse, he said. *But you already knew that.*

Yeah.

Can you communicate with Zaria, still?

Yes. She left markers on each level.

We found them. Tell her Tamp is determined to reach her, even if it destroys him.

Honey, I'm not sure that's a good idea. The rogue gods are practically next to her where she is. I didn't add that nobody might survive that final meeting. Not whole, anyway.

He understands the risk. I've already explained it to him—in detail. He loves her. She knows that. We've reached the third level, he announced. *This is worse than I thought. Hold on; attempting to split time.*

One more level and they'd find me. *Please*, I begged the universe itself. *Help him reach me.*

❧

Charles

The last mindspeech we heard from Randl was that he and Tamp had reached the third level. The next was where Lissa was trapped.

I hadn't heard him say that split time was successful past that point. I couldn't imagine how volatile those winds could be that they foiled even Lissa's attempts to escape.

All of Lissa's mates except Erland and her Falchani twins were now here with me, waiting to lend their power to pull her out.

Erland, Drake and Drew—they'd gone to help Breanne, and were now trapped in a separate vortex with her and Ashe—along with the High Demon army, Reah, Lexsi, Hank and too many others. If Randl were successful here, would we have enough time to make another attempt at the second pit? Many of them wore medallions, too.

Pull! Randl's mindspeech snapped into my mind.

Now, I shouted to all who stood about the pit. I guided the energy through Tamp's metal vine as it traveled far into the pit itself, until I felt the connection between it and Randl.

Through him, I felt Lissa—weak and vulnerable. *Heave upward*, I shouted to everyone around me. *Heave!*

~

Lissa

The moment I was flung out of the pit, followed quickly by Randl, Tamp removed the base of his vine from its clinging place in Russian soil and disappeared down the hole while Kalenegar shouted after it.

I was lifted into Merrill's arms and found myself weeping against his collar; "It's too late," I wailed. "I felt her fall the last time when Randl pulled me away. Zaria is in the hands of the rogues, now."

~

Charles

"If Zaria fell, then Bree and the others likely preceded her—that's what Lissa says happened—that Breanne and her group would fall first, and then Lissa and Zaria shortly after. I've attempted mindspeech through my medallion—they can't hear me. Too, the only one I've seen who could butt two universes together is Breanne, and we have no idea whether she'll be able to do anything of the sort," I explained to a small, tired corps of the powerful.

Nefrigar had transported us back to the Larentii homeworld; Karzac was tending Lissa and a few others and the rest of us were discussing the current predicament. Randl was a part of that group, although he'd remained silent so far.

The Larentii had gone to find sunlight to feed themselves after expending so much energy to get just one person back from the pit.

"I find it interesting that Lissa says the more she spent power, the weaker she felt—like the power was being sucked away by the vortex," Trajan said. This was Trajan the *Ko'Ahmari* speaking, not Winkler's second.

Winkler himself was nearby—Lissa was his mate and he was ready to take worlds apart because she'd suffered.

"That's right," Gavin agreed. "She said that her suggestion of going to mist and trying to blow the vortex apart was met by fear from Zaria. What do you suppose that meant?"

"I imagine," I began slowly, piecing it together as I spoke, "that the vortex was so strong that Lissa's mist particles would have been flung outward and she wouldn't be able to pull them together again."

"That's terrifying," Rigo growled. "No wonder it frightened Zaria."

"How many, Wisdom," Kalenegar appeared after replenishing his energy in sunlight, somewhere, "how many copies of Liron would it take to create two of these vortexes and defeat the amount of power held within them? He managed to take down the Mighty Hand and the Mighty Heart, in addition to the others."

"I have been working on that since we discovered how Liron recreated himself," I said. "It would take more than a thousand of him to do what he has done."

"You have answered my question as well," Nefrigar appeared beside Kalenegar. "And if we survive these events, how can we prevent it from happening again?"

"I think that should be determined by the Council," I said.

"What Council?"

"The one I intend to create if we manage to survive the next few days. If those who have fallen into the hands of the rogues are destroyed in their corporeality, then the God Wars are over and Liron has won the final round."

~

Breanne

Ashe's shield was holding—for now. What stood outside it, however, pounding giant fists against its surface—how had we not known?

Liron, his wings spread and shining in such a formidable, enormous form, was determined to reach us and destroy corporeal bodies. Nearby, Hank and his High Demons, all weary but still in Full Thifilathi, stood ready to do battle with what Liron had become.

Too afraid to ask Ashe how long he could hold out against such anger and brute force, I turned to the others who cowered behind Liron—the rogues who hadn't realized what Liron was doing until it was far too late.

Much like we'd been unaware and unsuspecting.

Their lives—and their free will—had perished while they'd been focused elsewhere.

Just as we'd been focused elsewhere. They'd be under Liron's thumb from now on, because they didn't have the strength to stand against him.

When had I thought that an alliance between Xenides and Baikov was a terrible thing?

This was worse. Yes, we'd imagined that we were dealing with a past version of Liron—but only a single version. This one had to be a thousand Lirons, at the very least.

Reaching out with my mind for perhaps the tenth time, I couldn't locate Lissa or Zaria. Were my sister and my daughter gone already, and I hadn't realized it? I should have hugged Zaria when I had the chance, and told her what I knew.

While I stood there, watching as Ashe's shield weakened under the constant pounding of Liron's fists, a strange thing happened.

Beside me, in barren soil, a small, green vine began to grow. I stepped aside, wondering how a small plant could appear in such an inhospitable place. I felt no malice from it—in fact, I only had good feelings from it, as if it were sentient.

I stepped back again, while Hank and his High Demons roared a challenge at Liron—he was about to break through Ashe's shield.

The vine exploded into a huge plant, and in its midst, Zaria was held. The plant lifted her out of its thorny center and set her down, whole and alive, beside me.

"Hi, Mom," she told me as the vine became her mate, Phrinnis Tampirus. "We tried to get here sooner, but you have no idea what those idiots have done to the ground in this place."

∾

Charles

"Do we fill in the pits? Are they a likely source of transport from the dark universe to this one?" Ildevar Wyyld asked. He and Kaldill Schaff had arrived together. It didn't surprise me; the friendship between the Founder of the Reth Alliance and the King of the Elves was a long one.

"Is there no one willing to travel through them to search for our missing?" Dragon sounded mournful. His youngest sons—both of them—had been with Breanne.

"I think that would be foolish, Warlord," Kalenegar said gently. "Unless you wish to meet the same fate."

"Even if we fill them in, we are still dealing with the one who created them to begin with," Nefrigar pointed out. "He can create more and will likely do so if we close these off."

"At least we know where these are," Aurelius sighed. "Any others he could hide, and we might have no idea where they were."

"How do we fight this threat?" Trajan asked. "We can throw everything we have against it, and it still won't be enough—unless I am very wrong."

"You're not wrong," I told him. Several quiet conversations that were taking place throughout the Archives suddenly stopped, leaving us in dead silence.

"Then we are truly lost," Rylend Morphis said, and in his voice were tears unshed for his father, Erland, and his mate, Reah.

"Do not be so swift to say those words," I held up a hand. "We do not know that they are true as yet. Liron is not here gloating, as you know, and if he had completely won, even the Larentii homeworld would not be a safe place of refuge from him."

"Then what do you suggest?" Ildevar asked.

"Here's my suggestion," I said, and laid out my plan.

~

Breanne

"I'm ready," Tamp kissed Zaria and grinned at her. On his chest shone a gold coin—his *Arpex*, Revalus.

On one of Zaria's shoulders lay three similar coins. I had no idea who they were, or from where. I had to trust that she knew what she was doing.

Tamp changed back to a vine, only this time, it was made of thick, clear crystal, with thorns longer than I was tall. He grew as Liron kept pounding against Ashe's shield. Ashe had gone to his knees, while Reah, Lexsi, Erland, Drake and Drew knelt beside him, their hands on his shoulders and arms, feeding him every drop of their energy.

"Fly, Tampirus," Zaria called out to him as Liron landed a shield-cracking blow.

Suddenly, the entire perimeter of Ashe's shield was filled with the crystal vine, all its massive, sharp thorns pointed outward.

The moment Ashe's shield failed, it dropped all at once, and Liron's next blows landed on Tamp's enormous thorns.

The scream Liron emitted was enough to deafen anyone, and we—and the rogue gods behind him, cowered for a moment.

Flee, I shouted at them in mindspeech. *Save yourselves from this abomination.*

Had I imagined they'd take my advice? They disappeared so quickly while Liron was distracted, I wondered if he'd ever find all of them again.

Liron, however, wasn't done with us.

Not by a long shot. After healing the wounds in his hands, he stalked toward us again, determined to eliminate the source of his troubles and pain.

"Go," Zaria lifted the gold coins from her shoulder and slapped them on the nearest of Tamp's vines. The vines turned to gold, and Tamp was removed in some way from the vines altogether.

He dropped next to Zaria, who clothed his nakedness with a thought.

"Who are they?" I whispered as Liron's arms raised and came down covered in metal, and clanged against the gold vines covering us.

"Three who came from this universe," Zaria replied. "They have to hold Liron off until I can search the Metal Library," she said. "Go see to Ashe and the others and hope these three have what it takes to keep Liron's fists away from us."

I ran, then, to Ashe, who was lying flat on the ground beside Erland. Lexsi and Reah wept as they tended to both.

~

Zaria

What Liron had done—had he known completely what it was that he *had* done? The Metal Library knew, and it was helping me in my search through its holdings, ferreting out the pieces needed to eliminate this virus within.

Hurry, it whispered to me, its metallic words ringing in my mind. I didn't bother answering, I merely moved as fast as my mind would allow, searching, searching—*searching*.

More than one thousand pieces had been corrupted. They all had to be found wherever they'd hidden themselves within the Metal Library. Whenever one was located, it was shoved out and lay floating about me, while Tamp and a curious High Demon watched.

Stand guard and allow nobody to get close to any of these, I warned the High Demon. Tamp already knew not to come close.

I am already doing so, he replied. I realized that this was Reah's new High Demon mate, Wardevik Weth.

The smart one, he informed me with a smile in his voice.

The ground around us shook, and somewhere, gold thorns tumbled down, ringing their metallic way through the supporting vine. Already, Liron was breaking into my three guardians.

Mom, I sent, *gather everybody to you and build a conduit. Get them out of here. I'll hold them off as long as I can.*

But, she began.

Please. If we can get out of this mess with only one or two heroes, then we're ahead of the game. Otherwise, nobody will remember any of us; it will all be Liron.

I understand. I'll gather them now.

I hoped she had enough energy to build a conduit from this universe to the other, and I hoped she'd have enough sense to shut it down the second they were all through. *Warde,* I sent to him, *go with Reah and the others. Time is short. Tamp, if you want to survive, I suggest you go with them.*

I'm not leaving, Tamp replied.

It was the response I expected, but I had to try. I had no guarantees that I could ferret out every single bit of Liron's existence from the Metal Library before Liron broke through my guardians and destroyed me.

We're all together, and I'm building the conduit now, Breanne told me.

Go. Hurry. With a crash, Liron broke through another level of thorns and was coming dangerously close. Small squares of gold, hundreds of them, floated about me, but there was too little time left, and too many of Liron still hidden within the Metal Library.

~

Breanne

Take them through first, I commanded the High Demons who carried Ashe, Erland and several others. They'd emptied themselves of power, attempting to buy us time. Most of them were still unconscious. I hoped healers would be waiting when we arrived—if we managed to escape. Behind me, another level of thorns and vines fell as Liron continued his assault.

The High Demons ran through the conduit as if the hounds of hell were after them. Actually, what they ran from was far worse than that. *Hurry,* I urged as a thousand High Demons raced through the connection I'd formed.

At least the Ra'Ak and the others we'd fought on Refizan had disappeared—victims of either Liron or the other rogues when they first arrived. Yes, that was poor payment for doing Liron's bidding, but they'd had little time to regret their bargain with him.

The ground shook beneath us again. Would it help if I could shove the others through? I was no longer worried about the damage to be done when they hit the other side; I worried that there was worse coming here.

Gathering as much power as I could, I lifted all of us—and shoved us through the portal before letting it fall shut behind us.

Then, on the green grass of a field outside Ordinandis, I fell to my knees and wept.

~

Zaria

He had almost reached us. Only one level of thorns remained.

Destroy what you have now, a voice whispered to me. I considered it —for a nanosecond—before Liron broke through my guardians.

CHAPTER 19

Queen's Palace, Le-Ath Veronis
Lissa

I was getting dressed for an infernal Council meeting five days later, as if nothing had happened and my heart wasn't broken.

So far, there was nothing on the Liron front, but that could change at any moment. Charles, Ashe and Breanne all said to go on with our lives as if nothing were wrong, to keep panic from the masses.

Let them be as happy as they can be in their final days, Breanne said.

My shoulders sagged as I studied myself in the mirror. For the first two days, I'd held hope that Zaria would reappear, and all would return to normal.

That hope had died, and there was no clock to point to and record an official time of death.

There'd been silence from Sirena, too. Too much silence. They had to be grieving—that was understood.

All of Zaria's mates had disappeared—likely to grieve in solitude and isolation. Except for Tamp. Like Zaria, he was now gone.

I'd studied Charles when he and the others came to say what they had. A deep well of emotion lay in his eyes that I'd never seen there before. I didn't remark on it. In fact, I'd said very little to any of them.

They were alive because of Zaria's efforts on their behalf. I hoped they realized the magnitude of that sacrifice.

"There's ah, something I meant to do for you while you were in the past, but things went out of control too fast," Breanne appeared and sat on my dressing bench beside me. Our mirror images stared back at both of us, now.

"What's that?" I pretended to busy myself by arranging my comb and hairbrush on the dresser.

"Come with me and I'll show you."

I really wasn't in the mood, and we both knew what had come of the last time she'd sent me anywhere. I was wallowing in the injustice of it, still. Nevertheless, I didn't try to stop her when she bent time and folded space.

I drew in a breath; it became trapped in my lungs as Bree led me into a hospital room in the past. Franklin had just stepped out to go to the bathroom, leaving Greg in the bed, half-asleep and half-watching a program on television, which hung on the wall opposite his bed.

Breanne had shielded her presence from Greg; I could tell.

"Lissa?" Greg's eyes widened as I walked in.

"Shhh, nobody is supposed to know I'm here," I held up a hand. "Don't tell anybody, not even Frankie."

"Because we don't want the vamps to know, do we?" A light appeared in his eyes.

"Nope. I can only stay for a minute, but I really, really wanted to come by and say hello."

Greg didn't even remark on the fact that it was daylight outside—the pain medication was dealing with that, and he wore the oxygen canula for the pneumonia he had.

He hadn't been in the hospital long, and I was grateful he was still mostly coherent. I approached the bed, leaned down and kissed his cheek before pulling away and smiling at him.

"We really should have taken you to Vegas with us—you'd enjoy it," he patted my hand.

"Honey, I'd give anything to do just that," I agreed.

~

Dallas, Texas, Past

William Winkler

"These belong to you—we apprehended the thieves," the bank president handed a large, sealed pouch to me. It was thick—as if it contained everything stolen from me. I tore into it immediately, spilling the contents onto his desk. Two million in cash takes up a lot of room. The ring and jewelry dropped out last of all. "I'm sorry it took nearly a month to locate it, but at least we have all of it back." The bank president was sweating, hoping I wouldn't sue over his poor security measures.

"We'll move this to a bank closer to home," Trajan began gathering money and stuffing it back inside the bag. "Pleasure doing business with you." He bared his teeth, meaning he was anything but pleased.

The last month, since the theft happened, was a bit of a blur, and I couldn't recall much of it. Kellee had just gotten back from a short beach vacation, and was now yelling at everybody in the house.

"Let's go." I handed the ring and jewelry boxes to Trajan, who added them to the bag.

"Ice cream?" Trajan asked on our way out the door.

"Yup. Let's go."

~

Vladimirsky Central

Ilya Kuznetzov

I didn't care that they'd captured me after I returned to Ukraine, or that there were people in my own country who'd sell their mother for the right price.

They'd sold me back to the Russian government, and I'd been imprisoned, although they couldn't fully prove that I'd had anything to do with the demise of both Baikovs. If only I could take full responsibility for that, I would be happy to report it to them myself.

When Charles took me back to my time, he said he couldn't interfere with the rest of my life—that things had to go as they would.

I said it didn't matter.

Zaria had not returned from the pit, and nothing mattered. Andrei was somewhere in the future, and I couldn't explain that to Katya. She thought he was dead at the hands of those who imprisoned me, and, as she wasn't allowed to visit, I couldn't convince her otherwise.

My cousins were transferred back to the Siberian Prison camp; I get the occasional message through Bespalov, who keeps an eye on them and Katya from afar. Katya is getting an education, and will learn things I shall never know.

As for me, after spending twelve years in this hole, I have cancer. They waste no time and spend no money on my illness, and I suppose it is my due. I am nodding off—sometimes the pain lessens and I sleep. I am almost there, now.

"Ilya?" A soft voice wakens me from my dozing.

"What?" She spoke in English, while I replied in Russian.

"Don't worry, I understand all languages," she told me. "My name is Conner," she added. A light shone faintly about her as she knelt beside my cot. Blonde hair hung about her shoulders, and she was beautiful.

Not as beautiful as my Zaria had been to me, but still lovely to look upon.

"Zaria asked me to come for you—and take you to the other side," she said.

"Where is she?" I struggled to rise.

"That I cannot tell you. She asked me to say this to you; *Ilya Kuznetzov, I will always love you, no matter who or what or where you are.* And she said to give you this, to take with you on your journey."

I was handed a feather, pure white, with the softest down close to the shaft. I clutched it against my heart as if I were afraid it would be taken from me.

"Come now—the feather is all you'll need where we're going." She pulled me to my feet, and suddenly I felt as light as the feather I so desperately clung to. Looking down, I saw my body lying on the cot—old and frail as it now was—the eyes closed, as if I were sleeping soundly for the first time in years.

"You don't need that anymore," Conner smiled. "Come with me."

"Where are we going?" I asked.

"To the other side," she said, and so we left the hell of Vladimirsky Central far behind us.

∼

SouthStar, Avendor

Ashe

Three months have passed, and still there is no sign of Liron. Was he rounding up his rogues again, after Breanne convinced them to scatter? Was he that much of a control freak, that he had to corral them before coming to do the same for us?

Trajan and I had taken a few days before gishi fruit harvest, to pick through everything that had happened from the moment Lissa went to Earth in the past to the second we arrived on Refizan and Bree had shut her connection down behind us.

We'd missed nothing, and then, when Charles came to join us on the last night before harvest, he'd gone over our notes and didn't add anything to them.

Nefrigar likely had a similar set filed in the Archives, but he hadn't said anything. After all, the Larentii had to be in mourning, much as the rest of us were. The Avii, too, had lost their Guardian, and Quin was likely inconsolable.

I found myself walking through the rows between gishi trees, shortly after this section had been harvested. A flock of white cranes flew overhead; at least fifteen or twenty of them. I stopped to watch as they lazily flapped long wings and soared northward.

Only a moment later, a white feather drifted downward, to land at my feet. Absently, I lifted it up to stroke its downy softness.

My mental shout was likely heard from one end of the universes to the other.

She's alive, I yelled to anyone who could hear me. *She's alive!*

*W*lodek's Mansion, Past
Charles

Two nights after the Annual Meeting, when Lissa disappeared after destroying Xenides, I sat at my desk in my usual place, going through two days' mail.

I almost missed it—the postcard at the bottom of the substantial pile of correspondence.

Addressed to me rather than to Wlodek or the Council, I studied it in surprise. On the front was the most unusual image of all—Lissa's coronet from the future encircling a white feather, both of which hovered over a pile of bones.

A shiver went through me as I gazed upon that image; Zaria had sent me a message. Turning the card over in trembling fingers, I read what she'd written.

Sometimes it's best to destroy the enemy in pieces, it said. *No blows can land if he has no arms.*

No new way of destruction can be devised if he has no head. Once he was completely destroyed, I built a conduit between universes and went in search of his treasure.

I am my mothers' daughter, after all.

More later—Z.

P.S. You named me Harriet after one of my grandmothers, didn't you?

She knew who her mothers were—at least two of them. Breanne could build a conduit between timelines and universes. Zaria could, too. Did she know about the third mother as well?

As for the treasure mentioned in her message, and the pile of bones depicted on the front of the card, Zaria was letting me know that she'd gone looking for Liron's cache of bones, bone dust, and his store of the drug itself. If he'd left those in the wrong hands, too many things could go awry.

"I hope you find those things, my daughter," I whispered softly. "And all your heart's desires ever after."

The End

BLOOD ALLIANCE, BLOOD DESTINY, BOOK 12

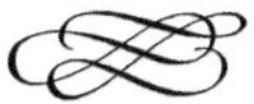

Excerpt

*R*ussian Embassy
Ambassador Bespalov

Zaria, I'm sorry I have not been able to find this information for you sooner. Many of my contacts and sources of information have either been arrested or have disappeared. I did finally speak with someone. He and his daughter worked as janitors at the facility you mentioned.

Regarding the one you name D'slay, the father swears that the filth disappeared and took his daughter with him, shortly before the facility was demolished. The father is still mourning her absence, and says that if Irina were in control of her own senses, that she would never have abandoned him.

If you wish to speak with Irina's father, his name is Viktor. You said you only needed first names, and I hope this is still true. The government is sending me into retirement in only a few months, and it is my hope that it will not be the same retirement home as that of our mutual friend.

Sincerely—B.

Queen's Palace, Le-Ath Veronis

    Lissa

    Lissa? Zaria sounded tentative, as if she thought I might scold her for not contacting me sooner. I knew through Ashe and Charles that she'd been more than busy tracing Sirenali bones, bone dust and Liron's stash of the Lyristolyi drug.

    Zaria? What do you need? I replied quickly, in an effort to quell her fears.

    Just to talk and run some things past you, she said, sounding weary.

    Want something to eat while you're here?

    That sounds nice. Can you feed four others besides me? Bleek, Tamp, Ilya and Edden are with me right now.

    Of course. Do you want to talk to anyone else while you're here?

    If Breanne is available, then yes. Also, if you can find Charles, his presence might prove useful.

    She didn't call him Father, or Daddy or anything else. I figured those were names he hadn't earned and might never do so.

    Like Griffin hadn't really earned them from me, either.

    Charles, Bree? I sent. *Your daughter wants to talk to you.*

    Be right there, Charles answered first, with Bree's acknowledgement coming shortly after.

    Damn, I wish they were this responsive whenever *I* wanted to talk to them.

Estimated Release date: Fall, 2018

www.ingramcontent.com/pod-product-compliance
Lightning Source LLC
Chambersburg PA
CBHW070432120726
47910CB00003B/751